Monsters
of the
North

Roy Sakelson

For Rachel, of course.

CONTENTS

Of all tyrannies, a tyranny sincerely exercised for the good of its victims may be the most oppressive.

C.S. Lewis
God in the Dock: Essays on Theology and Ethics

PROLOGUE: EDUBARD'S LEGACY

Asmodeus opened his eyes and stared at the cave's icy ceiling.

Something was wrong.

There were men walking in the snow on the earth's surface. He could hear them calling to one another, their deep voices muffled by the layers of rock and ice that had hidden his lair for so long. He did not know how they had found him and his sister this deep underground. Nor did it matter now. The language, plain and blunt, was unmistakable.

Sentinels.

Quieting his mind, he closed his eyes again and listened more closely. He felt the soft reverberations of footsteps on the tundra above. There were many of them, at least twenty. The voices betrayed a sense of urgency, excitement—and fear.

Asmodeus was used to inspiring fear in other living things. He smiled, shifting his weight from one skeletal leg to another. As a gholgor, he was sometimes mistaken for a man, a very tall, thin man who had seen too many winters. Only when he had drawn too close would you realize that he was far from human, for no man had such dead, sunken eyes or thin, pale lips. No man had such strange, bony hands with fingers as sharp as needles, and as strong as iron. No man had ever seen so much or lived so long. By the time you *had* noticed these things, it was already too late.

Yes, the sentinels were wise to fear him. Asmodeus himself had killed scores of these brave hunters in his time, striding quickly and silently from behind and sinking his claws into them to stifle their screams.

But he wasn't immune to fear, either.

The sentinels had tracked and killed many gholgors over the years, adapting and refining their tactics with each kill. Where Asmodeus and his kind had once been a common scourge to all living things, they were now rare, living in remote places such as deserts, jungles, and the icy tundra.

Aware of the danger the sentinels posed, Asmodeus and his sister, Lym, chose to live in the barren north, where human settlements were few. The cold temperatures had been difficult to endure at first, but they had learned to survive in the White Waste by lurking in the deep valleys that grew dark early, hunting only at night, and always returning by dawn to the cave in which they slept.

Still, nothing ever came easily here. The scarcity of food meant that Asmodeus and Lym had to work together. They chose peasants from small villages on which to feed, capturing hunters and fur-trappers who strayed too far into the forest. (Asmodeus especially liked to eat children for they were easy to kill and just as easy to digest.) But he and Lym had to be careful not to attract attention. Too many disappearances would create suspicion. That would bring sentinels, the sea-faring people, who knew exactly what gholgors were, and how to kill them. Now it appeared that day had finally come.

Asmodeus stirred, upsetting the pile of bones at his feet. The sound of the voices, sharp and clear, told him they had discovered the cave's entrance. It was just a matter of time before the sentinels found their way down into the darkness. He knew he had to move, quickly.

He turned to his sister. "Do you hear them, my love?"

"Yes," she whispered, her pale eyes glowing in the darkness. "Shall we greet them?"

He shook his head. "Too many to fight."

Asmodeus could hear her heart beating rapidly in the darkness. Her unblinking eyes, as hard as flint, stared at him, uncertain of what he meant to do. The sentinels would not flee. They never did. Instead, they would approach slowly, methodically, with their hateful torches and cruel, iron blades. She understood the danger just as well as he. "Then what shall we do?" she hissed. "Hide? We can conceal ourselves down here, remain safe."

"No," he said. "They will not stop until they have found us."

"Then how?" she asked, growing more anxious. "How can we defeat so many at once?"

"We must even the odds," he said. "We will surprise them by catching some of them from behind using the rear tunnel."

When digging the lair years ago, Asmodeus had insisted they create another outlet so that they could escape if the main entrance was blocked by snow or assaulted by enemies. Lym had objected at first, grumbling about the extra work. Now, the second entrance gave them hope.

"Of course!" she exclaimed. "We can circle back to the surface and kill the stragglers before they even see us."

They crept down the tunnel together in silence. Gholgors could see in the dark as well as trolls, and though they preferred to venture out at night, they could move well during the day with their long, loping strides.

Soon, they would reach the exit. This smaller opening led out to the sheer face of a cliff, which they would have to carefully climb to reach level ground. Not many creatures would attempt such a feat—but the gholgors were not like other creatures. Their sharp claws and long limbs made them not only formidable opponents but also excellent climbers.

They had almost reached the rear entrance when Asmodeus stopped abruptly. Lym halted, too, and looked at him inquiringly. Then she heard the voices. The sentinels had found the outlet as well! Worse, they were already inside. Asmodeus could see the dim flicker of torchlight on the walls up ahead as the men approached.

"Be wary, lads!" a voice growled. "This one is clever. It's not often we find multiple entrances."

"Clever or no," muttered another, "I'd like to see it outwit my iron."

"Don't go running off trying to be the hero like you did in the Moaning Isles, Dramon," said the first. "We stay together. My father wants us home before winter, all of us."

"Remember what Prince Edubard said, lad," cautioned a third. "Slow and steady. That's how we kill them. It's been a good year. Let's hope this is the last of the accursed creatures."

Asmodeus and Lym listened intently. The *last* of the accursed creatures? Could that be true? Had the sentinels really succeeded in killing so many?

Moving swiftly, the gholgors retreated. They were good at killing, but they did not relish this fight.

Asmodeus and Lym preferred to catch their victims from behind, or in the dark, alone. The thought of battling sentinels in an enclosed space, attacked from both sides amid torchlight, made them afraid, and they hated being afraid.

They returned to the largest part of the tunnel where they fed and slept, picking their way over piles of bones, clothes, weapons, and many other trappings that had been discarded over several decades. As they had expected, they could hear the sentinels approaching from both directions.

"Trapped!" hissed Lym, her voice quivering in fear. The likelihood that they would soon be fighting for their lives now seemed inevitable. "We must meet them here. Fight back to back."

"No," said Asmodeus, gravely. "We must break through the ranks. It is the only way. If we can reach the surface, we can easily outrun them, and then wait for night to fall."

"Very well," Lym replied. "At least we have one advantage. Didn't you hear the fools? They only think there's one of us. They'll be in for a nasty shock."

Asmodeus narrowed his eyes. "Only one of us . . ." he whispered, thoughtfully.

Lym turned. "What did you—?"

He raised one long claw and, quick as a snake, cut her throat. Her eyes grew wide in shock as she stumbled backwards, clutching at her wound with both hands and gurgling wretchedly on the blood that bubbled from her mouth. Still struggling to breathe, she glanced at Asmodeus in confusion. "Why?" she whispered. Before he could answer, she slumped to the ice and lay still.

"I'm sorry, my love," he said, crouching beside her and stroking her white face with one bloody fingernail. "One of us must survive."

Thinking quickly, he found an old sword amid one of the piles of discarded objects. Wiping it across her throat, it glistened with blood as he set it next to her. With any luck, the sentinels might think that one of her victims had killed her. But where could he hide?

Asmodeus raced back to the mounds of debris and, clearing away a small space, he began to dig into the icy ground of the tunnel. Few creatures had the strength to dig through solid ice, but Asmodeus, with claws like steel, and driven by desperation, made quick work. Soon, there was a hole just large enough for his body to fit.

A voice drifted through the shadows. "How long is this blasted tunnel?"

Asmodeus looked up, his eyes wide. The sentinels were just around the corner now. He had very little time. If they saw him, there would be no escape.

He climbed into the shallow space he had made, and hurriedly covered most of his body again with the ice. Then, using his long arms, he quietly gathered bones and other fragments of clothing to conceal himself before taking a deep breath and squeezing his head and arms under the surface of the stinking rubbish.

He was hidden, but not well. If a sentinel stepped into the pile of filth where he lay, the deception would be over. He had to trust in the hope that his sister's body would be enough to satisfy them. Otherwise, he was doomed.

Still and silent, Asmodeus waited. He did not have long to wait.

One of the sentinels, a man with a weathered face named Augred, turned the corner and raised his torch as he gazed in disgust at the foul lair. "Here!" he cried.

Another sentinel, a young man named Halam, rounded the corner. "This must be where it sleeps!" he shouted. He drew his sword and sprang into the cavern, ready for a fight. Instead, he saw a gholgor sprawled on the ground. Nearby, lay a blade, covered in blood.

Moments later, twelve sentinels approached from the opposite direction. Everyone seemed to be talking at once. The men were tall, pale, and fair with fierce, blue eyes. Most were clean-shaven, though some had tangled beards. Dressed in thick woolen cloaks and fur boots to protect themselves from the cold, they wore leather tunics and fleece leggings, forgoing the ring mail they normally used due to the freezing temperatures of the north. Each man held a torch and a large, iron broadsword, handling both with ease.

Augred, Halam, and the others gathered around Lym's body, inspecting it. "This one's big, though it's not been dead for long," declared Augred, pushing on the gholgor's head with his foot. "The corpse isn't rigid."

Sheathing his sword, he grasped the hilt of the blade that lay near the creature's neck. As one of the captains of the sentinels, he had killed three such creatures over the years, and knew that the task wasn't easy. He thrust the sword into the gholgor's side before drawing it out again, and gazed at the blade as it steamed in the cold air.

"The tale grows stranger," he said, surprised. "This sword is old, rusty."

A deep voice interrupted them from the other end of the cavern. "Have you killed the beast so quickly?"

Prince Edubard and six more sentinels appeared, holding torches and swords.

"No, captain," replied Augred. "We found it dead where it lies." He handed Edubard the sword and explained how they had found the body.

"It doesn't make sense," muttered Edubard, gazing upon the skeletal creature in the flickering torchlight. "Gholgors don't kill themselves."

He looked around at the bones and debris strewn across the floor in the dim light, expecting to see the body of some brave man who must have surprised the creature with a quick sword thrust before he died. But no corpse was visible, only the gnawed bones and entrails of victims several days old.

"Perhaps the beast was stabbed on the surface by someone who knew how to defend himself," suggested Augred. "It could have fled down here, hoping to survive."

Edubard looked skeptical. "Perhaps," he said. "It would have lost too much blood if it removed the blade immediately." He leaned over and inspected the creature more closely. "But it couldn't have had much hope either way. The wound is deep."

"The deeper the better as far as I'm concerned," replied Dramon, rubbing his hands together and smiling. "Should we care how it died?"

The prince glanced up at the young warrior. Edubard's eyes were troubled as if he were debating in his mind whether to pursue the matter further. Had the creature killed itself instead of attacking them? Perhaps it knew fighting would be hopeless, and that he, Edubard, feared nothing, and would show no mercy.

His name was hateful among the foul creatures of the world. He had inherited the dragon magic from his father, Childeric, and had used it ruthlessly to punish Valmar's enemies. Even his sentinels were a little afraid of him, but that suited him fine. Fear, he found, was a useful tool when it came to governing men.

"Perhaps I worry needlessly," he mused. "What we came here to do is done. Prepare a fire. We will burn the body here. Then we will return to Valmar. It has been far too long since I have gazed upon the green hills of my home."

"To Valmar!" cried Dramon. "Oh, how I have longed to hear those words, my lord!"

Edubard laughed. "Yes," he said, looking upon the young man. "To Valmar we shall return. But I'm surprised at you, lad. I would have thought you would be less than excited to put up your sword and return to your father's plow."

Dramon bowed. "I am quite out of practice with a plow, sire. I would much rather hold a sword. Before we left, were there not rumors of trolls on the move in the southern mountains?" He waved his blade through the air. "Perhaps I can be of some service, still?"

"We shall see," replied Edubard. He examined the piles of stinking debris that surrounded them. "First, you can all be of service by wading through this carnage, and making sure that there is nothing here of value. Who knows what we may find?"

Wordlessly, the sentinels spread out and used their swords to comb through the mounds of bones and other fragments of filth that covered the cavern's floor. A few muttered to themselves, disgusted by the odor that rose to their nostrils as they disturbed the soiled den. They found many old weapons, scraps of leather, fur and hundreds of bones (both animal and human) but nothing of value. With each step, they came closer to the place where Asmodeus lay hidden.

He heard the footsteps approaching. It was just a matter of time now until he would be discovered. He was sure he could kill at least one or two of the men before they recovered from their surprise. But what hope did he have once he had revealed himself?

A sentinel stopped just in front of the mound of bones that covered his body. The man's breathing was slow and relaxed as he swept his sword back and forth carefully through the pile of bones. Tensing his muscles, Asmodeus prepared to spring to his feet and attack.

To his surprise, he heard a familiar growl followed by a human scream. He did not need to see it to understand.

Lym was still alive.

While the sentinels were busy inspecting the cavern, she had somehow staggered to her feet and caught the closest, Dramon, unaware. Using one of her long arms, she had pinned his sword against his body and jerked him upward violently with the other, causing him to drop his torch. He struggled in her grasp desperate to free himself, but without fire or blade he could not hope to harm her.

The sentinels raised their swords and torches, and closed in around her warily, for she still had the strength of many men. The torchlight hurt her eyes even as her shadow danced on the walls behind her, making her seem like a pillar of darkness. Even now, injured and bleeding, she looked down upon them menacingly, hoping somehow to survive.

She raised her claws until they were touching Dramon's cheek and gazed at the sentinels surrounding her. The young man in her grasp did not dare to move.

"Let me go, and I will spare his life," she hissed.

The men hesitated and looked at their captain. Edubard stepped forward, still pointing his sword at the gholgor. "He is a sentinel," he replied coolly. "He has promised to kill you and your kind, or die trying. We all have. Do you think we fear you, demon?"

Lym gazed at Edubard with hatred in her eyes. There was no hesitation in his voice. He meant what he said. There would be no negotiation, no safe passage. With each passing moment, she would only grow weaker. Already she was growing dizzy. She had to act.

Lym smiled down at Edubard wickedly, her breath visible in the torchlight. "Then he will die trying!" she said, snapping Dramon's neck and flinging his body at Edubard.

The men cried out and charged toward the creature.

Augred was the first to reach her. Gripping his sword, he thrust it forward, attempting to skewer her. Before his stroke arrived, Lym jumped over all of the sentinels with remarkable dexterity, her limbs extending like a giant spider in the gloom. Some of the men crouched down and raised their weapons, fearing that she meant to crush them. Instead, she cleared them easily, and landed in a pile of debris at the far end of the cavern, scattering bones everywhere.

Lym sprinted down the tunnel toward the main entrance with astonishing speed. Nearing exhaustion, and bleeding badly, she willed herself to keep going. Only a few hundred feet more and she would reach the surface. There she could make her way into the shadows of the forest where they could not find her. In time, she would heal. Then, she would have her revenge. On the sentinels. On Asmodeus. On everyone.

She saw the moon's pale light ahead. She could feel the wind on her face. The entrance was near!

Suddenly, behind her, she heard something in the dim, cold tunnel from which she fled. It was faint but clear.

Die.

A human voice. One of the sentinels. Was he singing? Chanting? Compelled by a power she didn't understand, she stopped and turned. She saw nothing, not even the torchlight of the men sure to be following her.

The voice spoke again. It had grown louder, accompanied by a dull pain that arose inside her head.

Die.

The voice repeated itself, becoming deeper, stronger. It was harsh, even cruel. She rubbed her head and tried to keep going but her legs stiffened, slowing her progress. Why couldn't she run faster? The chanting grew even louder. She turned again, sure that she would see the owner of the voice. Instead, she saw only darkness. What was the source of this infernal song? When she made it to the entrance, the pain in her head had grown worse. Now, it was all around her, pulsing, throbbing. What was happening?

Die!

Before she could take another step, the pain in her head exploded and washed over her, running down her limbs. The chanting was deafening. It was all she could think about. With each syllable, her head seemed to shatter anew as she writhed and struggled. Conquered by the pain, she shrieked and stumbled as she fell to the ice.

She turned over on to her back and looked up, her chest heaving and falling.

The last thing she saw was a man standing over her, his face illuminated by the torch he carried. She did not know how, but she was sure he was her tormentor, the man they called Edubard. The man who betrayed no fear. It was he who chanted the magical words, the words that were worming into her brain, driving her mad, killing her. His blue eyes blazed as he gazed down on her without pity. He seemed to be enjoying her suffering.

Finally, she understood what he was chanting, even as she succumbed to death.

"Die," he said.

Die by the power of my voice,
that I, Edubard, may rejoice.
Die inside this icy tomb,
and go to your eternal doom.

More men appeared in the tunnel, looking at him warily, uncomfortable with the words he uttered. If Edubard noticed, he said nothing. He stared down at the gholgor, curled up and twisted like a dead spider.

"She has met her end," he muttered. "Burn the miserable creature." Turning away from the gholgor, he faced his men somberly. They kept their eyes on the ground, unwilling to meet his gaze. "Bring Dramon's body to the surface," he commanded. "We will bury him here in the White Waste before we set sail for Valmar in the morning." He turned to Augred. "Didn't he say he liked the hills?"

"Yes, captain," said Augred dutifully, glancing at Edubard before looking away again. "He came from a small village near the northern range of the Skelding Mountains. He . . . he liked high places."

"Very well," replied Edubard. "We will bury him in the hills here with a view to the sea. Let us work quickly. I wish to leave this foul place by first light."

***

Gholgors have keen ears, and Asmodeus overheard everything before he fled. When the men had followed Lym's flight, he quietly emerged from his hiding place and sprinted down the rear entrance, making his way up the cliff to the surface. It was evening. Clouds concealed the moonlight, allowing him to cross the tundra and reach the safety of the forest. He glanced back a final time before disappearing into the trees.

He was angry at himself for being sloppy, for allowing them to come so close to killing him. If his sister hadn't been there, he would now surely be dead. Still, questions crowded his mind as he crept through the deep snow. Who was that strange man, the one they called Edubard? He shivered as he recalled the cruel words, the rhythmic chant directed at his sister. He would remember that name. What sort of magic did the man possess to kill with a song? Only the oldest dragons were capable of wielding such power.

Despite these questions, Asmodeus smiled grimly. Two things he knew. First, the sentinels were unaware that he had survived. In fact, they suspected that Lym was the last of the gholgors. He was safe for now. Second, the sentinels, led by Edubard, were returning home to a land named Valmar.

He looked up and realized he had reached the foot of the mountains. The peaks rose up before him, steep and jagged, covered in ice. But he was not here to scale the cliffs. He was searching for a way *under* them. Finding a seam that led into the earth, he wound his way down into the bowels of the mountain until even the moonlight seemed like a distant memory. When he reached a large cavern, he stopped and permitted himself a smile. This place would be his new home. He would wait for the sentinels to leave before resuming his murderous ways. This time, he would be much, much more careful.

Picking his way down to the cavern floor, he froze. A stone edifice sat in center of the hollow, glowing faintly. It was tall and erect, like an accusing finger, at least six feet in diameter. He crept closer and realized it was a column, smooth and polished. Stranger still, someone had carved faces into the surface of the stone. He knew that certain men created such things, even worshipped them, fashioning images of animals or gods out of the earth. He had no need of either.

Still, these faces were different somehow. They certainly weren't human. There were five of them stacked upon one another, each ugly in its own way. The first face, the one closest to the ground, had large tusks, and looked angry, aggressive. Above it, another countenance, with a broad, flat nose, leered at him arrogantly, like some forgotten king. A third seemed to be laughing, but judging by its expression, it was a cruel, merciless laughter. The fourth, with round, full cheeks, seemed to have gorged on something unwholesome, while the topmost face simply stared at him with cold malice in its eyes. He was about to touch the object when he heard a voice whisper in the darkness.

15

Asmodeusss.

He sprang backward, and looked around wildly. Had the sentinels found him? Was this a lair of some kind? Were other creatures waiting in the shadows, ready to pounce?

Do not be afraid. Do you think you have come here by chance?

He looked back at the column. Was he going mad? Or were those faces addressing him?

"What do you mean?" he asked, suspiciously. "How do you know my name?"

We know all of our children.

The faces seemed to study him with wicked glee. He walked toward the column, drawn by some unseen power, and realized that he wasn't just imagining it. The eyes in each face were following him.

We have heard your thoughts, Asmodeus. We have felt your deep anger. Your undeserved suffering. We share it. That is why we have called you here. We wish to help you.

He thought of Lym's expression as she had looked up at him, hands clutching her throat, before she fell at his feet. "How can you help me?" he muttered. "I am alone now."

Not anymore.

A dull, grinding sound filled the cavern. He looked up to see the front of the column, the side containing the faces, swing slowly open like a door, revealing a narrow passageway. It was even darker than his surroundings.

Come with us, Asmodeus. We will teach you how to fight with more than just flesh. We will make you stronger than you ever imagined. We will make you a god.

Drawn by the promise of these words, Asmodeus crept toward the stone, and disappeared into the darkness. Silently, the door shut behind him.

1

THROUGH ANOTHER'S EYES

Kindle saw nothing but darkness.

As a dragon, he could generally see well at night. His eyes were capable of catching and amplifying the moon's soft light, which made it easy for him to swoop down and devour a mountain goat or unsuspecting boar. But something was wrong. He found himself flying blind, helpless in the cold night air. The wind whistled in his ears, and his face, specked with frost, was almost numb.

Slowly, colors began to grow out of the sky. A red wave, almost translucent, shimmered high above him, undulating in the darkness. Then green emerged, bleeding through the red, swirling and dancing before his eyes. Another surge of color, this one a sheet of blue, hovered like an angel's wings before deepening into a beautiful violet that seemed to complete the tapestry. Even as he gazed, the hues continued to shift, changing shape, before fading once more. Finally, the darkness returned, only this time it was flecked with beads of silver.

"Stars," he thought. "Those are stars. But where did the colors go?"

As he admired the night sky, Kindle heard what sounded like a cry from far below. Another howl, long and mournful, answered it. Despite his strange surroundings, he knew that sound well.

Wolves.

He looked down. A thick layer of clouds, pierced here and there by the rocky pinnacles of a mountain range, made it seem as if he were flying over a chain of islands suspended in air. He descended slowly through the mist. He didn't recognize these mountains. Few pine trees found purchase on the massive peaks. Fewer shrubs clung stubbornly to the countless bluffs below. Snow, ice, and rock dominated this place. To the south, the mountains gave way to foothills, where he could dimly see a forest. Beyond, lay the open tundra, a vast wasteland of icy plains, scoured by fierce winds.

He sensed movement in the valley below. Small, shadowy forms raced across a frozen river. Tilting his wings, he descended quickly and saw a pack of wolves. More than a dozen of the creatures, led by a particularly large, white wolf, were making their way across the ice and deeper into the mountains. Kindle observed them silently, hovering in the darkness.

A short time later, the wolves approached what appeared to be a cleft in the mountainside. This was no small cave or underground borough. It was much too wide to have occurred naturally. As Kindle flew closer, the mystery deepened. The huge archway through which the wolves passed was made of smooth, carved stone, and it blazed with green light. What else lived there?

He watched the last of the wolves disappear into the mountain before landing in the snowdrifts nearby. Driven by curiosity, he folded his wings and followed them.

He soon found himself standing in a vast, empty cavern. Green minerals, embedded in the walls, glowed with an unearthly light. Dozens of polished, granite columns supported this hall but Kindle noticed that as they extended upward, they became uneven in the shadows, revealing the rough stone of the earth from which they had been carved. He glanced around the chamber. The wolves were nowhere to be seen but many passageways led away from the hall, deeper into the mountain. Was that where they had gone?

He saw something glitter in the dim light near the center of the cavern. Walking towards the object, he realized it was an emerald throne, which sat atop a large, granite pyramid. Stairs had been carved into the sides of the structure, allowing one to approach, but something told Kindle that didn't happen often.

At almost the same time, two creatures, both wearing black cloaks, emerged from one of the passageways. They were speaking to each other in a language he had never before heard. When they noticed him, they didn't seem frightened. Instead, they shuffled out of his way and resumed their conversation. He didn't know what manner of creatures they were, but they were too small to be men. Before he could get a better look at them or ask them what they were, the creatures disappeared into another passageway.

Kindle examined the emerald throne more closely. It was marvelous in a way, cut with astonishing precision so that it reflected every beam of light, dazzling all who looked upon it. It was also large, too large for a man, and certainly beyond the skill of Valmar's craftsmen. Did a race of giants live under this mountain?

As he considered the possibility, he noticed his reflection on the throne's uneven surface. Thousands of small images stared back at him, sparkling in the ghostly light. Only, it wasn't *his* reflection. The dragon that gazed at him wasn't green. Instead, it had creamy white scales, with wings dappled here and there with blue spots. He shifted restlessly, unsettled by this revelation.

Then he heard a voice. It was hard, authoritative. He didn't know why, but the voice made him feel something he seldom felt—fear.

"Have you found him?" it demanded.

He was about to respond but the cavern abruptly disappeared. Instead, he was staring at the familiar courtyard of Ballan á Moor. Vine-covered walls and mighty towers surrounded him, but the courtyard itself was empty. He suspected that it was early morning, for the sun had not yet climbed high enough to warm the cobblestones on which he lay. He looked up at the clear, blue sky and listened to the seagulls calling to one another as the waves crashed on the beach below.

It had all been a dream.

He looked up and noticed Gwendolyn standing in front of him. She wore a green cloak, and was looking at him expectantly. Her long, black hair fell around a quiver of arrows on her back, and she held a longbow in her right hand.

"Have you found them, Kindle?" she asked, her blue eyes wide with excitement.

Still drowsy, the dragon stared at her, uncomprehending. She had grown considerably since they had met three years ago. Now almost fifteen, she was no longer a girl with skinned knees and disheveled hair. Instead, Gwendolyn was growing up. She had inherited her mother's beauty and her father's perseverance. Determined to be the best archer in the kingdom, she rose early almost every morning and made her way down to the courtyard to practice her marksmanship. Thanks to her dedication and natural skill, she could hit the bull's-eye consistently at fifty yards. But she wasn't used to finding Kindle asleep among the bales of hay.

"You returned from the Moaning Isles last night, did you not?" she said. "What have you learned about Uncle Wulfric and the others?"

Her impatience was understandable. Wulfric and the rest of the Steadfast Lady's crew had left Valmar in summer to explore the North Sea. It was the perfect time for an expedition. The country was at peace. The Low Road was being improved and expanded to strengthen ties with the giants. Three more ships had been completed, and with no sea serpents to hinder commerce, trade with the Moaning Isles was thriving.

So when Wulfric and the Steadfast Lady had ventured across the ocean, promising to return in autumn, Gwendolyn's father, King Argus, had been glad. He knew how much his brother loved the sea, and rejoiced to see the ship catch a strong wind northward. But autumn was almost over, and there was still no sign of them.

As the days grew shorter and colder, the people of Valmar watched the sea anxiously, fearing the worst. Not knowing what else to do, the king sent Kindle to Brae, the largest city in the Moaning Isles, to see if Lord Dravius, the archipelago's governor, had any knowledge of the ship's whereabouts. The Isles were a major center for commerce. Ships as far east as Quintharia regularly made port there to trade for olive oil and salt. If another ship had spotted the Steadfast Lady on the high seas, Lord Dravius would surely know. Unfortunately, neither he nor any of the foreign captains could give them news.

By the time Kindle had returned to Valmar it was well after midnight. Tired from his journey, he landed in the castle courtyard and fell asleep.

He was about to answer Gwendolyn when he remembered his dream. The wolves. The icy mountains. The pale dragon. The fell voice. It all seemed so real. What could it mean?

"Kindle," repeated Gwendolyn, looking at him curiously. "Are you okay?"

"Hmmm?" He looked at her and realized that she had been waiting for his answer for some time. "Yes, I'm fine," he replied. "Lord Dravius asked everyone about your uncle. No one could tell us anything. It appears that we were the last to see the Steadfast Lady."

She sighed and looked away. "Where could they be?"

"Where could who be?" asked Aethelred, appearing through a doorway with an apple in his hand. At thirteen years old, the boy was all knees and elbows. He had a shock of red hair (which seemed to stick up like grass despite his efforts to comb it) and a long, proud nose like his father. Like most teenage boys, he ate constantly.

"Uncle Wulfric," said Gwendolyn. "Lord Dravius hasn't seen him either."

"Don't worry, Gwen," he replied. "There's no better sailor than Uncle Wulfric. He'll turn up. They all will. You'll see."

"I wish I could be sure," she said, gloomily. "I hate feeling so, well . . . helpless."

Aethelred removed a small dagger that he kept concealed in his boot, and began carving the apple into smaller slices as he leaned against Kindle's flank. Unlike Gwendolyn, he had little interest in archery. Instead, he preferred a broadsword, and spent hours with the master of arms learning the finer points of using a blade. "I heard father say he's considering taking a ship north to look for the Steadfast Lady himself."

"Do you think he'll let us accompany him?" she asked.

"There's only one way to find out," said Aethelred, his cheeks bulging with fruit. "But first, you must come with me. Someone has asked to see you."

She looked at him, perplexed. "Who?"

He swallowed and wiped the dagger on his leggings. He was about to shove it back into his boot when he spotted the canvas target pinned to one of the hay bales that sat about ten yards away. "I'll tell you, but only if you can get closer to the bull's-eye than I can."

Gwendolyn smirked. "That'll be easy, especially since you never practice."

"Who says you need a bow?" He flipped the dagger in the air and caught it by the blade. Then, he flung it at the target, burying it just inside the circle of the bull's-eye.

"Pretty good," admitted Gwendolyn.

The boy lifted his chin, proudly. "You can't get much closer than that."

"Not much," she agreed.

Gwendolyn put an arrow on the bowstring and pulled it back until her fingers were touching her cheek. It had taken her more than a year to grow strong enough before her arm had stopped trembling from the draw weight. During that time, she had shot countless arrows, making small adjustments here and there, training her muscles to master the bow's dimensions. Now, her perseverance had paid off. She was deadly with a bow, especially at such a short range. Breathing slowly, she closed one eye, making sure her aim was true. Then, holding her breath, she grew still, and released the arrow. It landed an inch to the left of Aethelred's dagger—and dead center.

A perfect bull's-eye.

Aethelred clapped his hands. "Well done!" he said. "I knew you could do it."

Gwendolyn curtseyed, picking up her cloak with one hand while clutching the bow in the other. "Now, pray tell, who has requested the honor of my presence?"

"Polonius," he said. "He wants us to meet him near the entrance to the Low Road."

"Really?" she asked, growing serious. "Have he and the stonemasons finished? Do we finally get to see what they've been up to?"

"What else could it be?" said Aethelred. "But he said he wouldn't tell me until we were together. He said something about not wanting to repeat himself." The boy smiled. "At least no more than usual."

Kindle rose and flexed his wings before folding them again. "I must tell the king what I've learned from my journey," he said. "When I'm finished, I'll meet you there."

***

After returning her bow and quiver to her room, Gwendolyn met her brother in the castle's courtyard. Together they walked across the cobblestones beneath the archway of the south gate and hurried toward the center of town.

Ballan á Moor sat on the edge of a cliff that overlooked the sea. While its gilded spires and proud towers gleamed like jewels in the sun, it had not always been so. Only a few years earlier, a dragon named

Destiny had destroyed part of the castle and much of the village that surrounded it. Since then, the Valmarians had worked hard to repair the damage. Like Ballan á Moor itself, they had endured great hardship during that time, but as is so often the case with folk who choose to face their challenges, they had become stronger as a result.

Once the castle had been restored, they turned their attention to the Low Road, a great underground highway that connected Valmar's capital to Grimstad, the home of the Western Giants. The road provided a faster (and safer) way to trade goods between the two races, for the mountains and forests were filled with wild animals as well as other, fouler creatures that refused to be tamed. However, the trolls had damaged the tunnel that connected the castle to the Low Road, and it had required major repairs.

After speaking to the king, Polonius and the stonemasons began making changes to the tunnel. Instead of terminating underneath the castle as it once had, the Low Road's entrance would be accessible in the center of the village. Of course, this took time. The construction site stood for many months in the village square, covered in scaffolding, as the Valmarians worked to connect the new entrance with the tunnel below.

Though the children longed to see their progress, Polonius would not allow it. "You'll be the first to see it when it's finished," he promised. "In the meantime, it won't do for you two to be blundering about underground."

Now that day had come.

Gwendolyn and Aethelred made their way down the main road of the village, passing merchants preparing for the day's market. They walked past the bakery filled with freshly baked bread, shop windows displaying wheels of aged cheese, baskets of red apples, barrels of almonds and cashews, salted pork and fish that dangled from twine, and jars of honey neatly stacked on top of one another. Aethelred wanted to stop and sample some of the honey, but Gwendolyn wouldn't hear of it.

Finally, the children saw Polonius waiting for them in a large plaza. He was hard to miss, in part because he was a quarter giant, which made him the tallest man in the kingdom. Dressed in a brown cloak with a simple cord tied around his waist, he had a long, white beard that never seemed to grow any thinner. But the children knew better than to think him old and feeble. He could still move quickly, and was formidable in battle.

What really captured their attention, though, was not Polonius, but the strange building by which he stood. The scaffolding that had once surrounded the Low Road's entrance was gone. In its place stood a massive dome made of interlocking stones. The stonemasons had done their work well. The dome was perfectly round and smooth, save for a large, rectangular doorway framing an iron gate. The entrance was huge, twenty feet wide and nearly forty feet tall.

"That's the largest gate I've ever seen!" said Aethelred, admiring the structure. "But why make it so big?"

"Remember who we're dealing with," replied the old man. "We wouldn't want the giants stooping as they emerge from the Low Road. Besides, such a broad entrance will allow the villagers to bring along their carts and wagons." He swung open the gate, revealing a path that sloped downward. "Care for a tour?"

Wordlessly, the children followed him underground. The wooden retaining walls were lined with torches, which

Polonius had lit in anticipation of their arrival. After a modest descent, the path became level once again, and they found themselves standing in front of a series of broad archways supported by thick columns of stone.

"The arches must be under a lot of pressure," said Gwendolyn. "How can they bear so much weight?"

"It's called compression," explained Polonius. "The stones support each other, diverting the weight into the columns so that it doesn't collapse."

Gwendolyn looked up at her tutor, impressed by his knowledge. "How did you figure that out?"

"Geometry, of course." He gazed down on her, his eyes twinkling behind his bushy eyebrows. "The same subject that you sometimes dismiss as 'useless' if I remember correctly?"

She pursed her lips and folded her arms. "Now that I know it can be put to such good use, I may study harder."

"Glad to hear it," he said. "Now follow me. There's one more thing I want you to see."

He turned and continued underneath the series of archways, followed by the children. More torches lit the way, revealing walls with ornate, stone carvings. Aethelred was the first to notice the scenes depicting giants and men working together in friendship.

"I didn't know you were an artist," said Aethelred, letting his hand glide across the stone as he admired the skill it took to create images in such detail. "These are good." He pointed to one particular carving of an old man's bearded face that had a large nose protruding from the wall. "Forgive me, Polonius, but that looks like you!"

Polonius smiled. "I see you've discovered my little joke," he said. "You can think of it as a *signature* of sorts.

Mind you, many artists and stonemasons helped me build this entrance. I could never have done this alone."

When they reached the Low Road, the path flattened and widened, leading in both directions, accompanied by a narrow river that paralleled the tunnel. To their delight, they saw a wooden pier, with six small boats moored to the dock. Using the water, both men and giants could transport heavy loads up and down the river.

"You really did it, Polonius!" said Aethelred, excitedly. "Now we can even take a boat to the mountains!"

Gwendolyn frowned. "What if the Low Road should fall into enemy hands?" she asked. "Could it not be used to attack us?"

"Attack?" asked Aethelred. "Whom shall we fear? The trolls have retreated into the marshes, and the giants are our friends."

"Your sister's prudence does her credit," acknowledged Polonius. "All roads into Valmar should be defensible regardless of our present circumstances. But I have thought of that, too. Look up!"

They raised their eyes and noticed that a massive gate nested in the ceiling above. Save for the spikes that protruded from the ceiling, it was cunningly hidden.

"Is that what I think it is?" asked Gwendolyn.

"It's a portcullis," said the old man, proudly. "I devised it myself. If invaders were foolish enough to use the Low Road to attack us, they could be bottled up here below."

Aethelred looked around the tunnel, perplexed. "Where's the lever?"

Polonius smiled. "Remember the carving of my face you pointed out?" he said. "The one with the long nose?" The children nodded. "If you pull on it, the nose becomes a crank, which is connected to a series of gears behind the wall. Turn it six times clockwise and it lowers the gate."

"Amazing!" said Aethelred, his eyes shining with excitement.

Gwendolyn noticed the river. "What would prevent someone from diving into the water?" she asked. "Couldn't they swim under the portcullis?"

"Good question," said Polonius. "The gears also activate another gate underneath the river. Watch closely."

He walked back up the tunnel's entrance, pulled the nose out of the wall, and spun it six times. Not only did the portcullis lower silently from above, but a separate grill emerged from the side of the canal which fit into holes on the opposite side of the stream. This sealed off the rest of the tunnel while allowing the water to flow past.

Not for the last time, the children marveled at the old man who had taught them so much.

"With the Low Road improved and expanded, we can trade with the giants even more regularly," said Gwendolyn, looking at her brother. "We need to fill these boats up with blueberries and pay them a visit."

"Perhaps that's what has delayed the Steadfast Lady," said Aethelred. "Maybe Uncle Wulfric found a land filled with blueberries! Can you imagine how happy that would make the giants?"

"I hope he returns soon," said Gwendolyn. "It's been months . . . I'm starting to worry."

"If there's a man who can take care of himself, it's your uncle," replied Polonius, hopefully. "I don't think he *knows* how to worry."

2

A RUDE AWAKENING

Wulfric was worried.

He peered over the railing of the Steadfast Lady and shook his head. The shards of ice, floating on the water like pieces of a vast jigsaw puzzle, had grown more numerous by the day, making it difficult for him to find a way to the open sea.

"Spyglass!" he shouted. "Be quick about it!"

The slow, steady sound of ice crunching underneath the ship's keel hurt his ears as they journeyed northward. But that wasn't what really troubled him. It wasn't the thin sheets of ice that could rupture the ship's hull; it was the *icebergs*. Unfortunately, it was hard to tell the difference from where he stood. A piece of ice floating above the water could be much larger beneath the surface, flaring out in all directions, just waiting to tear a hole into any ship whose captain was foolish enough to sail too fast or too close to it.

A skilled sailor, Wulfric knew that patience was the ultimate virtue when sailing in northern waters. So he continued to take his time, giving the icebergs a wide berth, and sometimes even doubling back if he found the way to be too hazardous. If the ship's hull cracked, he knew the longboats would offer his crew of thirty-two men little chance of survival. Abandoning ship here meant they would simply die slowly from exposure rather than drowning in the icy waters.

"Where's my spyglass?" he demanded again, not taking his eyes from the ice that lay scattered across the water.

"I'm sorry, captain," said Melko, fumbling it out of his overcoat. "I couldn't hear you over the sound of this blasted ice. Is there no end to it?"

"That's what I'm trying to find out," replied Wulfric, taking the spyglass and holding it up to his eye.

Fog blanketed the northern horizon. Even if they were in sight of land, there was no way to know. Wulfric lowered the device and stared at the sky in frustration. It stared back at him, indifferently. It was up to him to find a way forward.

They had left Valmar more than three months before to explore the North Sea. But even by Wulfric's cautious reckoning, they had not come nearly as far as he had hoped. If they remained at sea much longer, they would risk being caught in the ferocious winter storms that were common in this part of the world. Still, the north beckoned. What was out here? What strange, new lands might he find?

He raised the spyglass to his eye once more. It was useless. The mist seemed as opaque as ever. Perhaps he should turn back, and try again next year? With no sign of land, it was madness to continue. He was about to give the order when the fog began to clear. Then, in the distance, he saw what he had been searching for.

"Land!" cried Wulfric. "Mountains! Ten degrees off the port bow! Land, I say!" He waved the spyglass around victoriously, barely missing his first mate's head.

"Are you sure?" asked Melko. "All I see are clouds."

Wulfric, his mood now much improved, smiled at the man's words. "Have a look yourself while I take the wheel." He handed Melko the instrument and adjusted the ship's course. "I know the difference between clouds and mountains."

Melko gazed into the spyglass and gasped. "I see them now, captain," he said. "White as the clouds themselves, but mountains they are."

Wulfric gazed north. "The question is—what will we find there, my friend?"

"Fresh meat, if we're lucky," said his first mate. "The men are tired of fish, lime, and hard biscuit. A few seals would be most welcome."

"I agree," said Wulfric. "However, I want to know what lies *beyond* the shoreline."

"Then, you still mean to go through with it?" asked Melko. "The landing party, I mean?"

"We've come this far, haven't we?" replied Wulfric. "Don't you want to know if the old tales are true?"

The first mate had difficulty hiding his skepticism. "If you're going to start telling children's stories again—"

"The gnomes were real, alive . . . once upon a time," said Wulfric, with a gleam in his eye.

"What makes you so sure? No one has seen one of those creatures for centuries."

"Perhaps not," said the captain. "But there is one who *has* seen something they left behind. What was the name of the merchant we met in Merovia? Bugby? Bartelby?"

"Bagby?"

"Yes, that's him! Bagby claimed to have met someone who saw a gnome not ten years ago."

"He was crazy," said Melko, dismissively, "not to mention drunk."

Wulfric smiled. "Sometimes, there is truth in wine, my friend."

"That still doesn't explain why you would trust his word. I overheard him tell Cillian that he was a fish in a former life." Melko paused. "Then again, he *drank* like one."

"It's true, he loved his rum," admitted Wulfric, rubbing his chin. "But one day, as I helped him finish a bottle in Moska, he gave me this." He pulled out a gold coin from his pocket and handed it to his first mate.

Melko examined it closely. "Is that a gnome's head?"

"What else could it be?" said Wulfric. "Ugly fellow, but he must have been important. They don't put just anyone's face on a coin."

"This could have been made anywhere . . . by anyone," objected Melko. "What makes you think this is real?"

Wulfric's expression grew serious. "Turn it over."

Stamped on the other side of the coin was a familiar mountain range. An enormous peak, with its top bent sharply to one side, rose up between two smaller mountains. Melko gasped and looked up. Though partially obscured by clouds, the same mountain range stood before him on the horizon. "The similarity is remarkable!" he said. "But why—"

"Why didn't I tell you before now?" guessed Wulfric. "Bagby said the creatures lived in the White Waste but I had to see it for myself, first."

"I don't suppose he gave you a map with that coin?"

Wulfric slapped him on the back. "No such luck," he said. "But it suggests that there were gnomes here once . . . and where there were gnomes, there could be gold."

Melko shrugged. "Even if they did leave piles of gold behind, it could be anywhere in those mountains," he said, looking anxiously at the ice that surrounded them. "And winter will be here soon."

"Where's your sense of adventure?" cried Wulfric, refusing to adopt his first mate's prudence. "We have come to *explore*, and that is exactly what I intend to do."

***

After they anchored the Steadfast Lady in a narrow bay, they gazed upon the mountains far to the north. The plains between the coast and the highlands looked much like the sea itself—blue and white, stretching away in all directions. Save for a few rocky patches of earth covered with moss and lichen, snow dominated the landscape. It was like they had entered a black and white world, where color was considered unnecessary, a luxury. Wulfric had initially hoped to hunt seals or sea lions to replenish the ship's food supplies. Instead, he saw nothing. Not even a seagull on the breeze accompanied them now.

The mountains didn't look any more inviting. Using his spyglass, he surveyed the summits, looking for any sign of civilization but he saw only more ice. The only thing that gave him hope was an alpine forest that sat nestled at the foot of those mountains. The trees promised protection from the wind and a closer look at the interior, but many miles of snow and arctic tundra still lay in between.

"How long do you think it will take to reach the trees?" asked Melko.

"Two days, perhaps," replied Wulfric. "Maybe three." He looked at his first mate. "But you'll stay with the ship. You're the best sailor we've got."

"But captain," protested Melko. "You're not going alone?"

"I'll ask for a few volunteers," said Wulfric. "We need to travel light and fast." He cast a quick glance at his first mate before gazing toward the mountains. "If we're not back in a week, you're to return to Valmar."

Melko frowned. "Without you? But—"

Wulfric pointed to the North Sea. "With each day that passes, the ice grows thicker," he said. "I will not allow our crew to get trapped here."

"Very well," replied the first mate, gloomily. "Just see that you *do* come back."

Wulfric chuckled. "I'll make it a priority."

***

The next morning, Wulfric and three others took a longboat ashore. Willom, a trusted lieutenant who had been a member of Wulfric's crew for years, was the first to volunteer. He seldom spoke, but was tough and reliable, and Wulfric trusted him implicitly. Fat, white-bearded Cillian, another veteran sailor, and his young friend Farin, a tall, lanky man that had not yet seen twenty winters, also offered to come. The two men couldn't have been more different in appearance and temperament yet they remained inseparable. (You may have witnessed this strange phenomenon about friendships in your own life.)

After waving to the crew, the four made their way toward the mountains. In addition to their swords, they each carried a horn of water, a week's worth of jerky, extra furs for warmth, and a small, canvas tent. Wulfric also brought a tinderbox, though he didn't really expect to find enough kindling for a fire. Even if he did, he doubted that he had the skill to keep the flames alive in the bitter cold.

After only a few miles, the low temperature began to take its toll. The men were dressed in thick, leather garments and fur cloaks, but the wind was relentless. It slowly chilled their hands and feet, hampering every step, buffeting them and numbing their faces. Still, they were men of Valmar. They wouldn't allow the elements to defeat them. Lowering their heads, they pressed onward.

By the late afternoon, they had travelled more than twelve miles. They stopped occasionally, looking for tracks or anything that would indicate civilization but they saw nothing. The snow swirled around their feet, the wind howled, and the mountains looked no closer. The tundra seemed to stretch on forever.

"Why would the gnomes choose to live in such a lonesome place?" asked Farin, as he trudged beside Cillian while Wulfric set the pace. Willom, as usual, followed last.

"Don't know about gnomes—but some bears love the cold," said Cillian. "Big 'uns, too. Over twelve feet tall they be when on their hind legs, and white as snow. They can run like the wind—and even swim like fish."

"Like fish ye say?" scoffed Farin. "Are ye tryin' to scare me or make me laugh? I s'pose they come with fins, too?"

"Now don't go mockin' me, lad," chided Cillian. "Bears can swim in Valmar, so why not here? How else are they s'posed to eat in these parts if they don't swim? Ice makes for a poor meal."

"It does, indeed," said Farin. "As does cold jerky." He licked his lips. "Maybe these bears dine on foolish fellows who go tromping about looking for gnomes that don't exist."

Cillian glanced ahead to see if Wulfric had heard his friend's words. If he had, he didn't show it. "Careful there, lad," cautioned Cillian, keeping his voice low. "Don't go disrespectin' the cap'n. He'll lead us home. Always has. Besides, ye volunteered to explore the mountains, ye did! Or have yer chatterin' teeth caused ye to forget that, too?"

"I remember, I remember," replied Farin, blowing into his gloves for warmth. "But what we hope to find is a mystery to me."

"*Most* things are a mystery to ye," said Cillian, "but that don't keep ye from sharin' yer opinions." Farin frowned in silence. "Look yonder now," continued the older sailor, motioning at the pine forest along the foothills in the distance. "We'll reach those trees by tomorrow afternoon, I reckon. They'll tame the wind, and help us quicken our pace into the mountains."

"Why?" asked Farin. "So we can see the rock and ice up close?"

"Gold," replied Willom. The old lieutenant had been walking behind them, listening to the conversation. "Have you not heard the tales? 'Twas the gnomes who first found the rich veins of gold in the north. They mined it for years, enduring the cold and the dark, and making themselves wealthy in the process."

"Then it's probably gone," said Farin. "Or why leave?"

Willom shook his head. "If the tales are true, they didn't leave willingly."

"What do ye mean?"

"It's been said that a darkness dwells in the north," replied the old lieutenant.

"Course darkness dwells here," said Farin. "It's *dark* half the year or more on account of the—"

"There ye go, interruptin' when a man's not finished!" cried Cillian.

"My apologies, lieutenant," said Farin, sheepishly. "What were ye sayin'?"

"According to the tales, none of the gnomes could see this darkness," continued Willom. "They *felt* it though, deep in the earth's bones, as if the mountain itself began to rot. A few of the creatures disappeared. Then more than a few, until they abandoned the gold altogether in great haste."

"It must have been terrible to abandon such a treasure," said Cillian.

"Terrible . . . and mysterious," said Willom.

A somber mood settled over the men as they trudged along in silence.

"Well," said Farin, at last. "After that tale, Cillian, yer white bears don't seem so bad."

"They be dangerous enough," said the old man. "But if ye want to take solace in something, just remember that if ye see one of the bears, you don't have to outrun it."

"What do ye mean?" asked Farin.

Willom simply smiled as he shouldered his pack. "He means you don't have to outrun the bear," he said. "You just have to outrun one of us."

***

As the sun began to sink behind the mountains, Willom peered at the dark clouds on the horizon.

"Captain," he said, trying to keep his teeth from chattering. "We won't reach the mountains tonight. Perhaps we should consider pitching our tents soon? The temperature will drop quickly once the sun has set."

Wulfric nodded in agreement. "You're right," he said, stopping. He looked around at the vast emptiness that surrounded them. "I had hoped to make better progress today but we will have to make do out in the open."

"I'll take first watch," said Cillian, removing his pack.

"No, I will," said Wulfric. "I'll wake you in four hours. We all need some rest if we're to make it to the trees tomorrow."

The men pitched their tents closely together for warmth and settled in for the night. Covered in furs, each man chewed his cold jerky, and wondered what the next day would bring. Would they find gnomes in the mountains? Long-abandoned gold? Or only more ice? Finally, the others fell asleep, leaving Wulfric alone to stand guard.

As he nodded off, Farin considered removing his shoes to rub his feet. But when he thought about what Cillian had told him about the bears, he decided to leave them on.

Just in case.

∗∗∗

It was not quite dawn when Wulfric awoke to the dull sound of marching feet. He had fallen asleep! He remembered sitting down for just a moment to rest his legs, but that was enough to allow his exhaustion to overwhelm him.

Cursing himself, he grabbed his sword and stumbled to his feet. He couldn't be sure, but he estimated about fifty creatures, cloaked and hooded, were trudging toward the camp, pulling a few sleds. They were no taller than children but some carried spears while others had crossbows strapped to their backs. Dressed in an odd assortment of wolf pelts and black leather, they approached in two separate columns. Stopping a short distance away, they cast off their hoods, and spoke to each other in a strange language.

They were all bald, with yellowish, lumpy heads that reminded Wulfric of ill-formed potatoes. Each had a large, bulbous nose that hung down like an elephant's trunk, and small eyes that disappeared into the folds of their faces. Strangest of all, the creatures bore black marks on each of their foreheads. Wulfric swallowed hard. He hoped it wasn't war paint.

He woke the others with a shout. Soon, his men stood beside him, clutching their weapons warily in the cold but they knew against such numbers, fighting was out of the question. Wulfric suspected they could outrun the short creatures but where would they go? They would die from exposure just as easily as they would a blade.

"That's close enough," he said, raising his sword and pointing it at the foremost creature, whose eyes were as tiny and crooked as a goat's. Wulfric realized this gesture was absurd for they had come no closer, but he didn't want to appear frightened. "Who are you?"

The creature took a few steps forward. "I am Kaag," he said, touching his nose before holding his hand out, palm upward, which Wulfric guessed was a customary greeting. "We are naradi."

"Naradi?"

"People of the tool," said Kaag. "In the common tongue, gnomes."

The men gasped. Was it possible? Even those who believed gnomes were real, like Wulfric, thought they had disappeared long ago, never to be seen again. Some said they were the estranged kindred of dwarves, for both were short, stout, and made their homes deep in the earth. But unlike dwarves, gnomes did not hoard treasure. They hoarded *knowledge*. They used it to design things, build things, tinker with things, producing all manner of gadgets and contraptions. Unfortunately, most of these inventions remained a mystery. You see, gnomes were as a rule shy and reclusive, and once finished with an invention, were content to put it on a shelf rather than to use it.

Others said that the gnomes were born from the earth itself, animated and given life by ancient, elemental magic. Their rough, creased skin and slow, ponderous movements made them look like small boulders rolling slowly across the tundra. Whatever their origin, they hadn't been seen for centuries.

"What do you want with us?" asked Wulfric, guardedly. The creatures didn't appear hostile, but he had to assume the worst.

"Want with you?" asked the gnome, perplexed.

"You approached us armed, and as we slept," he began.

"Ah," said Kaag. "I see. You are afraid of us?"

"Not afraid!" shouted Farin. He stepped forward and raised his sword. If the gnomes took offense at his words, they showed no sign of it. Instead, they stood as still as stone, examining Wulfric and his men with curiosity.

41

"Hush, you fool!" said Cillian, pulling Farin backwards.

"We mean you no harm," said Wulfric, quickly, hoping it wouldn't come to a fight. "We are explorers from a land called Valmar. If we trespassed on your land, we—"

"Trespassed?" said the gnome. Then a look of understanding dawned on his uneven, pock-marked face. "Of course! A southern notion. You think we *own* the land?"

Wulfric frowned. "You live here, do you not?"

"Yes, but we do not claim it exclusively," explained the gnome. "What purpose does that serve other than to create resentment? No, we do not own this land any more than the fish own the sea or the birds own the air. We are simply part of it."

"Where do you live?" asked Wulfric. "How do you survive in this wretched place?"

Kaag nodded towards the mountains. "We make our home in the Daggers. That is what we call the highlands to the north. We only come to the surface to hunt."

Wulfric spied a number of seal carcasses and large fish strapped across the sleds that accompanied the creatures. It had been too long since they had tasted anything but jerky. Kaag noticed the men looking at the fresh meat hungrily.

"The sun is rising," said the gnome. "When we saw you, we were about to take a short respite and eat." He rubbed his hands together. "Would you care to join us?"

Wulfric took a deep breath. The gnomes looked peaceful enough but if they really were hostile, there was nowhere to run. Besides, he was anxious to learn more about this strange folk, and how they had managed to remain hidden for so long.

"We would be honored," he said, with a slight bow.

The men watched as the gnomes busily prepared breakfast. One of the creatures dug a pit in the ice while another filled it with coal, arranging the pieces neatly at the bottom. When they had finished, a third took a vial of green liquid out of his jacket and poured it across the surface of the black, lumpy objects.

"You're wasting your time," said Farin, examining the process with bemusement. "It's impossible to start a fire in this cold."

Ignoring the young man, one of the creatures produced a rod of flint and scraped it against his blade. Farin watched as a few small sparks fell into the pit. Almost immediately, green flames began to grow. They climbed upward, impervious to the wind, fueled by something the men had never before seen. Farin smiled sheepishly at the gnomes. Clearly, they knew how to survive here.

Soon, seal meat was crackling over the fire as the group sat in a circle, warming themselves around the flames. While his men helped themselves to large slabs of fat (which is quite good if done correctly—just ask an Eskimo), Wulfric sought out Kaag.

"How many of you are there?" he asked. "Why have you remained hidden? Why do you choose to live here?"

Kaag's mouth seemed to pucker, which Wulfric guessed was a smile. The gnome produced a pipe stuffed with tobacco, and lit it with a small coal from the fire.

"It has been many years since we have seen men," he admitted, taking a short puff. "I have forgotten how curious you are. Curious and impatient." He cast a quick look at Farin before turning his eyes back to Wulfric. "You remind me of how we once were. So young. So deceived by the world. So divided by what it means." He took another puff on his pipe, and remained silent, as if meditating on these things.

Farin, listening intently with the others, couldn't help himself. "Just how old are you?"

Kaag looked up at the sun, which had appeared over the eastern horizon. "As old as the mountains."

Farin's eyes narrowed. "That's impossible."

"Impossible?" said the gnome. "Are the mountains impossible?" He motioned to the icy pinnacles that sat brooding in the distance. "For there they stand."

"Let him finish," said Wulfric, annoyed by the interruption.

"Long ago, when the earth was still young, we dwelled in an underground city, Feigaard, far to the east in the land now called Quintharia. The city's fame is still remembered as one of the world's wonders."

"I have heard of this place," said Wulfric, "though I had always understood it to be just one more tale told to those foolish enough to believe such things. In your language it means 'Fortress of Many Voices,' does it not?"

"It does indeed," said Kaag, who nodded approvingly. "Feigaard was real enough. It was built in the heart of the mountain out of living rock."

"Living rock?" asked Cillian.

"Yes," said the gnome. "The earth is not dead. It's alive, always moving, shifting, *growing*. You just have to be patient enough to see it. Long ago, our granite walls could heal themselves, regenerate, when besieged."

"Besieged by what?" asked Wulfric. "By whom?"

44

"All who coveted our inventions," explained Kaag. "The slimaks—I believe you call them trolls—were ever a threat. But so were boggarts, bygorns, tritans, truffleheads . . . and snopes." The rest of the gnomes shuddered and looked at one another in dismay. "The snopes, with their five legs and forked tongues, were particularly wicked. All attacked Feigaard over the years. All were repelled."

"Trolls I know, but the others—I've never heard of such things!" exclaimed Wulfric.

"Be thankful you haven't," said Kaag, taking another puff of his pipe. "We killed most of them many years ago. Only the slimaks seem to have survived. They breed too quickly." He exhaled slowly and watched the smoke curl upwards. "But while we were busy fighting the enemy along our ramparts, an even greater enemy was being born from within."

"Civil war?" asked Cillian.

Kaag nodded. "No foe had ever succeeded in breaching Feigaard's fortifications. But as the attacks continued, so did the debates about what to do. Eventually, two factions sprang up, dividing the city . . . and our race. Some argued that we should use our great wealth to pay for mercenaries. With their help, we could pursue our enemies beyond the walls, putting an end to them. Others argued that our wealth and ingenuity were precisely the problem. We had grown too rich, too decadent. If we gave away our things and chose to live simply, we would no longer be a target for plunder."

Wulfric noticed the silence in the camp. All of the gnomes were listening intently to the story, their small eyes sparkling out of the shadows of their hoods.

"Both sides made many eloquent speeches," continued Kaag. "Both claimed to know what was best for Feigaard. Many nights we watched our leaders deliberate, promising a solution to our problems, but in the end we turned against one another, and the civil war came. We learned too late that it was freedom itself that caused all of our trouble."

The gnomes muttered to themselves as they quietly recalled their own experiences during the war.

"It was a hard time," sighed Kaag. "As we fought amongst ourselves, our high walls still protected us from our enemies. But one night, the main gate was opened from *within*."

He stopped abruptly, as if afraid his voice would crack. The other gnomes stirred, gazing up at Kaag, wondering if he would continue.

"Those who opened the gates were never discovered in the chaos that followed—but it wouldn't have mattered," he said, mastering his emotions. "The slimaks ran through our city, murdering and plundering, setting fire to our homes and shrines, leaving not one stone on another. Feigaard, which had stood for thousands of years, fell in a single day."

Wulfric shook his head sadly. He remembered how the trolls had once threatened Valmar, and shuddered to think what would have happened had they been successful in breaching the walls of Ballan á Moor.

"I am sorry," he replied. "How were you able to survive?"

"A remnant of the naradi, some of which you see here, fought our way outside of Feigaard's walls and made it to the surface, into the morning light. That was what allowed us to escape," explained Kaag.

"I don't understand," Farin admitted. "What does the sun have to do with it?"

"Do you not know that slimaks hate the sun, venturing above ground only if necessary?" asked the gnome.

"Unfortunately, yes," said Wulfric. "We have had to fight trolls—er, slimaks, ourselves. They are a constant danger, and plague many lands."

"Many lands, but not all," said Kaag, looking around. "We rejoiced when we came here. Unlike Quintharia, this place—the Veerda—is free from our old enemies. Wolves and bears are nothing by comparison. We have sworn never to fight one another again, and the bitter cold has proven a greater defense than even the mighty walls of Feigaard."

"How did you learn to survive?" asked Cillian. "What do you do for food? For warmth?"

"The north is cold . . . always cold." Kaag rose to stoke the fire. "But deep under the Daggers, where we have tunneled, it is warm." He glanced up at them. "As you see, we live on seal meat and fish, mainly, and have even learned to make beer by fermenting a hardy type of weed that grows here in the north. In the mountains, well fed and well provisioned, we have grown strong again."

"You could not have known this place was so accommodating before you came here," acknowledged Wulfric. "Why did you choose to go north?"

To Wulfric's surprise, some of the gnomes laughed. "Did I say something funny?" he asked, looking around at the creatures with a furrowed brow.

"You'll have to forgive us," chuckled Kaag. "You must understand, we did not *choose*. Like you, we once thought in that way for that is what free creatures do. Now we know that we were guided."

"Guided?" said Wulfric. "By what?"

"Fate."

The men could not hide their looks of astonishment.

"Fate?" scoffed Wulfric.

Kaag nodded. "I understand that it is difficult to believe. I was once skeptical, too." He smiled and blew a smoke ring that quickly dissipated in the cold air. "But no longer."

"I don't understand," said Wulfric.

"As we tunneled under the Daggers, digging down into the roots of the mountain, we discovered something buried there. A shell of sorts, but much more than a shell." His eyes glistened at the memory before he turned to Wulfric. "We naradi pride ourselves on our craftsmanship. But when we discovered this *radu*—this stone—we knew that we had found an intelligence that surpassed our own."

"Stone?" said Wulfric. "I thought you called it a shell."

"It is both, and yet so much more," said Kaag, shivering as he spoke. "As we drew near with our torches, we discovered it contained a being."

"A man?"

Kaag shook his head as the gnomes surrounding them snickered again. "Nothing so weak," he said. "A force of nature. Perhaps an element—or a god. We call him Asmodeus. Like us, he comes from the earth itself."

Wulfric narrowed his eyes. "And this Asmodeus . . . means to do what, exactly?"

"He tamed the passions that made us weak, divided," said Kaag. "He will restore order, crush dissent, until there is only one truth, and one peace." The gnomes around him nodded approvingly. "Under his leadership, we have built a city even mightier than Feigaard."

He got to his feet and, raising both hands, gestured to the mountains. "Whereas Feigaard meant 'Fortress of Many Voices' this new city is called Skarsgaard or 'Fortress of One Voice.' The disagreements amongst the naradi are over. We are united. Soon, the strife that still exists between creatures everywhere will be a sad memory. Order, perpetual order, is at hand. That is what Asmodeus has promised, and we will help him fulfill that promise."

A disturbing chill ran up Wulfric's spine. "I thought you had grown tired of fighting?"

Kaag smiled. "I said we would never again fight *one another*. But if we must endure more violence so that others may know peace, we are willing to do so. When we have conquered all who oppose us, the world will be truly free. Free from responsibility. Free from fear. It is a small price to pay for such a noble achievement, is it not?"

As the gnome finished speaking, Wulfric and the others heard the sounds of barking in the distance. They stood up, and saw a pack of wolves harassing and harrying a group of men approaching from the south. The wolves didn't seem to be attacking the men as much as herding them.

Kaag said something in his language to the others and they spread out, clutching their spears. Were they under attack? Then Wulfric noticed that the gnomes stood facing the fire, surrounding him and his three men.

Wulfric looked at the others who were drawing closer. His eyes widened in surprise. Those were *his* men—the

Steadfast Lady's crew. Their hands had been bound. The wolves pranced around the group, yelping and snapping at the stragglers as they hurried forward. Another group of gnomes, also carrying spears, followed behind.

The men, driven mercilessly in the snow, were finally allowed to stop. Several of them sank to their knees, panting for breath, just outside the camp. Wulfric recognized his first mate among them.

"Melko?"

His face bloodied and bruised, Melko gazed up at Wulfric. "I'm afraid they were . . . quite persuasive, captain," he said, trying to catch his breath.

Wulfric turned on Kaag in a rage. "What is the meaning of this?" he cried. "What have we done that you treat my people thus?" As he spoke, he tried to draw his sword but a blow to the back of his head sent him sprawling. The others were also similarly disarmed.

"Men are so predictably violent," replied Kaag. "We would like it if you and your men came willingly. But willingly or no, you will return to the Daggers with us where Asmodeus is waiting to meet you. For as I said, we are all meant to be one."

3

RESCUE PARTY

When Polonius and the children emerged from the Low Road, they found Kindle waiting for them.

"Oh Kindle!" cried Gwendolyn as she ran up to him. "Isn't it magnificent?"

"It is, indeed," he said, admiring the dome's entrance. "What will you think of next, Polonius? Flying chariots?"

The old man smiled modestly. "An intriguing idea," he mused. "But if it comes to flight, there is nothing that can match you, my friend. How did you find Lord Dravius?"

"Very well, though he has not seen the Steadfast Lady," said the dragon. "I have just spoken to the king and queen." He gazed down at the children. "Your father has made up his mind. He means to look for the Steadfast Lady at once."

Kindle excused himself to hunt (dragons eat even more frequently than boys), and Polonius and the children returned to the castle, where they found the king in his study hunched over a map, consulting the queen and two veteran sailors. As they waited for them to finish, Gwendolyn and Aethelred learned that their father had ordered the kingdom's newest ship, the Fearless Finn, to be made ready for the long voyage to the North Sea. Built to protect Valmar's merchant ships, it was named in honor of the brave mermidian who had sacrificed his life to save the children—and what a ship it was. A two-hundred ton vessel, boasting three masts and over twenty cannons, it was the pride of Valmar. While not as fast as the Steadfast Lady, it was certainly the largest in the fleet.

Argus dismissed the sailors, and waved Polonius and the children forward. Assuming they would be forbidden from going on the journey, the children had prepared many arguments to the contrary. Regarding the king and queen with great seriousness, Gwendolyn started the assault.

"Father, we have plenty of experience at sea—"

"Uncle Wulfric taught us how to navigate by the stars," interrupted Aethelred. "I've also made great strides as a swordsman, if it should come to combat—"

"And I don't need to remind you how accurate I am with a bow," said his sister.

"Besides, they are our people, too!" pleaded the boy. "We—"

The king smiled and looked at the queen before holding up his hand. The children grew silent. "Well, of course you're coming," he said. "You're almost grown. Besides, you both have more experience than many of my knights."

Gwendolyn was astonished. "You mean it?"

Argus put his hand on her shoulder. "I have plenty of things to worry about," said the king. "The disappearance of the Steadfast Lady. The autumn harvest. Navigating the treacherous North Sea." He gazed at both children thoughtfully. "But you? You've proven yourselves time and time again. Besides, what would Kindle do without you?"

"He's coming, too?" asked Aethelred.

The queen smiled. "He agreed to accompany us this morning—as have I, for if Wulfric and the others are hurt, your father believes I may be of service."

"The gryphons taught your mother well," replied the king, proudly. "There's no better healer in the kingdom." He turned to his wife and looked at her affectionately. "Eldon tells me you're almost his equal in herbology."

"He exaggerates, my lord."

"Nonsense!" scoffed Argus. "Have you ever known a gryphon to spare one's feelings? I hope your skills won't be necessary but if they are needed, I want you by my side."

Thelda beamed at the compliment. "I can think of no place I'd rather be."

Argus looked up at Polonius. "Which leaves you, old friend," he said. "I trust you'll manage things while we're gone? We should return in six weeks at the very latest."

Polonius bowed. "Of course, my lord." He turned to the children. "I'm afraid your next geometry lesson will have to wait."

Gwendolyn and Aethelred smiled at one another, but their happiness quickly faded.

"Oh, I wouldn't say that, Polonius," said the queen, putting an arm around both of them. "I'll oversee their studies personally on the ship."

The children groaned.

"Pack your books quickly then," replied Argus. "We sail at dawn."

***

The Fearless Finn, aided by a strong wind, departed the next morning. Accompanied by twenty-eight experienced sailors, the children and their parents were confident they would find the Steadfast Lady. Perhaps it had something to do with the dragon who glided alongside of them. Not only could Kindle see for miles from the air, he could also scout ahead as they travelled north. But what would they discover? A damaged Steadfast Lady, floating listlessly among the waves? Or would they find her trapped in ice? They didn't know. Whatever the reason, they were anxious to find their countrymen, and bring them home. They sailed with a great sense of urgency, for every day that passed meant the possibility of stronger storms and rougher waters.

Argus spent most of his time on deck. Using a compass and rudimentary navigational charts, he would occasionally confer with his officers to determine which route Wulfric and his crew might have taken when they made the same journey. Other times he grew restless, ordering a sailor to trim a sail or alter course slightly, even if it had little effect. Most often, he would simply pace the deck in silence, gazing out at the vast horizon, hoping for some sign of the Steadfast Lady.

The children shared a room below the quarterdeck at the rear of the ship. Like the rest of the Fearless Finn, it was large for a ship's quarters, with two mahogany beds, adjoining closets, a washbasin, mirror, a table, two chairs, and a lantern that swung unceasingly from the ceiling. Perhaps the best part of the room was the fact that the rear wall contained a number of small, glass portholes, allowing for an expansive view of the sea.

Unfortunately, Gwendolyn and Aethelred had to be satisfied with this view for most of the first few days of the journey while Thelda, seated beside them, patiently guided them through a number of subjects. These included geometry, astronomy, navigation, grammar, rhetoric, and philosophy.

True to her word, Gwendolyn tried a bit harder in geometry now that Polonius had shown her how useful it could be. Using her slate and a few axioms, she scratched out her sums, discovering the areas of triangles and circles that were previously unknown to her. To her surprise, she rather enjoyed it. Geometry reminded her of a puzzle. With a limited amount of information, she could deduce much more about the shapes in front of her, and fill in the blanks. She thought of the columns and arches that supported the Low Road, and wondered if someday she would have the skill to improve it just as Polonius had done.

However, when the lessons turned to philosophy, she became frustrated.

"I don't understand," she said. "What's a fallacy again?"

"A mistaken belief, founded on a poorly reasoned argument," explained her mother.

"You mean like confining us to our room while everyone else gets to enjoy the fresh air on deck?" grumbled Aethelred.

"Very funny," replied Thelda. "Though you've provided a good example of a fallacious technique."

"I have?"

"You tried to win support for your idea by exploiting my feelings of pity," she said. "Though it may win you points for rhetoric, it doesn't give me a good reason to excuse you before you've finished your lesson."

"I still don't understand why we need to *study* philosophy, mother," grumbled Gwendolyn, crossing her arms, and leaning back in her chair. "Isn't it obvious that we're all born with the ability to reason?"

"Yes," replied Thelda, "but we can be misled. Sound reasoning must be practiced because poor reasoning needs to be answered."

Gwendolyn still looked skeptical.

"Think of it like geometry," explained Thelda, noticing her daughter's slate was filled with shapes and numbers. "You used axioms to find angles previously unknown in that triangle, correct?"

"You mean like 'things which are equal to the same thing are also equal to one another?'"

"That's right," replied Thelda. "A good philosopher begins with what she knows, and then uses it to discover the unknown—or at least things that may not be immediately obvious."

"Such as?"

The queen thought for a moment. "Well, let's start with a general observation. Can we agree that all women are mortal?"

"Of course," said Gwendolyn.

"Okay," said the queen. "And I am a woman, am I not?"

"Obviously."

"If both statements are true, then we can deduce that I am mortal."

Aethelred shrugged. "That seems pretty easy."

"It does," admitted his mother, "but we must be careful. We often make untested assumptions which can lead us to false conclusions. For instance, let's say that I told you we brought a raven on board, and it's in your father's quarters right now happily pecking away at a pile of seeds on his desk. What color would you say it was?"

The boy didn't hesitate. "Black," he said.

Thelda smiled. "How do you know?"

"All ravens are black," explained Gwendolyn, impatiently. "Everyone knows that."

"You mean all the ravens you've ever *seen* are black," replied Thelda. "Does that mean that there can't be a white raven?"

Gwendolyn looked puzzled. "No, but isn't it reasonable to assume it's black . . . you know . . . based on experience?"

"It is," said her mother. "But we must always remember to acknowledge our assumptions, even if they are reasonable. Which brings us to the most important philosophical lesson of all."

"What's that?" asked Aethelred, intrigued.

"We must recognize the limits of our own knowledge. It's fine, even admirable, to admit when you don't know something. But claiming to know something with certainty if you don't—that's more dangerous than ignorance. Philosophy helps us identify what we know compared to what we simply *assume*. It's important to remember the difference."

***

The children didn't spend all of their time studying. They were permitted to walk the deck in the afternoons where they could stretch their legs and enjoy the sun's warmth on their faces. As they settled into this routine, they quickly became friends with a few sailors, peppering them with questions. The men were impressed by their knowledge, and were happy to explain in detail when to trim the sails, why the hull needed to be cleaned of barnacles regularly, how to gauge the speed of the ship, and many other things. Thanks to a steady north wind, they had already travelled more than four hundred miles which was even better progress than Argus had dared to hope.

One afternoon, as the sun began its slow descent toward the western horizon, casting the ship in golden light, Gwendolyn and Aethelred found their father on the quarterdeck.

"How many more days until we reach the North Sea, father?" asked Aethelred.

"Two weeks if the wind holds," he replied, glancing at the children before gazing out to sea. "However, I'm not overly familiar with those waters, nor was your uncle."

"Perhaps it's time to send Kindle on ahead," suggested Aethelred, looking up at the dragon floating in and out of the clouds above. "He has to be bored pacing us."

"I was going to ask him to save his strength until we've gone a bit farther," explained the king. "But winter is almost here, and I'd like to know what we're sailing into."

"Why not start now?" said Gwendolyn. "Today?"

"What?"

"He can take Aethelred and me north—just for a couple of hours."

"I don't know" began Argus, doubtfully, looking up at the sun. "It's already past noon."

"All the more reason not to waste time," she replied.

"What if the Steadfast Lady is just beyond the horizon?" added Aethelred.

"Very well," Argus conceded. "Be quick about it. I expect you back before sunset."

***

Clinging to the dragon's shoulders, the children watched the Fearless Finn slowly disappear over the horizon. Soon, it was just the three of them above the vast, blue sea. They felt the dull throb of Kindle's heartbeat against their chests as well as the great muscles at work underneath his scales. They looked at each other and smiled. Never did they feel more alive than when they were flying with Kindle.

The only problem was the wind. As the dragon raced across the sky, the wind blew straight into their faces, causing their eyes to water if they attempted to stare directly ahead. They solved this by looking from side to side, which offered some respite, while allowing them to scan the sea in multiple directions.

"Do either of you see anything?" asked the dragon.

"Water," replied Aethelred. "Lots and lots of water."

"Wait," said Gwendolyn, squinting into the beams of the sinking sun as she pointed straight ahead. "What's that?"

Beating his wings, Kindle climbed higher. On the horizon, they could see a small island almost totally covered in fog. Here and there, tall mountains rose out of the mist before disappearing again like ghosts, obscured by the white haze. They all recognized the place immediately.

Cloud Isle.

It had been nearly two years since they had seen the island. Aethelred's hands tingled as he remembered his strange encounter with a creature he met there that called itself the Malodoi. It convinced him that by using its power, he would become strong, invincible. Instead, it tried to enslave the boy to its will, physically becoming a part of him until another being, Oorano, expelled it— and restored Aethelred's life.

Still, Aethelred was anxious. He felt as if he were trespassing here, as if something slumbered on the island that was better left undisturbed. Sensing the boy's uneasiness, Kindle slowed his pace, unsure of whether or not to proceed. Gwendolyn's eyes, however, sparkled at the discovery.

"Why are we slowing?" she asked. "Can't we get closer?"

"I don't think father would want us coming back here alone—" began Aethelred.

"We wouldn't set foot on it," she insisted. "We'd just investigate the shores. Perhaps we'll find some mermidians! Wouldn't that be wonderful?" Her face brightened. "Or maybe the Steadfast Lady has made anchor there. How will we know if we don't go closer? You know, beyond the fog."

Reluctantly, Aethelred agreed.

"Very well," said Kindle. "We'll take a look."

As they approached the island, the fog seemed to grow thicker, as if someone had drawn a veil across the sky, refusing to let them pass. The white tendrils clung to them and then slowly dissolved but not before the children felt a chill enter their bones. Soon, they emerged through the wall of fog and into weak sunshine.

Cloud Isle was just as they had remembered it. The trees, with their strange roots sinking into the water, grew so closely together along the island's edge that it was difficult to see the interior. The jungle was equally impenetrable. A few palm trees sprouted out of the rest of the vegetation while some brightly colored parrots flitted in and out of view.

The children glanced at each other knowingly as they spied a few giant snail shells embedded in a small, sandy cove. The shells were similar to those they had used to walk along the ocean floor when they helped the mermidians defeat the sea serpent. But that seemed like ages ago. Now, they saw no sign of the Steadfast Lady or anyone else

"We can't simply give up," pleaded Gwendolyn. "We have to keep looking, right Aeth?" She noticed for the first time that he looked worried. "Are you okay?"

He nodded. "I just don't think we should stay too much longer," he replied. He hated to show fear in front of his sister, but he felt like something was watching them.

"But don't you want to know the secrets of this place?" she demanded.

Aethelred didn't need to be reminded how they had once found an ancient ring of stones on the island. At first, the stones appeared to be normal. But he soon realized that nothing about this place really made sense. The stones turned out to be ethereal, mere projections, as if rooted in another world. He remembered touching one of them and being transported to a place where trees and snakes could talk, and where a thing that claimed to be his friend was really his enemy. Mostly, though, he remembered being afraid. He had no desire to experience it all again.

He looked up and found his sister staring at him. "Aren't you curious?" she asked.

The question seemed to echo in his mind, as if he had heard it before. "Not curious enough to postpone our search for the others," he said, firmly. "We mustn't forget them."

She gazed up at the large mountains that encircled the island. "Who said anything about postponing our search?" she replied, innocently. "I want to find them as much as you do. Perhaps they're up there . . . in the mountains?"

"I thought you just wanted to investigate the coast?" said Kindle. "We've circled the island. If the Steadfast Lady was anchored here, we'd have seen it."

Gwendolyn shrugged. She knew it was unlikely to find anyone here but her curiosity had grown considerably in just a short amount of time. It was as if the jungle was beckoning to her, calling on her to discover its secrets. Was the ring of stones still here? What other mysteries did Cloud Isle keep? She was about to plead for one more chance when her brother spoke.

"Please, Gwen," he said, putting his hand on her shoulder. "Let's go back."

"Why?" she asked, annoyed. Was she the only one who wanted to continue the adventure? Why was her brother always so hesitant?

Aethelred clenched and unclenched his right hand as if remembering an old wound. "Can't you feel it?"

"What?"

"This island," he replied. "It feels alive somehow."

"Well of course it's alive," said Gwendolyn. "The jungle has grown since we were last here, and the birds seem to be doing quite well. As for the—"

"That's *not* what I mean," he said. "I feel like we're, well, we're intruding."

"On whom?" demanded Gwendolyn, looking up and down the empty coast and trying to sound indifferent. "The snails?"

"On your brother's memories at the very least," growled Kindle, sensing the boy's discomfort. "I know what it's like to be haunted by something that you'd rather forget."

"Fine," sighed Gwendolyn, casting a last glance at Cloud Isle before the fog shrouded it once again from view. She was determined to return one day, with or without the others.

As Kindle turned back toward the Fearless Finn, Aethelred asked him a question. "What do you mean? What would you rather forget?"

"I've been having a dream lately," explained the dragon. "It always starts out the same. It's cold and dark, and I'm flying in the night sky. The stars are beautiful, but I don't recognize the constellations. Colors appear in the darkness, swirling and dancing, setting the heavens on fire. I see other strange things but mostly, I feel alone."

"But you're not alone," replied Gwendolyn. "You have us."

"What if you hadn't found me?" he continued. "Would I have chosen to be like my mother? Would I be wicked?"

"I think you'd be exactly who you are," said Gwendolyn. "Our friend."

Aethelred nodded in agreement. "Not a bad mode of transportation, either."

Gwendolyn punched him in the shoulder.

"What?" he said.

Kindle climbed higher into the air as the sun sank toward the horizon. He was grateful for the children. They had taught him so much. Still, he felt that his dreams did not bode well for the future. He couldn't explain it, but he guessed that a trial was coming—a trial that he wasn't sure he would pass.

4

FOOTSTEPS IN THE SNOW

Ten days later, the Fearless Finn reached the North Sea. The strong southerly wind allowed her to travel faster than they had anticipated, and she skipped lightly over the waves. But things soon changed. With every league, the air became noticeably colder, and the water more treacherous. Small chunks of ice began to appear on the surface, forcing Argus to trim the sails. The children now awoke to frosty portholes.

When they strolled the deck in the afternoons, they marveled at the sea life that surrounded the ship. The animals were quite different from those in Valmar's waters. Creatures that looked like seals (only larger, with thick whiskers and huge tusks) surfaced from time to time, gazing up at them curiously before disappearing again beneath the waves. Occasionally, the children spotted enormous whales which dove in and out of the water. Colored black and white, they travelled in packs and had sharp teeth. Argus explained that he had seen them before as a boy, and that his father had called them "the wolves of the sea."

The whales never came too close, which may have had something to do with Kindle. The dragon paddled in front of the ship, making a way through the ice floes that seemed to grow thicker and more numerous by the day. His thick hide made him impervious to the cold, and he enjoyed lowering his head and smashing the large, frozen sheets as he propelled himself forward with his tail.

As amazed as they were by the sea life, Gwendolyn and Aethelred were equally impressed by the towering icebergs that floated nearby. Some were as large as small islands, while others barely rose a few feet from the water. Nevertheless, large or small, Argus wisely ordered his crew to lower the main sails, slowing the ship while Kindle led them through the water.

After only a few leagues at this slower pace, Aethelred became frustrated. "Why can't we go any faster, father?" he asked. "I understand that we have to be cautious around the larger icebergs, but all I see ahead of us now is a little ice."

"A little ice, you say?" scoffed his father. "Don't be fooled by appearances, Aethelred. We can only see part of every iceberg. Most of the ice is *below* the water. I assure you, they can be as strong as stone. If it weren't for Kindle, we would be forced to go even slower."

"But our hull is thick, made out of solid oak and ringed with iron cleats," persisted the boy. "It may be scratched by the ice . . . but breached?"

"Breached and sunk," said the king. "Extremely cold temperatures cause things to become brittle, including iron cleats. The colder something is, the less flexible it becomes, making it easier to crack."

Suddenly, a voice called out from the crow's nest. "Land!" shouted the sailor. "Land to starboard!"

Everyone rushed to the side of the ship. Barely visible, was the dark, uneven horizon that could only be land.

Walking to the bow, the king peered down at Kindle who remained in the water directly ahead of them. "Kindle," he asked. "Would you be so good as to fly ahead and see what there is to see? We'll wait here until you return."

"Certainly," replied the dragon. He sprang into the air, the cold water streaming off his scales, and soared away.

The children remained on deck and huddled together for warmth, awaiting his return. Looking back, they saw a trail of dark blue water behind them where Kindle had broken the ice. The rest of the sea had almost frozen. If the Steadfast Lady *had* made it this far, it would be almost impossible to return without Kindle's help. Had Uncle Wulfric really come this way? If so, how long could he and the other men survive here? As if responding to the children's thoughts, the wind moaned ominously.

After less than an hour, Kindle reappeared. He was flying swiftly, anxious to tell them his news. "I have found the Steadfast Lady!" he said, hovering above them. "She is anchored along the coast, trapped in the ice, several miles to the west."

"And her crew?" asked Argus, hopefully.

The dragon shook his head. "There's not a soul aboard."

The sailors began to mumble. "This land is cursed," said one, as he spit into the sea. "We should turn back before we share the same fate."

"Nonsense," replied Argus. He strode to the railing of the forecastle and addressed his men. "These are your countrymen and mine. We will *not* abandon them."

"But sire, we haven't prepared for a journey inland," explained another sailor. "We lack the necessary provisions."

Others nodded.

"Did I say anything about leaving the ship?" asked Argus. "We can sail along the coast before the ice grows too thick."

With Kindle continuing to lead the way, they meandered northward. The sea was almost totally frozen now. Narrow ribbons of blue separated the large, flat sheets of ice that floated calmly on the water, disturbed only by the dragon's limbs. Kindle allowed them to avoid the larger icebergs, some of which rose out of the water like silent cathedrals, pushing them out of the way with his head. Nevertheless, the ship's hull scraped past large chunks of ice regularly, creating a dull, grinding noise that set everyone's teeth on edge.

After sailing in this fashion for most of the afternoon, they finally saw the Steadfast Lady. She sat in a narrow cove about a mile away, trapped in ice. Save for a few hills, the land surrounding her was flat, interrupted only by the mountains far in the distance, which rose up like an enormous wall. Unfortunately, the sun began to fade before they could reach the ship. Soon, it was too dark to navigate. The Steadfast Lady sat tantalizingly close, but Argus did not dare go farther until dawn.

The king gave orders to drop anchor, and paced the deck impatiently. "Why?" he mumbled.

"My lord?" said one of the sailors, Brim, who stood nearby.

"Why would they leave the ship?"

"It's no mystery," said Brim. "Isn't it clear that when the Steadfast Lady became trapped, they had no choice but to seek shelter in the mountains?"

Argus shook his head. "It isn't clear to *me*," he said. "Look." He pointed at the ice between the Steadfast

Lady and the narrow seams of water that separated them. "Can't you see the cracks?"

"Yes," said the sailor. "But I don't understand—"

"This ice is still thin," explained Argus. "Thin enough to break with axes. With a little work, they could have reached the open sea. They could have *escaped*."

"Then why didn't they?"

"That," replied Argus, "is the mystery."

As if mocking him, a cold gust of wind came sweeping down from the north, blowing ice into his face. Argus wiped it away, and examined the mountains in the distance with suspicion. "Where are you brother?" he muttered.

***

The next morning, Kindle plowed through the rest of the ice that separated the two ships, and they reached the Steadfast Lady. Just as the dragon had reported, it was empty. The ship sat frozen in the water about a hundred yards from shore. After debating whether to walk across the ice to reach her, Argus decided it was too dangerous. He could still see patches of blue. If the ice cracked and someone plunged into the frigid sea, even for a moment, it could be fatal. Instead, he had a longboat lowered into the water. The king, along with three sailors, crossed the short distance by breaking the ice with oars, and used ropes to climb aboard the Steadfast Lady.

After they had inspected the ship, the mystery deepened. The ship's supplies were gone. Food, cutlery, rope, tools, weapons, clothing—even her sails were missing. Only the cannons remained, apparently too heavy to carry. As he stood gazing into the mountains from the ship's deck, Argus saw tracks leading north.

When they returned to the Fearless Finn, Argus explained to the crew what they had found. The king tried to sound optimistic even as he remained worried.

"Valmarians are survivors," he insisted. "Especially Wulfric and his lads. If they could avoid the Merovians for three years at sea, they can certainly survive a little cold weather. In the meantime, we have work to do."

Gwendolyn furrowed her brow. "Work?"

"If the Steadfast Lady remains where she is too much longer, the ice will thicken, and eventually destroy her hull," said Argus. "If we work diligently, we can free her by carving a path to the sea before that happens." He turned to Kindle who floated in the water below. "Would you be willing to soften the ice with your breath?"

The dragon nodded.

"What about Uncle Wulfric and the others?" asked Aethelred. "Are we going to wait for them to return?"

Argus shook his head and addressed Kindle once more. "After you've melted the ice, we need to see where the tracks lead." He paused. "Time is short, and we're not prepared to march into those mountains on foot."

"Of course," said the dragon. "I'd welcome a little company."

"You wish Gwendolyn and Aethelred to accompany you?" asked the king.

The dragon nodded and looked at them. "Three pairs of eyes are better than one."

"Very well," said Argus. He turned to the children. "Put on a few extra layers—and don't take any chances."

By that afternoon, Kindle had used his breath to soften the ice considerably, which allowed the crew to make good progress. Using axes, they cleared a path from the Steadfast Lady to the sea in the longboats.

After a brief rest, Kindle soared into the air with the children. They had dressed warmly for the journey, but Gwendolyn and Aethelred were unprepared for the bone-chilling cold of this place. Their fingers quickly became numb in their leather gloves, making it difficult to grip Kindle's scales. Still, they pressed on, following the footprints that led across the plains. The vast, barren landscape made it seem as if they were making no progress. The mountains still looked as remote as ever.

After nearly an hour of following the footprints, Gwendolyn saw a dark smudge on the snow.

"What's that?" she asked, pointing.

Kindle spiraled slowly downward and landed near the remnants of what had once been a fire. Sliding from the dragon's back, the children rubbed their hands together for warmth and examined the scene.

A few pieces of charcoal were all that remained in a hastily dug hole. A short distance away, strips of blackened meat lay nearby. Footprints, faded but still visible, were everywhere, suggesting that the group had lingered here for some time.

Gwendolyn's face brightened. "We're getting closer."

Aethelred didn't seem to hear her. He crouched down in the snow and traced one of the footprints with his finger. "Strange," he mumbled. "These seem different from ours."

"What do you mean?" she said, walking up to him and looking over his shoulder.

"Look," he replied. "There are two types. See? Some are smaller and wider than others, leaving deeper tracks."

Kindle nodded. "You're right. They're closer together, too, suggesting a shorter stride."

"You mean the Steadfast Lady's crew is travelling with others?" wondered Gwendolyn.

"That's not all," explained Aethelred, rising to his feet. "Most of these tracks continue north . . . but some go in another direction." He was right. They soon discovered that while most of the footprints led into the mountains, some of the shorter, heavier tracks led east.

"How are your wings doing in this cold, Kindle?" asked Gwendolyn. "Can you take us closer to the mountains?"

"I could," said the dragon, "but the sun will be setting soon. The temperature is already dropping, and we shouldn't risk getting caught out at night."

"Of course," said Gwendolyn. "We'll return to the ship and tell the others what we've found. At least we know where they've gone."

"Then we can set out tomorrow morning," suggested Aethelred. "We'll have the entire day to find them."

By the time they reached the coast, it was nearly twilight. It had also begun to snow, making it difficult to see. Without the sunlight, the temperature plunged, causing the children to clutch the dragon's scales closely for warmth. Kindle, too, was unprepared for this extreme cold. Though his body radiated heat, the air chilled the thin membranes of his wings, making it painful for him to fly.

Aethelred was the first to spot firelight in the distance. "I'm surprised to see them working so late," he said, his teeth chattering. "After the help you gave them this morning, Kindle, I thought they'd be finished by now."

Suddenly, they heard the frightened cries of men. Kindle streaked through the snow to see what was wrong. Six Valmarians sat huddled together in a longboat among the ice floes separating the Steadfast Lady and the Fearless Finn. Nearby stood some of the largest wolves the children had ever seen. The men had just finished broadening a lane of water to the sea when the beasts materialized and surrounded the small boat. They snarled and snapped at the sailors, rushing toward them and retreating among the treacherous sheets of ice as the Valmarians threatened them with axes. But the wolves, driven by hunger, would not be discouraged so easily.

One of the beasts, a great, white creature with yellow eyes, crept closer and waited for the next sailor to swing his axe—and then seized his arm in its jaws. Before the others could move, the wolf pulled the man over the boat's edge and dragged him across the ice. The rest swarmed the poor sailor and would have killed him, but Argus had already climbed down from the Steadfast Lady and sprinted across the ice.

Reaching the wolves in a few strides, Argus drew his sword and attacked. He killed one with a quick thrust to the chest before turning and decapitating the leader. Abandoning the sailor, the wolves retreated a short distance, unsure of whether or not to continue. Inspired by their king's bravery, the other five sailors jumped out of the longboat and rushed to his side—but quickly realized their folly. With so much weight, the ice began to buckle and crack beneath their feet. The wolves, sensing an opportunity, attacked once more.

Things would have gone badly if not for a shadow that descended out of the gathering darkness.

Kindle had reached the battle.

With the children still clinging to his back, the dragon dove into the midst of the wolves, crushing two with his claws while scattering the others with his tail. Terrified, they sprinted away—but Kindle wasn't finished. He circled back and overtook them, forming a fireball in his throat. To his surprise, he could only produce a weak flame. As the wolves escaped into the darkness, he heard Gwendolyn's voice.

"The men need your help!"

He looked over his shoulder and realized that while some of the Valmarians had safely reached the longboat, others still clung to large chunks of ice. If they fell into the water, they would surely die. Flying back to the longboat, he plucked the sailors from the sheets of ice and returned them to the deck of the Fearless Finn.

"Is everyone accounted for?" said Argus, breathing heavily while examining his men.

The others looked around quickly. "Yes, sire."

The king exhaled slowly and looked up at Kindle and the children who hovered overhead. "Those brutes crept up on us like shadows."

Aethelred smiled from the top of the dragon's back. "Now some of them *are* shadows, in a manner of speaking. I doubt they'll return." He looked at Kindle. "Why didn't you turn them into ash?"

"I tried," he insisted. "I'm—I'm not sure why I couldn't produce a steady flame."

"It must be the air," said Argus. "It's too cold. You should have seen how much oil we needed to keep our torches lit. Nevertheless, thank you for saving our lives."

Kindle set the children down on the deck next to the king and then settled into the icy water nearby as the sky grew dark. The water was cold, even for the dragon, but still manageable. (A dragon's hide puts a whale's blubber to shame.) The snow, however, only seemed to intensify as evening approached. The children told everyone about the camp that they had discovered, and the two sets of tracks that led in different directions.

"Curious," said Argus. "But it still doesn't explain why they would abandon ship."

"Perhaps they were taken prisoner," suggested Gwendolyn.

"By whom?" asked Thelda, shivering and looking into the darkness. "Who would choose to live in this wasteland?"

Argus stroked his moustache. "My father told me that men had once made a home in the north long ago," he said. "They had dwindled to only a handful of nomads, even in his time. Even if it's true, how could so few take Wulfric and his men by force?"

"We will try to learn that tomorrow," replied Gwendolyn. "If the storm breaks, we should be able to catch up to them quickly." She peered overboard. "Right, Kindle?"

The dragon looked up at her kindly. "Unfortunately, my wings aren't as thick as my hide," he said. "It might be difficult to fly long distances in this cold air, especially if it snows."

"Why didn't you say so, earlier?" she asked, feeling guilty. "You must rest."

"We all must rest . . . and take shelter from this storm below deck," ordered Argus. "I'll have sentries posted throughout the night. Then, we'll continue our work. We should be able to clear a path to the open sea by tomorrow."

"What about Uncle Wulfric and the others?" asked Aethelred.

Argus lowered his eyes. "I don't know," he replied. "But I'll not leave them to die here."

***

When the children awoke the next morning, they heard shouts and the rush of feet on the boards above. They dressed and hurried above deck with their mother—and were astounded by what they saw.

Though the storm had passed, its effects had been devastating. All of the previous day's work had been undone. The ice that trapped the Steadfast Lady was now thicker than ever. The water surrounding the Fearless Finn itself was nearly frozen, undulating only slightly around the ship's hull.

But that was not why the crew was agitated. Many of the sailors were arming themselves as they looked northward.

Gwendolyn frowned, trying to peer beyond a line of broad shoulders. "What's going—?"

"Hush," said the queen.

The children squeezed through a few sailors and followed her gaze. More than a dozen sleighs, each pulled by a team of four polar bears, approached rapidly. Yoked together by heavy chains, the beasts slobbered and panted as if they had been driven mercilessly across the ice. Inside the sleighs, a small army of strange, hooded creatures, watched them stoically. All of them, Argus noticed, carried long spears.

He glanced down, relieved, at the thin ice that surrounded the Fearless Finn. Whatever the creatures were, they would have to risk plunging into the sea if they came any closer. Nevertheless, his hand tightened around the hilt of his sword as they stopped at the edge of the ice and gazed up at the Valmarians in silence. Kindle examined them warily as he floated in the icy water.

One of the figures stepped off his sleigh and pulled back his hood. Even from a distance, it was clear that he was incredibly ugly. His large, hairless head and deformed nose made the sailors gaze with a mixture of fascination and disgust.

The creature addressed them with a strange cordiality. "On behalf of the gnomes, welcome to the Veerda, Argus of Valmar!" he said. He paused and smiled mysteriously. "We have been expecting you." He eyed Kindle. "*All of you.*"

Gwendolyn and Aethelred exchanged glances. Expecting them?

Masking his surprise, Argus observed them guardedly. "Gnomes do not live in the north," he said, with a stony glare. "In fact, I thought gnomes no longer existed at all."

The creature and his fellow companions grinned. "As you can see," he said, extending his arms, "we are quite . . . alive."

"What is your name, and how do you know mine?" demanded Argus. "More importantly, what has become of the Steadfast Lady's crew?"

"My name is Kaag," replied the gnome. "As for your other questions, Wulfric said that you would come. He even told us about Kindle. A dragon who has made peace with men? A rare friendship, indeed!"

"Why haven't my men returned to Valmar?" asked Argus. "Have you taken them prisoner?"

"On the contrary," said Kaag. "They remain with us quite willingly underneath the Daggers, as does everyone who has found the truth. Come, you can ask them for yourselves. I assure you, our sleighs are comfortable, with ample room for everyone. If we leave soon, we can reach Skarsgaard before dark."

"The Daggers?" asked Argus. "Skarsgaard?"

"Forgive me," said Kaag. "The Daggers are what we call the mountains to the north. As for Skarsgaard? Well, it is our home. There, you will find food, warmth—and the rest of your people. Will you not come with us?"

Thelda leaned close to Argus. "Surely, it is a trap."

"You're probably right," said the king, still staring at the ugly creatures. "But what choice do I have? This may be our only chance to find the others." He took a deep breath. "Besides, Kindle will be able to protect the rest of you."

He raised his voice for all to hear. "I will return with you to Skarsgaard."

"Just you?" Kaag frowned. "Perhaps it would be better if everyone came."

"Why do you need all of us?" asked the king.

Another gnome stepped forward and looked up at the dark clouds. He was shorter than the others, and his eyes seemed different, less crooked. The children noticed that instead of carrying a spear, he held a small book. "Last night's storm was a trifle compared to the weather that is to come," he explained. "Those who remain here will not survive without stronger shelter. We would rather that you all come . . . and live."

"Be silent, Jorgan!" shouted Kaag. "I am in command here!"

The smaller gnome, chastened and subdued, mumbled an apology and said no more.

Were the gnomes telling the truth? Argus couldn't be sure. But if last night's storm was any indication of the changing weather, it was unfair to ask his people to remain. His choice was clear. Either follow the gnomes into the mountains or return home without Wulfric and the others. Argus sighed and looked at Thelda, who nodded at his unspoken question.

"Very well," he said. "We will come." He glanced at Kindle. "All of us."

Kaag seemed to expect the dragon's company. "Excellent. As you will see, Skarsgaard can accommodate many beasts . . . of all shapes and sizes."

The children didn't know why, but those words sounded ominous.

5

STRANGE REUNIONS

In order to spare his wings from the cold, Kindle trotted along briskly next to the sleighs as they raced toward the mountains. Remarkably, the bears didn't seem to fear the dragon, nor did they need prompting on which direction to go. They seemed to know the way home instinctively.

Despite the day's unexpected events, it was a rather dull journey. The arctic tundra remained as bleak as ever, with little contrast between the ice and sky, except for the occasional fox peeking out of its den. Still, Gwendolyn and Aethelred were glad for the chance to examine the beasts that pulled the sleighs more closely. Twice the size of the brown bears that lived in Valmar, these creatures were almost as tall as horses, possessing huge muscles that rippled continually underneath a thick coat of white fur. They also had claws the size of daggers that left deep tracks in the snow. But they didn't seem dangerous. In fact, the bears seemed docile, even meek, obeying the gnomes without question as they raced across the plains.

They hurried for a reason. Jorgan's prediction about the weather had proven true. Dark clouds covered the sky, and it had begun to snow. The wind had grown stronger, biting at their faces and hands, forcing the Valmarians closer together for warmth.

The Daggers rose up slowly before them. The mountains were fittingly named, for the peaks and spires that ran from east to west looked sharp and sheer against the leaden sky. The thought of attempting to scale these mountains seemed impossible. If life was hard on the plains, it would be doubly so in the highlands.

The sun had almost disappeared over the horizon when they reached the pine forest among the foothills. Using a narrow pass, the bears descended into a valley before climbing again along a trail carved into the side of the mountain. Afraid of heights, Aethelred tried not to look down. Instead, he let his eyes drift upwards. He noticed many small, dark holes in the craggy surface that stared at him like angry eyes.

About halfway up the slope, they reached a plateau as the path widened into a broader road. Directly in front of them, carved into the face of the mountain, stood a stone archway framing a large entrance. The interior glowed with green light but there were no guards in front of the doorway, nor even a gate. The bears, knowing that food and rest were near, surged forward and passed through the entrance.

As the Valmarians would learn, Skarsgaard was more than an underground city. It was a fortress. Using their ingenuity, the gnomes had carved hundreds of holes into the mountainside and fitted each with glass. These windows allowed them to gaze across the White Waste while keeping out the freezing wind. They had also built a vast network of roads and tunnels, which they used to come and go in all directions.

Gazing up at the mountain, Argus looked confused. He called ahead to Kaag, who travelled in the sleigh ahead of them. "If this is your home, why are there no guards posted? Why are there no battlements, no gates?"

"What would be the purpose?" replied Kaag, his fat nose quivering in the cold. "The elements serve as our protection."

As the sleighs passed underneath the archway, Kindle paused and looked around. Why was this place familiar? He sensed something, a presence, curious but wary, trying to probe his thoughts. Closing his eyes, he focused on the being. *Who are you?* He waited for an answer, but none came. The presence soon vanished. "It's shielding itself from me," he thought. "But why?" Opening his eyes again, he noticed the last of the sleighs disappearing into the mountain. He ducked his head and followed.

Once underground, they saw the source of the strange, green light. The tunnel walls were marbled with emeralds, which glittered in the darkness. The air had also grown warmer. A few men unbuttoned their jackets while the children removed their scarves. Despite their unfamiliar surroundings, everyone was thankful to leave the open tundra behind.

Soon, the tunnel split into three directions. The polar bears, accustomed to this routine, stopped, allowing the gnomes and Valmarians to dismount. "We're almost to the Receiving Room," said Kaag. "Follow me."

A few of the gnomes led the polar bears through the tunnel to the right while Kaag and the others directed the Valmarians to the left on foot. Passing underneath the archway, they entered a vast, oval cavern. As Kindle followed them, his eyes widened. He remembered this place from his dreams.

If Skarsgaard was an underground city, the Receiving Room surely had to be one of its great halls, a place where all of the gnomes could assemble at once. Giant pillars of granite supported the massive cavern, rising from floor to ceiling. Similar to the tunnels, the room was illuminated by large veins of glowing emeralds embedded in the rock.

As their eyes adjusted to the surroundings, they realized that the cavern was two stories tall. A balcony encircled the walls about twenty yards above. In addition, many entrances led in and out of the chamber on both levels, making it appear like a giant ant nest. On the floor where they stood, hundreds of wooden tables and benches sat empty, positioned around a raised pyramid that supported an emerald throne.

Flanked by the rest of the gnomes, Kaag turned to them and smiled. "Welcome to Skarsgaard," he said. "You must be weary from the journey." He motioned to the tables and benches nearby. "We will have food and drink brought to you."

Argus was about to tell him that he hadn't abandoned his ship in the ice to eat a hot meal, but he managed to control himself. "I would much rather see my men," he said, evenly.

"Of course," replied the gnome, looking past him. "Here comes one now."

The king turned and saw Wulfric approaching. His brother was alive . . . but he appeared very different. His head had been shaved, and he wore a black cloak. As Wulfric drew near, Argus noticed another feature. He bore two black marks on his forehead just like the rest of the gnomes. Were they bruises? Argus squinted. Paint, perhaps? Had the creatures forced him to adopt their customs, staining his skin with some sort of dye?

Ignoring his odd appearance, the children rushed up and threw their arms around him. "Oh, uncle!" Gwendolyn cried, smiling up at him. "How we've missed you!"

Instead of greeting them warmly as he usually did, he pursed his lips and offered a curt nod. "It's good to see you," he said.

They stepped back and stared at him in wonder. "Why are you wearing that strange cloak?" asked Gwendolyn.

"And what happened to your forehead?" said Aethelred, studying his uncle's face. "Is that a tattoo?"

"A tattoo?" Wulfric reached up and touched his head, self-consciously. "Ah, yes. I'd nearly forgotten. I must look quite different to you." His eyes narrowed as he smiled. "I *am* different."

Argus looked at Thelda, bewildered by Wulfric's answer. What had the gnomes done to him that would cause him to change so dramatically? Had he been tortured? He looked healthy enough. There was nothing to indicate he had been mistreated.

Argus stepped in front of the children and spoke softly, so that Kaag couldn't hear him. "Don't worry," he said, putting his hand on Wulfric's shoulder. "I'm here now."

He paused, waiting for his brother to acknowledge the words with a wink, a quick nod—something. Instead, Wulfric stared at him with the same cold passivity with which he greeted the children. "Why didn't you return to Valmar?" continued Argus. "Where are the rest of our people?" He lowered his voice to a whisper. "Have you been prevented from leaving?"

Wulfric observed him coolly before responding. "No, nothing like that," he replied. "We choose to remain here . . . in the presence of our lord."

"Your lord?" sputtered Argus. "Have you gone mad?"

"Not at all," said Wulfric.

The king was speechless. He expected to find his brother in chains, perhaps even beaten. But aloof? Surly? That just wasn't Wulfric's way.

"Come, man! Don't you recognize us?" He turned toward Thelda and the others. "We're here to—well, to rescue you!"

"As you can see, I don't need rescuing," replied Wulfric, calmly. "But *you* do."

"Me?" Argus began to grow angry. He hadn't sailed for weeks across treacherous waters to listen to coy answers. "Look here, where are the rest of our people?"

"Wherever our lord wishes them to be," said Wulfric.

Before the king could respond, Thelda reached out and took her husband by the hand. She didn't understand why Wulfric was acting this way, but she knew they had to be patient. Anger would achieve nothing. They needed information.

"Does your lord have a name?" she asked.

"Playing the peace maker as usual, my lady?" Wulfric smiled slightly. "His name is Asmodeus. In time, you, too, will come to see his great wisdom."

"If I remember correctly, there was a certain sorcerer from Merovia who thought himself wise," said Argus, trying to contain himself. "Do you remember what happened to *him?*"

Thelda squeezed the king's hand in warning.

"Asmodeus is nothing like Sköll," replied Wulfric, dismissively. "His motives are pure. He doesn't act out of selfish ambition, only benevolence. He will reconcile us with the Merovians, the gnomes, the trolls—"

"The trolls?" gasped Gwendolyn. "Who would want to make friends with them?"

"That's just what I thought at first," replied Wulfric, glancing down at her. "But Asmodeus says we mustn't think in those terms. Everyone wants what is good, even the trolls. They are just mistaken in how they attempt to achieve it."

"Nonsense!" cried Argus. "Have you been bewitched?"

"Quite the opposite," said Wulfric. "For the first time, I see clearly."

The king was about to say more when he heard a strange voice.

"Did I not tell you, Wulfric, that they would doubt me, just as they doubt all of their prophets?" The voice's tone was charming and even indulgent in its kindness. Everyone who heard it felt momentarily guilty for harboring suspicion about this place.

Everyone except Aethelred.

Before he even saw the voice's owner, he felt the hair rise on the back of his neck. His palms began to sweat. He had experienced this before—an overwhelming sense of dread, making him want to run away, as if he were back on Cloud Isle. What was it about the sound of this voice that made him so anxious? Reluctantly, he turned and looked up along with the rest of the Valmarians.

A pale, skeletal figure sat on the throne, dressed in a black cloak while holding an emerald staff in one hand. At first, the children thought he was a mummified corpse but his hard eyes told them otherwise. His cloak, old and shabby, hung open at the chest, revealing a body that was impossibly thin. His flesh, sickly and ashen, stretched across his large frame, causing his ribs to stand out grotesquely in the green light. He was much too tall to be a man, and much too gaunt to be a giant. Save for a few strands of oily, black hair pulled behind his ears, he was mostly bald, and the Valmarians fancied they could make out his skull beneath his colorless scalp.

Peering down at the Valmarians, he regarded them with boredom, studying their faces slowly. When he came to Aethelred, however, he stopped. His dark eyes seemed to blaze and swirl in their sockets as he shifted uneasily in his throne.

Defiant, Aethelred returned the creature's gaze but soon found that he couldn't look away. Asmodeus's eyes held him fast. They also seemed to grow larger, blocking out the light as they regarded him warily, accusingly. The boy tried to cry out but his voice, like his eyes, were no longer his to control. Mentally, he was being taken somewhere else, somewhere he didn't want to go. He felt his sister take his hand and the eyes slowly faded, receding back into the creature's face.

Despite the ordeal, Aethelred had learned something important. There was more to Asmodeus than most realized. It was as if a veil had been drawn over the creature's face, leaving his true nature in the shadows.

As the boy tried to make sense of what he was seeing, he heard his father speak.

"Asmodeus, I presume?"

Almost reluctantly, the creature turned to the king, nodding his head in acknowledgement. "You presume correctly," he replied. "You and your people are welcome here. We wish you only peace." He paused, glancing at Kindle. "Though I wonder why you would venture to a place as wild and inhospitable as the White Waste when you come from a land of so much beauty and abundance."

"The land I come from has many things," said Argus, looking at him from underneath his eyebrows while resting his palm on the hilt of his sword, "and is often underestimated by those who would do us harm."

Asmodeus smiled as he took the meaning. "Yet you allowed Wulfric and the rest of these men to come here, to our home, in search of . . . what exactly?"

"To explore," explained Argus. "We did not know the north was inhabited."

"You do now," said Asmodeus, his sunken cheekbones shining in the green light.

"Yes, we do," said Argus, "and I thank you for your hospitality. Now, if you don't mind, we'll be on our way." He glared at Wulfric. "All of us."

Asmodeus shook his head. "I'm afraid that's impossible."

"What do you mean?" asked Argus, frowning.

"You wouldn't get very far in the bitter cold of the mountains, especially now that night has fallen. Not many creatures can bear those temperatures. Besides, you are our *guests.*"

Asmodeus seemed to notice that Kaag and the other gnomes were still holding their spears. He addressed the creatures, angrily. "Have I not told you before that it's forbidden to bring weapons into the Receiving Room? You're making our guests feel anxious!"

Most of the gnomes scurried back into the tunnel from which they had entered, leaving only Jorgan. The poor gnome had apparently forgotten to bring his spear. He waited awkwardly, unsure of whether or not he, too, would be dismissed.

"Won't you stay a while?" continued Asmodeus, turning back to Argus. "We could learn much from one another. Isn't that the point of exploration? To learn?"

Argus glanced at his family and his men. While they were armed, they also looked tired and hungry. Did they still have the strength to fight? Asmodeus certainly didn't look trustworthy, but he was right in this case. They wouldn't survive in the cold very long if they tried to depart now. Instead of leaving immediately, Argus would use this time to find answers. Tomorrow, he would politely say goodbye and return to the ships with Wulfric and his men. And if they encountered problems? Well, there was always Kindle.

"Very well," he said. "We will spend the night. I'd like to see the rest of the Steadfast Lady's crew." He turned to Wulfric. "Where are they?"

"They are well, I assure you," replied Wulfric. "You will see everyone at dinner. You can ask them anything you wish."

"Anything," agreed Asmodeus. "We will prepare a feast in your honor! We have never hosted a *king* before." He pointed his staff at Jorgan who stood nearby. "He will show you to your rooms."

The gnome, grateful to be acknowledged, bowed. "At once, my lord." He turned to the others and started toward a small opening. "This way, if you please."

Gwendolyn ignored him and glared at Asmodeus. "What about Kindle?"

He smiled indulgently. "He is much too large to follow you," he said. "Besides, he and I have other matters to discuss . . . matters which I believe he will find very interesting."

She was about to respond when she heard the dragon's thoughts. *Do not fear. He cannot hurt me. If you are in danger, all you need to do is call.*

Gwendolyn peered into his eyes. *But what about the mountain? Surely not all of these tunnels will be large enough to let you pass! How will you reach us if we are separated?*

She saw the dragon smile. *I was* born *in a mountain. Earth and stone cannot hold me.*

"Very well." Reluctantly, she turned and followed Jorgan and the others into the passageway, leaving Kindle alone with the strange figure.

***

Kindle stared up at Asmodeus. Was it his presence he had felt when they entered Skarsgaard? If so, the creature had hidden it well. The dragon tried to probe his mind, but found only darkness. Asmodeus rose, and slowly made his way down the stairs of the pyramid toward him.

I'm sure you have many questions," he began. "Questions about your friends' safety, particularly the two young ones." He glanced at the dragon. "I noticed the way you looked at them. There's a bond there, quite strong, too."

"I'm glad you recognized it," replied Kindle, with the slightest hint of a growl. "If they were to be hurt in any way, I would be very angry."

Asmodeus laughed grimly. "I have no doubt," he said. "But surely there are others with whom you have felt a connection?" He twirled his staff idly in his hand.

"What do you mean?"

"Come now," he chided. "Did you not sense another mind when you first entered the mountain?" Kindle looked uneasy as Asmodeus smiled and came closer, stopping at the dragon's feet. "Yes, she knew you were coming. Wouldn't you like to meet her?"

"I came here to find the Steadfast Lady and her crew—"

"Of course. But have you not also come to solve the riddle in your dreams?"

"My dreams?" Kindle's eyes narrowed. "What do *you* know of my dreams?"

"It isn't simply your imagination," he replied. "The one you seek is *real*." He pointed at the southern end of the cavern with his staff. "She is waiting for you."

Kindle noticed a large archway that led into another cavernous hall. Unlike this one, however, it was not illuminated by emeralds. It was shrouded in darkness. As he wondered whether or not to trust Asmodeus, he heard a voice in his mind.

Kindle.

He closed his eyes to concentrate. The voice was pleasant, earnest.

How long I have waited to meet you.

He was overcome with curiosity. *Who are you?*

Come and see.

The dragon's eyes snapped open. He looked for Asmodeus to provide some explanation, some reason, but the creature was gone.

Kindle desperately wanted to see who or what waited for him in the hall beyond, but he hesitated. He had said he would remain here. What if they needed him? Then he took a deep breath—and felt a familiar sensation. The cavern's warm air had made it possible once again for him to breathe fire. He could feel the heat even now, swirling and pulsing in the gland beneath his throat. If

Gwendolyn called him, he would turn this mountain upside down to find her.

Making his way across the cavern, he passed underneath the archway and found himself surrounded by darkness. Using his night vision, he scanned the hall. The room was empty. However, it contained yet another passageway that led into a larger tunnel . . . and even more darkness. Determined to solve this mystery, Kindle followed the path downward. He saw many openings on either side, dark and drafty, tempting him to explore other parts of the mountain but he continued forward. He somehow knew that what he sought lay at the end of this tunnel.

As he descended, the air slowly changed, growing stale, cold. Ice began to appear. The scent of gnomes, so pungent in the cavern, had disappeared. He guessed that here, this far underneath the earth, even those creatures did not venture very often. Soon, the tunnel's smooth, polished walls gave way to rough excavations of stone, and the adjoining passageways, once so common, ceased. His breath, cloudy and white, appeared in the air before him. How far had he gone? He didn't know. But he sensed that it was very cold now. Unnaturally cold. If it weren't for his great scales, he wouldn't have been able to go on. Certainly, a man or even a gnome couldn't endure such temperatures for long. But where was the one whom he sought?

You are close now.

Kindle stopped. "Where are you?"

He saw something flickering in the darkness. Quickening his pace, he continued forward and discovered an archway filled with light. He paused before entering. Even though the voice seemed sincere, Kindle was still suspicious.

You will come to no harm, I promise you.

He sighed. Whatever it was, it was powerful enough to read his mind. Why couldn't he discern its thoughts?

He stepped across the threshold. The place pulsed softly with green light. Unlike the warmth of sunlight or firelight, these rays were cold. They dazzled him, dancing on the walls, making everything seem hard, definite.

Slowly, his eyes adjusted. He was standing in a long, narrow chamber. Something large moved at the far end of the room and approached. He crouched down, defensively, but the rays shone directly into his eyes, making it difficult to see what it was.

Then the creature stepped in front of the light. A cream-colored dragon, slightly smaller than Kindle, gazed at him in curiosity and deep gladness.

"We meet at last," she said.

***

As Jorgan led the Valmarians deeper into Skarsgaard, they couldn't help but like the gnome. He chatted away merrily, answering questions and pointing out places of interest, describing the great caverns and halls with pride. Despite being a bit absent-minded, he seemed very different from Kaag and many of the others. He was proud of what the gnomes had built, and anxious to share what he knew.

The underground city was indeed a place of unexpected splendor. The streets and halls were filled with gnomes and, unlike what one might think, far from damp and gloomy. Emeralds, embedded in the walls, bathed everything in green light. Some passages led to grand boulevards and enormous chambers while others were so narrow only two people could pass abreast. It would be easy to get lost in this labyrinth if one didn't know the way to the surface.

Despite their suspicions about Asmodeus and his intentions, they were impressed by the austere beauty of this place. Countless sculptures and fountains adorned the squares through which they passed, commemorating the various accomplishments of famous gnomes. In one plaza, statues of great mathematicians, engineers, and architects looked down at them in silence as Jorgan described each with reverence.

"That's Sharga the Great," he explained, pointing to a sculpture of a particularly fat gnome holding an astrolabe. "She was one of the first gnomes, and invented many things, including trigonometry." He pointed to his left. "The shorter figure next to her is . . . Wando—no Vando! Sorry, I always get them confused. He gave us the aqueducts. We still use his techniques to this day." He motioned to another statue of a gnome with a smaller nose and long beard holding a series of small gears. "Yorgo, of course, invented the astronomical clock. Or was it the pulley? Oh . . . I can't remember. My mind seems to be slipping lately. But he was very smart, despite the rumors."

"Rumors?" asked Thelda.

"Yes," said Jorgan with distaste. "You see, because of his beard, some suspect he was part dwarf . . . but that has never been proven."

"What about artists?" said Gwendolyn. "Don't you celebrate them, too?"

The gnome looked at them, surprised. "Artists?"

"You know," explained Aethelred. "Painters, poets, musicians. Surely you must have those?"

He nodded. "Yes, I understand what you meant. I just didn't expect such a question." He lowered his voice. "You see, most in Skarsgaard believe that unless creativity is applied—that is to say, functional—it's useless. Art is considered a luxury we can no longer afford." He smiled slyly. "But there *are* some among us who disagree."

He pulled out a small book from the folds of his cloak. "I've been writing poetry lately. It's quite wonderful, playing with words. A few of us meet regularly to share our work with one another but we do so in secret." He looked around to see if he'd been overheard. "We wouldn't want Asmodeus to think we're being disobedient." Jorgan put the book away and led them underneath another archway.

Unlike the plaza from which they had just come, this chamber was conical. It tapered upwards, filled with a spongy, blue substance that grew in enormous stalks, anchored to ropes hanging from the ceiling. Jorgan explained that this was called *durma*, a type of edible moss that made up a large part of the gnomish diet.

As they continued onward, it became clear that no one who lived here was idle. Some gnomes dug for precious metals; the children saw them crawling in and out of tunnels, covered in dust. Other chambers revealed workshops filled with gnomes who tinkered with strange devices. They even passed a classroom where Gwendolyn thought she saw a few formulas scratched out on the wall as a large, ugly gnome taught a younger group the finer points of geometry. "At least we have that in common," she thought.

When they saw the Valmarians, most of the gnomes stopped what they were doing and stared, whispering to one another furtively. The children didn't sense malice in their looks, only a deep curiosity. A few even smiled at the children, nodding their head in greeting. Gwendolyn and Aethelred dutifully smiled back. Still, they didn't feel safe here. They simply wanted to return home with their uncle and the others.

"How much farther?" asked Argus impatiently, glancing around the cavern. Though he had grown to like Jorgan, it had been a long day. "Or are you planning on showing us the *entire* city?"

The gnome chuckled. "Oh, no," he said. "That would take days. I'm not sure anyone has seen all of Skarsgaard. It's forbidden to travel too broadly through the tunnels."

"Forbidden?" asked Thelda. "Why?"

"Do you know, I can't quite remember?" admitted the gnome. "I think it has something to do with rockslides. In any case, Asmodeus has declared it unsafe."

He led them across a large square and through another passageway before stopping in front of a long hall with many doors on either side. "Here we are. I hope you and your family will find these accommodations suitable?"

Jorgan opened the door nearest to him and stood back, allowing Argus to look inside. The room, lit by more emeralds protruding from the walls, contained a round table, four stools, four beds, and a fireplace. On the opposite side of the room, another door led into a bathroom, complete with indoor plumbing, which the Valmarians had never before seen. They also noticed four black garments hanging from hooks in the wall.

"You can change into the cloaks we have provided," explained the gnome. "After you have had some time to rest, I will return to escort you to the feast." He turned to the others and gestured at more doors in the hallway. "Now, if you'll follow me, I'll show the rest of you—"

"Are those prison uniforms?" asked Argus, still examining the cloaks suspiciously before gazing around the room. "And are these rooms to be our prison cells?"

Jorgan shook his head. "The cloaks have been provided for your benefit. It must be . . ." he paused, searching for the right word. "It must be *uncomfortable* for you to look so different compared to the rest of us. Perhaps, if you adopted our ways, it would be more pleasing for everyone? As for your lodgings, these rooms have no locks."

Aethelred looked down at the door handle and found his words to be true. It was a simple knob; nothing prevented them from leaving.

The king shrugged. What choice did they have? "Do as he says," he ordered. "Stay in your rooms until you're called—but remain vigilant . . . and don't even think about putting on one of those absurd cloaks. We will return to the ship with everyone tomorrow. You have my word."

He looked out at the dozens of faces watching him expectantly. The sailors were trying to maintain their courage, but they were clearly intimidated by the number of gnomes in this city. Though armed, how could the Valmarians possibly defend themselves if the gnomes became hostile? He wished he knew why Wulfric had changed. He needed time to think, to solve this mystery. If that meant pretending to be more confident than he really was, so be it.

"You will come to no harm," said Jorgan, addressing the others. "I will return soon. I believe there's a feast tonight in your honor." He looked at them, confused. "Or did I already say that?"

The children nodded, and had to lower their heads to suppress their smiles. Despite his forgetfulness, they found him quite charming.

As the men followed Jorgan to the other rooms, Argus sighed and closed the door. He was finally alone with his wife and children. Unclasping his sword belt, he put the weapon on the table and sat down on one of the stools. "I don't understand," he said. "What has happened to Wulfric to make him behave so strangely?"

"And why did he have those two marks on his forehead?" said Aethelred.

Thelda sat next to her husband and put her arm around his waist. "He must be under a spell," she sighed. "He would never consent to remain in such a place." She looked at the others with fear in her eyes. "We must be careful. If this creature enchanted your uncle, he'll probably try to do the same to us."

Gwendolyn walked over to the fireplace and found a few coals, kindling, and some flint already prepared for them. "So why doesn't he just do it?" she asked. "Why all the smiles and hospitality?" She struck the flint and watched as a few small flames began to appear. "Why these rooms instead of a dungeon? What if Wulfric, and the gnomes for that matter, aren't under a spell at all?"

"Didn't you hear your mother?" said Argus. "Wulfric wouldn't believe this nonsense for a minute. As for not taking us prisoner, perhaps Asmodeus thinks he can learn more from us if he treats us well."

"What exactly *is* Asmodeus anyway?" asked Aethelred, remembering how difficult it was to see him clearly, as though a dark fog continually swirled around the creature's body.

"I don't know," admitted the king. "I've never seen his like before."

"What about his staff?" Gwendolyn said. "It looked like it's made out of emeralds, the same used to illuminate the city." She looked at the stone in the middle of the ceiling and watched it pulse with green light. "Perhaps that's the source of his power."

"Let's not jump to conclusions," said Argus. "Maybe there's a simpler explanation: Wulfric was protecting us. Remember, we still haven't been allowed to talk to him *alone*."

"You're right," said Aethelred. "Maybe they threatened him? Told him they'd hurt him, or us, if he told the truth."

"We still haven't seen the others," said Thelda, softly. "Perhaps he's protecting *them*."

As they pondered these possibilities, Argus began to despair. Could they convince Wulfric and the others to come with them? Even if they were successful, how would they make it back to the coast?

Then Gwendolyn thought of something that sent her father's doubts scattering. "We mustn't forget that Kindle is here with us," she said. "There aren't many friends better than a dragon in such circumstances. Whatever we have to face, he'll face it with us."

The others nodded.

"That is indeed a source of comfort," admitted Argus.

Gwendolyn didn't share her next thought. "Yes, a great comfort . . . as long as he doesn't change like Uncle Wulfric."

6

A SINGLE BANNER

When Jorgan returned to escort the Valmarians to dinner, he was surprised to find them standing in front of their rooms dressed in their native garb—and still armed. The gnomes did not dare to disobey Asmodeus but the Valmarians would not be intimidated. With the exception of Gwendolyn and Thelda, they all carried broadswords. The queen preferred a long dagger hidden in the folds of her dress while Gwendolyn carried a bow slung across her shoulder, along with a quiver full of arrows.

Jorgan looked at them, doubtfully. "The Receiving Room is a place of peace, dialogue," he explained. "Asmodeus forbids weapons."

"He'll have to make an exception," replied Argus.

The gnome shrugged. "As you please."

Returning to the cavern, they found it crowded with gnomes of all kinds. Fat gnomes and thin gnomes. Tall gnomes and short gnomes. Young gnomes and old gnomes. The creatures all stood or sat huddled together, talking quietly amongst themselves, their large noses bouncing softly as they spoke. When they saw the Valmarians enter, they grew silent, staring at them with their small, round eyes.

Argus ignored them and glanced up at the throne. He had expected to find Asmodeus there, ready to chide him for coming to dinner with his sword. Instead, the chair was empty. More troubling, Kindle was missing. The cavern was large, but a dragon was hard to miss.

Before he could ask where Kindle had gone, the king spotted a group of particularly tall gnomes, cloaked and hooded, standing at the opposite end of the Receive Room. He gazed closer—and his heart sank. They weren't gnomes at all but Wulfric and the others! Like their captain, the rest of the men had adopted the ways of this place. They had shaved heads, which made them look pasty and colorless as if they hadn't seen the sun in months. They also bore the same mysterious marks on each of their foreheads.

The children hurried forward, followed by Argus, and Thelda. Though their uncle had treated them coldly just a few hours ago, he had promised answers. Perhaps this time he would be different, more himself.

Gwendolyn and Aethelred looked up at him expectantly, hoping for a smile, an embrace. Instead, he gazed down upon them with the same detachment as before. In fact, all of the men regarded them with similar expressions of apathy.

"Ah," said Wulfric. "You've come."

"Of course we've come!" said Argus, stepping in front of the others. "Do you think we had a choice?"

"Quite right," mumbled Wulfric. "Choice is an illusion."

Argus glowered. "That's not what I meant." He looked around at the rest of Steadfast Lady's crew and recognized Wulfric's first mate. "Melko? For pity's sake, please tell me you haven't fallen under the same spell. What have they done to you?"

"Asmodeus has received us," he replied, "as his children."

"His children?" scoffed Argus.

"Is it so hard to believe?" Everyone looked up to find Asmodeus on his throne, which startled the Valmarians. "I consider all of these creatures my children. I care for them, guide them . . . and when necessary, discipline them." He smiled at Argus and Thelda. "Do you not do the same?"

The king was about to reply but Asmodeus continued, his voice growing sharper as his eyes fell on Jorgan. "And if they fail to obey our commands? What then?" He glared at the forgetful gnome. "Did I not tell you they were forbidden to return here with weapons?"

Jorgan looked up, frightened. "You did? I mean, yes, of course! You did, my lord. I'm sorry, I tried to explain to them—"

"Do not bore me with your excuses!" he thundered, pointing at Jorgan with one of his long, bony fingers. "Take him away." Two gnomes hurried forward and led Jorgan out of the room.

"He shouldn't be punished," said Argus. "It was my decision, not his. Besides, if we are truly your guests, then what do you have to fear?"

"Fear?" Asmodeus said, his eyes smoldering. "I fear *nothing*."

Thelda put a hand on her husband's arm as she addressed the pale creature. "Then there is no cause for concern," she said. "You must forgive us. We are strangers here, and do not yet understand your customs.

Perhaps as we talk, we can build the trust that seems to be lacking between us?"

"Very well," said Asmodeus. "I will overlook this transgression."

Argus bristled but Thelda squeezed his arm. "Patience, my lord," she whispered. "Now is not the time to fight. Now is the time to learn something to our advantage."

Reluctantly, the king agreed. "Where do we sit?"

Asmodeus rose from his throne and raised his long, thin arms. "As you see, there is plenty of room for all." He smiled. "We have prepared a place of honor for you and your family. Won't you follow me?"

As the gnomes and men seated themselves, Asmodeus descended from his throne and led Argus, Thelda, and the children to a long, rectangular table. "We will be able to talk here more comfortably."

He clapped his hands and dozens of gnomes appeared carrying platters of food and drink. They served great heaps of durma, the blue moss that Jorgan had pointed out earlier, as well as tuna and sea bass, along with larger, coarser cuts of meat. Beer, too, was plentiful.

"What is that?" asked Aethelred, pointing at a pile of dark, rubbery flesh.

Kaag grabbed a piece and put it on his plate before sitting down heavily next to the boy. "Eel," he grunted. "It's quite good, especially raw." He took a long draught of beer and wiped his chin.

Aethelred wrinkled his nose. "I think I'll stick with fish."

Despite the strange company, the Valmarians were famished. They ate quickly while Asmodeus, still clutching his staff, sat nearby, studying them closely. The food didn't seem to tempt him in the least.

"Where is Kindle?" asked Gwendolyn. She had used her mind to call out to him several times, but he still hadn't responded, and she was beginning to worry.

"He is . . . exploring," explained Asmodeus. "He will be back soon, I assure you."

"That's not reassuring," said Argus. Thelda kicked him from underneath the table. "I mean, I hope he is able to join us. He must be hungry, too."

"Oh, there is plenty of food," said Asmodeus. "Now that I've taught the gnomes to stop fighting amongst themselves, they have all the food they need."

Though he found sitting at the same table as Asmodeus disturbing, Aethelred was intrigued. "How did you teach them to stop fighting?"

The creature examined his staff. "When I found them, they were much like men: dishonest, anxious to avoid danger, and covetous of gain. I realized that before they could be happy, they needed discipline." He looked up at Argus, gazing at the king with his dead eyes. "I needed only to kill the strongest among them before the rest acknowledged my authority."

"You *killed* some of them?" asked Thelda, astounded that he would admit to such an act.

"Would you prefer a lie?" he replied. "Do you think it would be more compassionate to watch them persist in their petty disputes?"

Argus scoffed. "Might makes right, is that it?"

"To put it crudely, yes," admitted Asmodeus. "Isn't Valmar governed in a similar fashion?"

"We don't kill or imprison those who disagree with us," said the king.

"Don't you?" replied Asmodeus. "Your brother has told me about your country's history." He looked at Wulfric, who sat nearby, silently observing the conversation with interest. "You've killed men, trolls, dragons, and other creatures who threatened you." He smiled, twirling his staff. "Why, Wulfric claims to have killed scores of Merovians by leading a sea serpent towards them, a particularly gruesome way to die. Wouldn't you agree?" He glanced at Argus, clearly enjoying himself. "Then there was Edubard, who killed using only his voice. A curious skill. He was your father, I believe?"

Argus narrowed his eyes. "What of it?"

"Can't you see?" replied Asmodeus. "We are both killers, you and I, but with one important exception. I have *evolved*. I don't kill merely to survive. I kill so that others can be saved."

"Saved from what?" asked Gwendolyn.

"From themselves, of course, and the illusion that plagues them—the illusion of good and evil." Asmodeus turned to her. "Most creatures aren't evil. They're confused, sick. Instead of fighting amongst themselves, they could build a better world. A world of order filled with peace and plenty for all. I have chosen to help them."

The children regarded him in wonder. They had to admit there was something compelling in his argument. If he were successful in uniting all creatures, there would be no more wars, no more rivalries, no more inequality. There would only be Asmodeus and those who conformed to his will.

Argus wasn't convinced. "Without freedom, even the most peaceful society is still a prison," he said.

Asmodeus sighed as if he had explained this to others many times before. "Only because you still don't understand that freedom is not a gift, but a burden."

"A burden?" asked Aethelred, confused.

"Ask yourself—why do you *want* to be free? To achieve what you desire? To be independent?" He snorted. "Pure selfishness. No, Aethelred. The freedom you claim to cherish isn't a virtue. It prevents you from being happy. Where there is no freedom, there is no suffering, no violence."

"No hope," said Thelda.

"Hope?" he said, smiling at her. "Hope is simply another word for desire. I have taken from my children their hope, their pride, and have given them humility."

"You talk of humility, equality, but the only thing the gnomes seem to share is fear."

He shook his head. "What makes you so sure my ways are so unjust compared to Valmar's?"

"Yes, yes," said Argus. "You've already mentioned my father but I can only speak for myself. If you expect me to apologize for killing trolls or dragons that have attacked my people, I'm afraid you'll be disappointed."

"I do not speak of dragons or trolls!" said Asmodeus, his voice cracking in anger as he tightened his grip on the staff. "Your father tried to *exterminate* an entire race of creatures . . . creatures who did nothing to threaten Valmar. Wulfric has already told me of Edubard's crimes."

Argus furrowed his brow. "I don't know what you're talking about." He turned to Wulfric. "What have you told him?"

Wulfric observed him calmly. "Have you forgotten?"

"Forgotten what?"

"About the journeys our father made when we were children," he explained. "We were younger than Gwendolyn and Aethelred are now, but have you forgotten how he abandoned us?"

Argus looked down and paused. "I remember," he said, finally. "Our mother had died near the end of the Giant Wars, and he was filled with grief. He left us for a time, sailing over the ocean with his knights to try to forget her death, and his pain."

"That is what he *told* us," replied Wulfric. "But did you know that he and his knights—his sentinels— travelled the world, seeking out and killing certain kinds of creatures?"

"How do you know that?" asked Argus, folding his arms.

"Because *I* was one of those creatures," said Asmodeus, shaking in anger. The children stared at him in disbelief as the gnomes began to murmur among themselves. "It is true," he continued, raising his voice and addressing the gnomes as much as the Valmarians. "Edubard and his men killed many of my kind, including my sister. They asked no questions, gave us no chance to explain ourselves." The gnomes glared at the Valmarians and the murmuring grew louder.

"Why would he do that?" said Argus, puzzled.

"Fear, intolerance," said Asmodeus. "He hated us because we were different." He stared directly at Argus. "It was only when I watched him use his magic to kill my sister that I realized that the people of Valmar will always attack those who are not like them."

"That's not true!" insisted Gwendolyn.

Asmodeus ignored her and rose to his feet, pointing his staff at Argus. "We must never tolerate the ignorant, the violent, the intolerant. Rather, we must force them to adopt our ways." The gnomes nodded their heads in approval. "I will take Valmar's sins upon myself. I will teach it a better, a more civilized way. When I reach your shores, I will give the rest of your people the king they deserve." Mastering his anger, he smiled again. "So you see? Violence is necessary . . . if peace is to last."

Aethelred raised his voice so that all could hear. "Men don't claim to be perfect," he said. "My grandfather certainly wasn't." He looked at Asmodeus. "But I know someone who is."

The creature stared at him with contempt. "Who might that be?"

Aethelred swallowed. "Oorano," he replied. He glanced at Gwendolyn before facing Asmodeus and the others. "It was Oorano who saved me from this sort of talk about my right to happiness." He flexed his hand, remembering how the Malodoi had deceived him, had become part of him before Oorano had purged him of its influence.

Upon hearing Oorano's name, Asmodeus's countenance changed. For just a moment, his benign mask gave way to one of hatred before returning to a studied indifference. "Oorano, you say? The 'maker of the stars'?" He smiled and looked at the gnomes sarcastically. "I know you're young, Aethelred, but it's a bit too early for bedtime stories, even for you." The gnomes laughed and nodded in agreement.

"It's no story!" said Gwendolyn, angrily. "I was there. Aethelred speaks the truth."

"Has anyone else seen this so-called immortal besides these two children? Heard his voice?" Asmodeus turned to Argus and Thelda, smugly. "Did *you* see him?"

Argus shook his head. "No," he said. "But my son is not a liar."

"Oh?" said Asmodeus, as if he knew more than he would acknowledge. "Is he not?" He stared at them, his black pupils seeming to bore into their souls. "Has your son not *lied* to you? Has he not *stolen* from you, even put your lives in danger?"

Aethelred's face flushed crimson as he remembered how he had behaved when he had used the wand. He was indeed guilty of those things. Wulfric must have told Asmodeus all about it, and now the creature was setting a trap for his parents.

"I am guilty of those things," admitted the boy. "I also would have died if it weren't for Oorano. It was he who took me into the fire . . . and delivered me from it."

"Took you into fire?" said Asmodeus in mock astonishment. "That doesn't sound particularly *merciful*. What a strange god!" The gnomes laughed again. "But enough! I do not wish to embarrass you. I will even tolerate your imagination up to a point, but you must not pretend to have any special knowledge of the gods. As I said, I will not tolerate intolerance."

At this, the gnomes repeated his words. "We will not tolerate intolerance! We will not tolerate intolerance!" Their ugly faces shone with animated zeal and the sound of their voices filled the cavern as they chanted in unison.

The children looked around, frightened. Until the feast, the gnomes had seemed dull but peaceful. Now, they realized just how dangerous these creatures could be under Asmodeus's command.

To everyone's surprise, Gwendolyn laughed, startling the gnomes into silence. She regarded Asmodeus with contempt. "You will not tolerate *intolerance*?" she replied, incredulous. "Who exactly do you find intolerant?"

Asmodeus looked at her as if she'd asked a stupid question. "Those who refuse to obey me, of course."

"I see," said Gwendolyn. "If one disagrees with you, he is intolerant?"

"By definition," said Asmodeus.

"That's absurd!" she cried, scowling. "What makes you so sure of yourself?"

He had never considered the possibility that he could be wrong. "I am guided by pure reason, immune to the selfishness that plagues other creatures," he said. "I am never wrong."

Gwendolyn looked around at the gnomes. "Can't you see that your 'lord' is a fake? I don't know what trick he has played on my uncle and the rest of you but you must know that we mean you no harm. We only want to go home."

"That's just what Edubard said when he was here with the rest of his sentinels," hissed Asmodeus. "And yet here you are, back with more of your people. Surely, if you leave, you will return with an army."

Gwendolyn stopped trying to reason with him. Instead, she climbed up on the table, scattering food and beer, and looked around at the hundreds of gnomes who surrounded her. "You don't have to live in submission to this . . . this thing," she said, pointing to Asmodeus. "You don't have to be afraid."

She noticed one of the gnomes sitting at a table nearby, gazing up at her pensively, as if seriously considering what she had to say. "You there," she said. "Would you really remain a slave?" He glanced away, unwilling to meet her gaze. She looked down at the gnomes at her own table and saw Kaag. "Do you really choose to live in this wretched place governed by a master you fear?"

Kaag cleared his throat. Had he seen through Asmodeus's cruelty? Would he acknowledge the enchantment that rested heavily on this place?

"That's just it," said Kaag. "We aren't afraid anymore, at least not of each other." Gwendolyn's heart sank as he continued. "We're happy now that Asmodeus tells us what to do. It makes things easier." Most of the gnomes in the cavern nodded in agreement.

"Then there's nothing left to discuss," she said, pulling her bow from her shoulder and fitting an arrow to the string. "You can choose to be slaves, but I'll remain as I am." Aethelred drew his blade as he climbed up and stood next to her while the gnomes retreated, unsure of what to do next.

As if clearing away a fog, Argus stumbled to his feet. It was clear that Asmodeus was mad—mad but with a twisted logic that he used to justify his actions. (You may have met such people yourself.)

Drawing his sword, he stood next to his wife. "All true Valmarians!" he cried, raising his sword. "I call upon you to forsake this place and return with us!"

Thelda and the others rose and drew their weapons as they gathered around the table on which the children stood. Argus glanced at Wulfric and the Steadfast Lady's crew. His words appeared to have had no effect on them. They scarcely moved as they watched him curiously. There was no fear in their eyes. In fact, there was nothing at all.

Asmodeus drew back as the Valmarians raised their weapons. Now, he stood in front of the rest of the gnomes a short distance away. "Do you see?" he said, pointing at Argus with his staff. "Do you see how rashly they act when frightened?"

Ignoring the creature's words, Argus focused on the staff. He had been watching it for some time, noticing the way it glowed and sparkled as Asmodeus twirled the object in his hands. A thought occurred to him. What if it were to be broken?

"You claim to bring peace . . . but I simply see one more of the world's many tyrants," said Argus.

Asmodeus smiled. "And you?" he asked. "What are you, oh mighty king? An invader with a sword in his hand, nothing more! But that will soon change." He turned to the gnomes nearest to him. "Take him!"

Before they could reach him, Argus ran down the length of the table directly toward Asmodeus, kicking over bottles and breaking plates before leaping into the air. Raising his blade, he brought it down hard. As he expected, Asmodeus used his staff to parry the blow. The rod shattered, leaving him with only a small shard in his hand.

Asmodeus stumbled backwards, stunned by the king's audacity. Breathing heavily, Argus raised his sword again and glanced at Wulfric and the others. His heart leaped as he watched them rise and approach. The spell had been broken! They would rally to him! Then he noticed their faces. They walked towards him warily, with clenched fists and grim expressions. They were coming to help Asmodeus.

"Did you really think that breaking my staff would change anything?" asked the pale creature. "No, you have only proven how quickly men resort to violence. Indeed, it is the only language you understand."

Tired of his words, Argus charged the creature. Slashing at him with three mighty strokes, his attack would have felled a giant—but Asmodeus's skin was as hard as stone. When the king stepped back, he realized his adversary wasn't even bleeding.

"Are you quite finished?" said Asmodeus.

Before Argus could respond, the creature snatched the blade from his hands and leaped into the air. He landed on the table where the children stood and raised the emerald shard to Gwendolyn's throat while pointing the sword at Aethelred. "How much violence would you like to witness today?"

"Stop!" cried Argus. He addressed his men. "Put down your weapons." Swords clattered to the ground. Reluctantly, Gwendolyn and Aethelred did the same. Picking up the blades, the gnomes gathered around the Valmarians.

Asmodeus smiled. "You see?" he said. "You *can* act civilized." He turned to the gnomes. "Prepare them for the initiation. They'll soon share our perspective once I provide them with the proper . . . vision."

The gnomes smiled knowingly while Argus and Thelda looked at each other in dismay. The Valmarians didn't understand what he meant, but they knew it couldn't be good.

As they were led away, Asmodeus pushed Gwendolyn and Aethelred into the hands of another gnome who stood nearby, a particularly ugly creature whose eyes were lost in the folds of his face.

"Take the children to the lower dungeon, Norr," he said. "I will attend to them separately."

The gnome picked up Gwendolyn's bow and quiver. Strapping it over his shoulder, he also recovered Aethelred's sword. "Come along, you whelps," he grunted.

When the king and queen realized that Gwendolyn and Aethelred were being led elsewhere, they cried out, struggling against their captors, but sharp blades were pressed to their throats.

"Keep going!" cried Kaag. "Or would you rather we run you through?"

Forcing them into a small tunnel, the gnomes disappeared with the Valmarians, leaving the children alone with Norr.

They looked up at the gnome, uncertainly. His face resembled a rotten onion, and his breath smelled no better. He smiled, revealing a mouthful of blackened teeth. "Don't worry," he said. "The dungeons aren't that bad . . . if you don't mind the rats."

7

FINAL PREPARATIONS

Norr shoved the children deeper into the tunnel. "You'd better not run," he said. "I'd hate to get blood on such a perfectly clean blade. Now, move!"

The path rose and meandered as they walked, and they soon lost all sense of direction. Unlike the cavernous halls and wide plazas through which they had passed earlier, this tunnel was crude, featureless . . . and empty. They saw no other creatures on the journey.

A jumble of thoughts filled Gwendolyn's mind. Dungeons were usually in the bowels of a castle. Shouldn't they be going downhill? Yet she guessed that they had already climbed hundreds of feet. The thought of being locked in a cell wasn't pleasant but being separated from their parents made it even worse. What did Asmodeus have in store? Gwendolyn knew she needed to find Kindle—fast.

Quieting her mind, she tried to communicate with the dragon. She called to him repeatedly, begging him to respond—to come—but she was met with silence. Had he been bewitched? The thought made her sick. If Asmodeus could gain control over him, there was no telling what he could do. No, she decided. Kindle wouldn't succumb to that. There must be another reason. He would come. In the meantime, she had to be brave for her brother.

She glanced at Aethelred as they continued up the passageway. He smiled back at her weakly, his breath appearing in small clouds as he labored to keep up with Norr's quick pace. The air had become much colder. She even sensed a breeze. Were they near the surface? That would certainly explain the change in temperature.

They finally came to a stone archway covered in frost. Norr nudged them forward. "Through there," he ordered. Passing underneath the archway, they entered a large, rectangular hall. Overhead, emeralds gleamed brightly, filling the place with light.

"Here we are!" said the gnome. "Home sweet home."

The children examined their surroundings, and realized that this must be the dungeon. Ten small cells, five on either side of the hallway, stared back at them. Each chamber had a gate with thick, iron bars but most of the gates were open. The dungeon wasn't needed very often. Most gnomes obeyed Asmodeus without question.

A shallow fire pit sat in the center of the room, built to warm the cells. The children noticed a few spare cloaks hung on the wall, apparently there to provide the guards with extra layers for warmth, if necessary.

Norr motioned to the nearest cell. "In you go," he said. Shivering, the children peered in doubtfully—and felt Norr's rough hands shove them inside. Before they could turn around, they heard the lock click into place.

Gwendolyn glared at the gnome through the iron bars. "What is to become of us?"

Ignoring her, he leaned Aethelred's sword against the opposite wall. Then he removed Gwendolyn's bow and quiver and set it beside the blade.

"Once Asmodeus is finished with the others, you'll know soon enough," he said. "Until then, I'd better keep you warm. It wouldn't do for him to find you frozen. No, that wouldn't do at all."

Reaching into his cloak, Norr produced a dagger and a piece of flint. He hunched over the pit and struck the flint across the knife repeatedly, his breath appearing in the cold air. "Yes, a nice fire is exactly what this place needs."

Gwendolyn looked around the cell. She didn't want to wait for Asmodeus to appear. They needed to escape. Perhaps they could still reason with the gnome, and convince him that they posed no danger?

"Asmodeus is using you," she said. "All of you."

"You'll get no argument from me," said Norr, surprising her. "Of course he's using us . . . using us to perform a mighty work. We're united now under a single banner."

"A banner of slavery!" shouted Aethelred.

The gnome struck the flint against the dagger once more, and a few sparks fell into the coal. A small flame flickered to life as he looked up at the children.

"Do you still not understand? We tried to govern ourselves, but we failed. Too many voices. Too many arguments. No, my poor, little fools, unity is what makes us strong."

Returning the instruments to a pocket in his cloak, he rose and rubbed his hands together before holding them out towards the flames. "Now, if you'll excuse me, I have a few other . . . guests to look after. I'll be back soon."

He smiled, sarcastically. "Don't go anywhere." Before they could respond, he was gone.

Aethelred turned to his sister. "Where's Kindle? Why haven't you called him?"

"I've tried," she snapped. "I don't know why he doesn't answer."

The boy pursed his lips and stared at the gate. "Then it's up to us to find a way out of here."

She looked at him skeptically. "How?" she asked. "Even if you had your sword, there's no way you could break these bars. Or have you recently learned how to walk through walls?"

Aethelred smiled mischievously. "He took my sword, but he didn't take *everything*."

Reaching into his boot, he withdrew a small dagger. Its pearl-white handle gleamed in the light as he held it up for her to see.

"What can you do with that?" she asked.

"Pick the lock, of course!" he said. "Stand back." Holding the blade firmly in his hand, he slid his arm through the bars and inserted the steel tip into the keyhole. Turning it gently back and forth, he expected to hear a click.

Only, he didn't.

Patiently, he tried again and again, changing the angle and twisting the dagger in many different directions. Unfortunately, it had no effect. The lock seemed impenetrable.

"Here," said Gwendolyn. "Let me try."

He handed her the knife and watched her struggle in a similar fashion. Frustrated, she gave up, and passed it back to him. "Got any other brilliant ideas?"

"Hey, don't blame me!" he said, defensively. "You couldn't do it, either!"

As they bickered, they heard a familiar voice. "Gwendolyn? Aethelred? Is it really you?"

They peered into the hallway. Locked in a cell at the far end of the room, Jorgan stared at them from between metal bars. The poor gnome looked like he had been beaten. His face, normally thin, was swollen and red.

"What happened to you?" asked Gwendolyn. "Why didn't you say anything earlier?"

"I didn't want to risk another beating," he replied. "Though I suppose I deserved it for not following Asmodeus's orders." He touched his face and winced. "Oh! It's all my fault. I knew I shouldn't have allowed you to bring those weapons to dinner."

Aethelred snorted in disbelief. "You blame yourself?"

"Of course," said Jorgan. "If I had done as Asmodeus ordered, there would have been no conflict between our two races. You'd both be headed back to Valmar with your people tomorrow, not here with me."

Gwendolyn shook her head sadly. "No, Jorgan," she said. "Asmodeus only *pretends* to want peace. I don't think he ever planned to let us go."

"I know his methods can be a bit . . . harsh," acknowledged the gnome. "I've even been having doubts lately about his leadership, but my mind isn't what it used to be. I can't really seem to focus anymore." He shook his head, as if clearing away the fog. "Still, he must have his reasons. If you just give him time, you'll come to see him as a visionary."

Aethelred stared at the ugly scrapes and bruises on the gnome's face. "Does that vision involve beating those who don't do his will?"

The gnome looked down, ashamed. "I still don't understand all of his ways," he mumbled. "If I could just talk to him, I could explain what happened . . . make things right."

"I'm afraid the only thing we'll be seeing is the inside of this cell," said Aethelred. "At least for the time being."

"Not necessarily," replied Jorgan. "You hold the key in your hands."

The boy looked down at the knife and frowned. "We've already tried to pick the lock," he said. "It doesn't work."

"Why pick the lock when you can unseat the gate from the hinges?"

Aethelred looked at the gate's construction—and laughed. "Of course!" he said.

Using the dagger's handle, he pounded it against the pin that ran through the knuckle of one of the gate's three hinges. After only a few blows, it loosened slightly. Striking it a few more times, he was able to remove it by hand. He did the same to the other two hinges, and the gate collapsed into the hallway.

"Well done!" said Gwendolyn. Picking up her bow and quiver, she slung it over her shoulder and grabbed Aethelred's sword. "Here you—Aeth?" To her surprise, he had crossed the hallway and began hammering away on the hinges that supported the gate to Jorgan's cell. "Aeth, what are you doing?"

The boy stopped and looked at her. "Setting him free, of course. If it weren't for him, we'd still be stuck here."

"But can we trust him?" she whispered, looking at the gnome suspiciously.

"We don't really have a choice," he said. "Don't you remember the maze of tunnels that we took to get here? We need someone to guide us back to the others."

Soon, the gate to Jorgan's cell was leaning against the wall. The gnome stepped into the hallway. "Thank you," he said. "You're a genius! I would have never dreamed of removing the hinges! Oh, bravo!"

Arching an eyebrow, Gwendolyn glanced at Aethelred before addressing the gnome. "But you just . . . Oh, never mind. We need to find our parents—and Kindle," she said. "Can you help us?"

"Of course," said the gnome. "Where are they?"

"If we knew that, we wouldn't need your help, would we?" she asked, frustrated.

"Well, where did you last seem them?"

"In the Receiving Room," said Aethelred. "Asmodeus said something about an initiation."

"Ah, the initiation, of course!" cried Jorgan, triumphantly.

"What's it all about?" asked Gwendolyn.

Jorgan's face went from happy to confused. "I—I don't remember," he said, frowning. "It's the strangest thing." He tapped his forehead. "My memory, you know . . . goes in and out."

"Can you get us back there?" said Aethelred.

The gnome nodded vigorously. "Oh yes. That's easy. We just need to stay on the main path. We mustn't wander, you know."

Gwendolyn held out her arm. "Lead on, then."

Jargon had almost reached the archway that led out of the room when Aethelred noticed the black cloaks hanging on the wall. "Wait," he said. "If we're seen, we'll simply be recaptured. We can use these to blend in."

The boy grabbed one of the cloaks and pulled it over his shoulders. It covered his body well enough. If he kept his head down and remained silent, he might even be mistaken for a gnome. He drew the hood over his head. "Keep your face covered," he said.

He handed another one of the garments to his sister. Removing her bow and quiver, she put it on, and her expression immediately changed to disgust. "It smells like someone died in this thing," she said, examining the thick material.

"Just make sure *you* don't die in it," he replied. "Now let's get out of here."

Despite his short legs, Jorgan set a brisk pace, leading them through the underground labyrinth. The children would have been lost without him. Skarsgaard was filled with all different manner of tunnels but when they came to places with multiple paths, he never hesitated, knowing the way instinctively. Occasionally, they stopped and glanced behind them, expecting Norr or someone else to raise the alarm but they saw nothing.

After a while (the children were never sure how much time passed under the mountain), the air had changed again. It had grown warmer, almost stuffy.

"How much farther?" panted Gwendolyn. She had developed a stitch in her side, and struggled to keep up.

"We should reach the plaza, soon," said Jorgan. "Then we'll come to the Receiving Room."

Gwendolyn slowed. "Do you mind if we stop for a bit?" she asked, clutching her ribs. "I could use a rest."

"Of course," said the gnome.

They stopped, and the children leaned against the wall. Aethelred wouldn't have admitted it, but he was glad for the respite, too. He was also thirsty.

"You don't happen to know where we could get some water do you?" he asked.

The gnome shook his head. "No," he replied. "But I always try to carry a bit of wine." He reached into his cloak and handed him a small flask "Will this do?"

Aethelred licked his lips. "Thank you." He took a long drink and then offered some to his sister. "Gwen?"

He noticed that her eyes were closed. "Gwen?" Her eyelids fluttered open. "Hmmm?" she asked. "Oh." She took a drink and handed it to Jorgan.

"You were trying to call Kindle again, weren't you?" asked Aethelred. "Any luck?"

"No," she said. "I feel like my mind is being blocked by—"

They jumped as a high-pitched scream erupted from the tunnel. The children had never heard such a sound before but whatever made it had to be large.

"What was that?" whispered Aethelred, alarmed.

Jorgan shook his head. "I don't know," he said, putting his flask away. "Judging by the sound, it's close."

Gwendolyn started to creep forward.

"Um, Gwen?" said Aethelred. "What are you doing?"

"We have to keep moving," she said. "I don't want Norr catching up to us." Without another word, she continued up the tunnel. Jorgan and Aethelred looked at each other and followed her.

They found Gwendolyn standing in front of another junction. Four different tunnels converged on this spot, creating a crossroads. The gnome pointed to the large passageway directly in front of them. "The Receiving Room is that way."

"What about these other paths?" asked Gwendolyn, looking in both directions. "Where do they lead?"

"I'm not sure," replied the gnome, scratching his head. "There are many lanes and corridors in Skarsgaard. I try to stick to the main tunnels."

Another screamed pierced the air, startling them. It came from the narrow tunnel to the right. Now that they could hear it more clearly, they knew that whatever made that noise wasn't a man or a gnome. It had to be a beast.

They stared at the tunnel. Warm air flowed from its opening, but it was not pleasant or inviting. It stunk of damp fur and rotting flesh. They noticed that the passageway was dark, too. The green light that illuminated most of Skarsgaard tunnels did not shine here. Instead, the path glowed with torchlight.

"We have to find out what's making that noise," said Gwendolyn.

"We do?" asked Aethelred, doubtfully.

"It'll just take a moment," she replied. "Besides, Kindle might be down there. The cloaks should disguise us as long as we're careful." She glanced at Jorgan. "Just hunch down a little. Try to stoop like a gnome."

"We stoop?" asked Jorgan.

They entered the tunnel. As the path descended, the foul odor grew stronger. Covering their noses, they turned a corner—and froze. Directly in front of them was a large cavern filled with gnomes. The creatures worked in silence, unaware that they were being watched. The children noticed that a network of metal tracks crisscrossed the cavern like a spider's web, leading in and out of the void through different passageways. Many of the gnomes moved along these tracks on pump trolleys. They sped back and forth, propelling themselves by pushing a lever up and down while towing other, smaller cars filled with dead animals.

At the opposite side of the room, one team of gnomes emerged from a tunnel on a trolley and stopped in the center of the cavern. They unloaded carcasses—seals polar bears, fish—and sped away. Another group drove large, iron hooks into the bodies before stringing them up to the top of the cavern using ropes and pulleys.

Jorgan and the children strained to see why the dead animals were being hauled to the top of the cavern. Unfortunately, it was so high and narrow, the torchlight couldn't pierce its darkness.

Aethelred stared in astonishment. "What are they doing?"

"Drying the meat, maybe?" replied Gwendolyn.

"No," said Jorgan, wrinkling his large nose. "Can't you smell? It's already rotten. Gnomes wouldn't eat that."

"Perhaps they're feeding something," she said.

"Feeding what?" asked Aethelred.

He didn't have to wait long to learn the answer. Another shriek, fierce and wild, caused them to cower against the wall as something hurtled out of the shadows above. It moved so quickly that it took them a moment to realize what it was.

A giant bat, as large as a gryphon, descended out of the darkness. Beating its wings, it hovered over one of the gnomes who stood near the edge of the cavern. He had just removed a torch from the wall when the bat snatched him up in its claws. The gnome didn't even have time to scream.

Gwendolyn and Aethelred waited tensely, expecting the others to come to his aid. Instead, they shrugged and resumed their duties. Sometimes the bats wanted fresh meat. He should have been more careful, and there was nothing they could do for him now. The poor gnome still clutched his torch as the bat returned with him to the cavern's ceiling.

The torchlight revealed that it was not alone.

More bats hung suspended from the uneven rock, crowded against one another. The creature took its place among them and began to feed as the gnome struggled in its grasp. Now the children understood. The gnomes were responsible for *feeding* these bats. But what purpose did the beasts serve? As Jorgan and the children wondered at these strange events, a last, despairing cry came from above as the gnome's torch fell to the ground, shrouding the ceiling once more in darkness.

Jorgan tapped each of the children on the shoulder. "I've seen enough," he muttered.

Shaken by what they had witnessed, they returned to the crossroads. Jorgan walked ahead of them, dazed, speechless.

"What was that place?" asked Aethelred. "Did you know about those creatures?"

"Why didn't the others help him?" demanded Gwendolyn, staring at Jorgan expectantly. "They acted like nothing happened."

Jorgan stared straight ahead, saying nothing. His face was ashen.

Aethelred turned to his sister. "I think he's going to be sick."

The gnome sank to his knees and lowered his head. "I don't understand," he croaked. "They left him to die."

"Then you didn't know about the bats?" asked Aethelred.

"No! Yes!" Jorgan put his head into his hands. "Oh, I can't seem to *remember*." The children regarded him skeptically. "You must believe me!" he pleaded, looking up at them. "I've seen things in these tunnels—bad things. I try to forget, but if I can't, I figure it must be for a good reason." He paused. "But this . . . . I don't think I'll be able to forget this."

Gwendolyn's eyes softened. "Good," she replied. "Because you shouldn't." She turned to Aethelred. "Even if we find the others and make it out of this mountain, we won't get far if Asmodeus has creatures like that to do his bidding. We have to find Kindle."

As if reading her thoughts, the boy spoke. "What if they've enchanted him?" He looked down as if ashamed to ask. "Why can't you reach him, or at least hear his thoughts?"

She didn't know why. She had called out to the dragon several times in her mind but silence was her only answer.

Aethelred swallowed hard and spoke in a whisper. "What if he's . . . dead?"

Gwendolyn's eyes flashed. "Don't be silly!" she said, angrily. "You're letting this place get the better of you. Do you doubt him so easily?"

"I'm—I'm sorry," began Aethelred.

She sighed. "No, I am." She crossed her arms and looked up the tunnel. "I shouldn't have lost my temper. To be honest, I've been wondering the same thing. I don't know why he doesn't answer me."

Her eyes fell upon the passageway immediately across from them. "What about that tunnel, Jorgan?" she asked. "Where does it lead?"

She looked around, and realized the gnome was gone.

"Where did he go?" she asked.

"Maybe he went to tell Asmodeus where we are," said her brother. "Do you think he would betray us?"

She pursed her lips. "I don't know," she said. "He just seemed so . . . well, so different from the others. In any case, it's too late to worry about him now." She nodded at the tunnel to the left. "Let's try this direction. At least it doesn't stink."

The path sloped downward, allowing them to travel quickly. Soon, they smelled fresh air, and Aethelred thought he heard a strange clanking noise. (Imagine a thousand hammers striking a thousand anvils at different speeds, and you'll have some idea.) Finally, they saw the unmistakable gleam of sunlight in the distance. It was weak but real, making the green light of the emeralds look ugly by comparison.

When they reached the end of the tunnel, they found themselves standing at the top of a staircase that overlooked an enormous cave, the mouth of which was far away. A patch of sky gleamed in the distance. Had they really found a way out? Then the children looked down. Hundreds of gnomes sat together on long benches that spanned the cavern. Some were assembling small metal rings, while others busily polished larger, caste-iron cylinders. It didn't take long for Gwendolyn and Aethelred to understand the purpose of this place.

It was a workshop.

To the right, small groups of gnomes, five or six each, huddled around ships in various states of completion. The children recognized the half-finished frames of hulls, piles of rigging, and canvas cloth that would eventually make up the sails. Strangely, these vessels did not appear to be made of wood but of strong, fibrous reeds lashed together, forming a dense web. A few gnomes hung suspended from ropes, hammering nails into one of the decks. Others stoked coals in a large pit while blacksmiths forged the metal bands and ribbons used to support the structures.

"Why make them so small?" said Gwendolyn, gazing at the ships that sat ordered neatly in rows all over the workshop. "They'd be lucky if eight creatures could squeeze into one of those vessels when they're finished."

"How will they transport them to the ocean?" asked Aethelred, equally confused. "Where are the masts, or the keels, for that—?"

A roaring noise erupted near the mouth of the cave. The children crouched lower, expecting to see some beast, wild and angry, emerge from its cage. Instead, they saw a strange machine as large as a house, belching smoke into the air. Peering closer, they marveled at its construction. The object had dozens of valves and pistons that all worked furiously, generating a great deal of noise and heat. A narrow, metal cone rose out of the top, spewing hot air and, occasionally, flame.

Was it some sort of torch? A cannon? Whatever it was, the gnomes didn't seem to think the machine remarkable. Holding a large, canvas cloth covered in rope, they placed one end of it over the cone. Slowly, the material began to swell, growing large and round. As it expanded, it floated upward like a balloon. Before it could reach the cave's rocky ceiling, a team of gnomes held it down by pulling on the thick ropes that encircled it, while others attached it to one of the finished frames.

"What in the world—?" began Gwendolyn.

Aethelred gaped. "Impossible."

"What is it?"

Airships!" he whispered. "They're building *airships*."

It was true. The canvas balloon, held fast to the basket with many strands of rope, slowly rose into the air until it rested against the cave's ceiling. A propeller, which the children originally mistook for a rudder, was mounted on the back of the frame to power the craft.

Gwendolyn and Aethelred regarded the gnomes with a new sense of admiration. The creatures may have been foolish enough to follow Asmodeus, but they clearly possessed a great deal of engineering skills.

"Polonius would love to see this," said Aethelred, shaking his head in disbelief.

"Let's hope he never does," replied his sister.

"What do you mean?"

"Don't you see?" She turned and looked at him, exasperated. "This is how Asmodeus plans to invade Valmar!"

8

A WAKING DREAM

Many years earlier, a small group of gnomes led by Jorgan had discovered a stone column in the middle of a cavern deep under the Daggers. They would have ignored it entirely if not for its strange carvings. Gathering around the tall object in the torchlight, they were amazed to find a series of faces staring back at them. Five faces to be precise, all stacked on top of one another. Each bore a different expression. Some looked evil, grinning down on them wickedly. Others appeared angry or in pain. None of them looked happy.

The stone wasn't made out of granite like the rest of the mountain. In fact, they did not recognize the material at all. This vexed them mightily, for gnomes pride themselves on being able to identify all manner of stone. They could tell the difference between quartzite and quartz at a glance, and the variations between sandstone and limestone at a touch. So when the texture and density of the column proved foreign to even the oldest of them, it caused quite a debate.

Some like Jorgan thought the stone was evil, and that it was best left undisturbed. Others, like Kaag, believed that it was a remnant of an ancient civilization, and that the faces were some sort of mysterious language or code waiting to be translated. A few believed it was a sign, an omen, from the god of the mountain, welcoming the gnomes to the Veerda.

After much discussion (and over Jorgan's objections), they decided to carry the stone back to their workshop to inspect it more closely. The task wasn't easy. It was almost twenty feet tall and six feet in diameter, but gnomes love a challenge. It took sixteen of them to hoist the column out of the cavern. Cursing and grumbling, they finally reached their destination: a narrow cave that looked out on the valley below.

Setting the object down gently, they prodded it and poked it, arguing about what to do next. Where had it come from? Should they dismantle it? Or simply keep it as a curiosity?

Finally, Kaag grew impatient. Using a wooden mallet, he tapped the stone from top to bottom. It sounded hollow. "Give me a hammer," he said. The others watched as he attempted to smash open the column. Despite his mighty blows, he didn't even make a scratch. In fact, the hammer cracked in his hand. The graven image leered back at them, cold and silent, daring them to guess its secrets.

Jorgan shook his head. "We don't know who made this thing," he said. "Until we do, it would be wiser to leave it alone."

"Nonsense," said Kaag. "I'll find out what's hiding in there, one way or another. Bring me a pick!"

As they fumbled for more tools, the column flickered and began to glow.

The gnomes looked at each other, mystified, as the stone changed color, becoming pale, then green. Harsh, radiant beams shone out from the column, pulsing in a rhythmic pattern, causing them to grow light-headed. They shielded their eyes as the light grew hard, casting shadows across the cavern. Still, they could dimly see the surface of the object swing open, like a door. They gasped and shuffled backwards as two pale hands appeared, grabbing the edges of the stone.

A figure emerged. It unfolded its long legs and arms slowly like a giant insect before rising to its feet. Its skeletal frame was wet, glowing with a silvery substance that throbbed with energy.

"Who are you?" spluttered Kaag, looking up at the tall, thin figure that stood before him.

The creature stared down at them. "A child of the earth," it whispered. "Like you."

The gnomes looked at one another in confusion. "You're not like us," said Jorgan. "You're not a naradi. What are you?"

"Come closer," said the pale figure, its voice growing stronger as it approached. "I will *show* you what I am."

***

Kindle stared at the dragon's silhouette in disbelief. Her scales were white save for her wings, which were specked with blue. She watched him with interest but he did not detect malice or deceit in her eyes. Still, there was something familiar about her.

"I've seen you before," he said, recalling the memory. "It was *your* reflection I saw in my dreams."

"Yes," she admitted. "You have seen through my eyes just as I have seen through yours."

"How?"

"Projection is but one of our powers," she said. "I will teach you that—and many more."

Kindle couldn't contain his curiosity. "Who *are* you? Where do you come from?"

"My name is Argent," she said. "As for the rest, perhaps it would be easier to show you."

In his mind's eye, Kindle saw an image. It was Argent, flying high above an alien mountain range, darting in and out of the clouds. She followed another dragon in the distance. "I was born in Merovia almost two hundred years ago," she explained. "My mother's fire set me free from my shell, but I found myself imprisoned again shortly thereafter."

"Imprisoned?" asked Kindle. "By what?"

"Her hatred," replied Argent. "It was she who taught me to hate and fear other living creatures, especially men. It was she who taught me to kill."

Kindle saw Argent descending on a mountain village like a tornado. The villagers, spying her in the distance, screamed as they ran. Some picked up children and fled into small, crude cabins. Others ran for the forest, hoping to find shelter among the trees, but none escaped. Argent devoured them all.

Kindle looked up at her, horrified.

"I was taught that only gold mattered," she continued, regarding him uneasily. "Gold—and survival."

Another scene appeared in Kindle's mind. This time it was a large, fortified city that stood between two rivers. Strange, narrow turrets capped with black marble rose from behind thick walls. Hundreds of men, armed with bows, stood on the ramparts gazing up at Argent as she hovered over the city.

They shot many arrows at her only to watch in dismay as her alabaster scales turned them back. Then she dove, flying along the top of the ramparts, smashing the men with her tail, and sending them hurtling over the edge. More arrows rained down upon her but with no effect. She took a deep breath and a torrent of ice erupted from her mouth, freezing flesh and stone alike. Soon, nothing moved. The city lay in icy ruins.

"You breathe . . . ice?" said Kindle.

Argent nodded. "My mother told me it was a rare gift. It's particularly effective when I'm near water due to the moisture in the air. You should have seen what I have done to navies, entire fleets." She paused, remembering another horrible scene. "As I grew older, I became increasingly unhappy." She smiled self-consciously. "I longed for . . . ." Her voice trailed away.

"Longed for what?"

"Meaning, I suppose." She looked up at him. "Something that involved more than killing and robbing men of their treasure." She sighed wistfully. "My mother told me I was a fool. That I should be happy with my gifts, and leave introspection to men. For men, above all, deserve death."

"Men have many faults," admitted Kindle. "But there is still much good left in them, particularly the young." He thought of Gwendolyn and Aethelred. Why had he not thought to check on them? He was about to reach out to Gwendolyn in his mind when Argent spoke.

"This place, what the gnomes call the White Waste, was not always so isolated," she explained. "Men once lived here. When I left my mother, I came here, though at the time, I didn't know why."

Kindle saw Argent soaring through the skies. Below, many small towns, separated by hundreds of lakes, dotted the icy landscape. The dragon made her way into the mountains, where she built a lair of her own, eventually filling it with piles of gold and other treasures stolen from the settlements she tormented.

"I had plenty of everything," she said. "Plunder, food, safety. Everything except a purpose." She sighed. "It was here in this cold, lonely place that I rested, weary of the amusement I once found in killing other creatures. Weary of *myself*."

"How long have you lived here?"

"I've lost count," she replied. "Years can seem like days to our kind. I killed. I ate. I slept. Then *he* discovered my lair."

Argent shared a new memory. Asmodeus stood at the mouth of her cave, arms crossed, watching her with great interest as she dozed on an enormous pile of gold. A smile played on his lips but he said nothing.

Finally, the dragon's nostrils twitched. She opened her eyes and lifted her head slowly. "You're a brave one," she said, surveying him. "Before I kill you, may I ask you for your name?"

"Asmodeus," said the creature, betraying not the least bit of fear.

"You must be quite a climber to reach me here so high in the mountains. How did find this place?"

"It was hidden well," he admitted. "But you must realize that after so many years of raiding towns in the northern valley, word would get out. It was only a matter of time before I found you."

"Congratulations . . . but what exactly are you?" She paused, inspecting him more closely. "You don't smell magical. You're too tall to be a man, and giants tend to be quite fat. I have eaten both, you know."

"I am neither," said the pale figure.

"A white troll, then?"

"No."

"Well, you must have come from somewhere," said Argent, exasperated. "I don't remember your kind, though I suppose I must have plundered your city, killed your family?" She sniffed. "Are you here to reclaim your gold?"

He began walking towards her. "You have done me no wrong nor do I seek your treasure," he said. "I have come here to give you peace."

"There is no peace for me—not in this life," she said, with a growl. Argent rose to her feet. "Now, whatever you are, rest in peace!"

She opened her mouth and sent a storm of ice racing toward him. It smashed into his body, throwing him backwards violently toward the mouth of the cave. (Imagine being pierced by a thousand pieces of glass, and you'll begin to understand how dangerous an ice dragon's breath can be.) He lay there, broken beyond all healing. Scornful of the creature's impudence, she lowered herself back into the pile of gold and prepared to go back to sleep.

Then, impossibly, he began to move. Argent opened her eyes, astonished to see Asmodeus rising to his feet. The frost still covered him in some areas but it melted quickly, sliding from his body in large, slushy chunks. The splinters of ice had not harmed him, either. They had not even pierced his skin. Most astonishingly, he glowed with a shadowy aura that seemed to absorb all traces of light.

She watched, dumbstruck, as he walked toward her, reaching out his hand. "You cannot kill me," he said. "I will show you a world where you will never have to kill again."

The scene faded from Kindle's mind and he found Argent looking at him proudly. "Asmodeus gave me peace that day, and all the days since," she explained. "When the gnomes found the Steadfast Lady along the coast, he said that others would follow. That *you* would follow . . . and you have."

"What do you want with us?" asked Kindle, drawing back from her. "What do you want with me?"

"To give you peace, of course," said Argent. "You and your friends."

"I already have peace."

"Come now," she said, reproachfully, taking a step toward him. "I have shared your thoughts. There is no need to lie to me. You love the people of Valmar, especially those children. (You have been thinking of them even as we spoke.) Nevertheless, you remain restless, do you not?"

Kindle sighed. She was right. He had tried to hide these thoughts from himself, but he still felt lonely. That is, until now. Here was a dragon, another creature just like him, offering understanding, fellowship, belonging. Just as important, she had forsaken her wicked nature. She appeared to have found peace, and simply wished the same for him.

"Asmodeus taught me that we are all one," she continued. "When you surrender your will to his and allow him to use your gifts to tame the desires of others, you will be happy."

Kindle bristled at her words. "Surrender my will to his?" he asked, recoiling. "Tame the desires of others? That sounds more like tyranny."

"Only because you assume that freedom brings happiness."

"What?"

"Don't you understand?" she said, frustrated. "You are restless precisely *because* you are free."

"What will I get if I choose to follow him?"

"Happiness," she said, beaming at him. "Don't you want to be happy?"

Kindle examined Argent closely. There was nothing in her thoughts that suggested she was lying. She was at peace with herself. Still, what she was saying couldn't be true, could it? Would Asmodeus really offer him answers?

He needed time to consider her words. As Kindle wrestled with his thoughts, the light behind Argent seemed to shine even more fiercely. He grew dizzy as it pulsed hypnotically, throbbing in his eyes and ears, making it difficult for him to think.

"I hear your thoughts," said Argent, softly. "You desire happiness, too, but you are afraid of what it means. Trust me. He alone has the power to make the world as it should be. He alone has the power to rule over all other creatures."

Kindle seized on something that had been eluding him. "Power," he said, resisting the urge to close his eyes. "Yes, that's it. There's a power here. What is it?"

Argent stepped aside, revealing a stone column at the other end of the chamber. It pulsed with a strange, green light, forcing Kindle to narrow his eyes. At first, he thought it was just another column supporting the cavern. Then he realized that five faces had been carved into its surface, stacked upon one another like figures in a totem pole. They were all distinct from one another yet looked alike, sharing the same wicked thoughts. Animated by the light, they seemed to look down at him, laughing contemptuously.

Argent smiled. "This is why I have called you here," she explained, hypnotically. "My words are but a poor substitute for the source of his power. Come closer. The stone will tell you all you need to know."

9

MADE TO SEE

Aethelred's eyes grew wide as he glanced down at the airships.

"Invade Valmar?" he repeated. "Why?"

"Don't you remember what Asmodeus said?" asked Gwendolyn. "He claimed that he would 'save us from ourselves' but I think he always meant to punish us."

"The last war," mumbled Aethelred.

They were interrupted by a shout from below followed by a small explosion. A thick plume of smoke rose into the air. When it cleared, a gnome's lifeless body, charred and blackened, lay at the bottom of a crater in the cave's stone floor.

The rest of the gnomes put down their tools and gathered around the grim scene. A few shook their heads while others murmured in confusion. Soon, a figure approached. Dressed in a red cloak, he pushed through the mass, shouting at the others to make way. Judging by the tone of his voice, the children guessed that he was in charge.

When he reached the edge of the small crater, he looked down at the body that lay at the bottom. "What happened here?" he barked, glancing up at the rest of the gnomes. Instead of answering, they kept their eyes fixed on the ground.

He pointed to one of the shorter gnomes. "You there, Crum isn't it?"

After hesitating, Crum stepped forward. He was small even for a gnome. His cloak trailed along the ground almost comically and his nose waddled from side to side when he walked. Unlike the figure in the red cloak, however, his eyes seemed meek, introspective.

"Yes, Captain Sneed?" he asked, glancing up fearfully.

"What do you have there?"

Crum looked down. He was holding a round, black object that resembled a bowling ball. (Though bowling wouldn't be invented for another hundred years, the trolls played a similar game with the skulls and bones of their victims on rainy days.)

"It's an explosive, sir," replied Crum, holding up the shiny sphere as the other gnomes backed away slowly. "Kalrash handed it to me a moment before he dropped the other one." Crum motioned with his chin to the dead gnome at the bottom of the crater. "He told me he'd found defects in the fuses. He was just about to take them outside . . . to disarm them, I think."

Sneed's eyes narrowed. "You mean to tell me you brought armed explosives in here?" he growled.

"Not me, captain," Crum mumbled. "Kalrash."

"Serves him right, then," sneered the captain. "You know the rules! We don't equip the airships with munitions until they're ready." He turned to the others. "Do you hear me?" he said, raising his voice. "No bombs near the ships until I say so!" They nodded at him, dumbly. "Now clean this up quickly! The master wants us to witness the initiation!"

The gnomes hurried to do as he ordered. "As for you, Crum, make sure you get that bomb back to the explosives department—and don't drop it!"

"Yes, sir," said the gnome. "Right away!" Holding the object carefully, he shuffled away and headed toward the stairs that led to the ledge on which Gwendolyn and Aethelred stood.

Seeing him approach, they ducked back behind the tunnel's opening.

"Initiation?" said Gwendolyn. "What did he mean by that?"

"How should I know?" whispered Aethelred. "But when Crum reaches the top of the stairs, he'll spot us and raise the alarm. We need to go . . . now."

"No, he won't utter a word, not if you're quick enough," she replied. She hoisted her bow over her shoulder with both hands like a club.

Aethelred looked at her in alarm. "Please tell me you're not going to do anything stupid."

"We need that bomb."

"Why?" he demanded. "So we can die like that other poor creature?"

"We can use it to call Kindle."

"What about the one that just exploded?" he asked. "Wouldn't he have heard that, too?"

Gwendolyn shook her head. "He's not around here. I may not be able to hear him but I can always sense his presence when he's near. We need to return to the place where we last saw him, the Receiving Room."

"Then what?"

She peeked out from behind the tunnel's entrance. Crum was halfway up the stairs, holding the bomb carefully as his nose bobbed back and forth. He would pass through the archway in a matter of seconds.

"We detonate the bomb," she explained. "If Kindle can't hear my thoughts, perhaps that will be enough to get his attention."

"But—"

"No time!" she said, raising the bow above her head. "Mind the explosive!"

Crum appeared underneath the archway. He trudged along slowly, his pudgy face pointed downward, focused squarely on the round object in his hands. Gwendolyn brought the bow down hard on the gnome's head. He pitched forward and crashed to the floor, the explosive slipping from his fingers. Aethelred dove, catching the bomb just inches from the ground. Gwendolyn exhaled and helped him to his feet.

"That *was* stupid," he said.

She shrugged. "Only if it hadn't worked."

After dragging Crum's body into the passageway, she turned to her brother. "There's no telling when he'll awaken, so we should move fast. Keep that bomb hidden underneath your cloak and let's go!"

It was a difficult time for the children. Already cold and tired, they returned to the crossroads where they had last seen Jorgan and continued on, trusting that their cloaks would disguise them long enough to reach the crowded passageways of Skarsgaard. There, they could blend in with the other gnomes as they searched for the Receiving Room.

Eventually, the tunnel turned and widened. They stopped and smiled wearily when they recognized the main avenue through which Jorgan had guided them earlier that day. In the distance, they could even see the great stone archway that led to their destination. Would Kindle be waiting for them in that enormous cavern?

As Gwendolyn considered the possibility, she noticed that something was wrong. The streets, normally crowded with gnomes, were deserted. The plazas and squares sat empty. It was as if all of the citizens of Skarsgaard had disappeared.

She looked at Aethelred. Where was everyone?

Before she could ask him, hundreds of voices cried out, but whether it was in fear or joy, she could not tell. The sound came from the passageway in front of them— which led to the Receiving Room itself.

"Well," said Aethelred, with a half-smile, "at least we know where everyone is."

They approached the archway and peeked inside. The place was filled with gnomes. Fortunately, the creatures were all facing the center of the cavern, as they peered up expectantly at the platform that held Asmodeus's throne. Though it was empty, they repeated the same words over and over again in their strange language, as if trying to summon him.

The children couldn't see the entire chamber from where they stood, but it appeared as though Kindle was still absent. Were the rest of the Valmarians missing as well? Gwendolyn wanted to take a closer look. It was risky but she was tired of running. If Kindle or the rest of her people were in there, she would stand with them.

She started forward.

"Gwen?" said Aethelred.

"Just keep your hood on and follow me," she replied.

"Gwen, wait."

She stopped and turned impatiently. "I know it seems stupid, walking in there like this, but judging by their

145

excitement, I'm pretty sure they won't even notice us. Besides—"

"Listen for a second!" He pointed to another tunnel to the left of the main entrance. It contained a stairwell that led upward. "Remember the balcony that rings the cavern? Why don't we try these stairs? If I'm right, we can see everything that's going on, but we won't be stuck in the middle of all of those gnomes if we're discovered."

"Why didn't you say so?"

When they reached the balcony, it was just as Aethelred had predicted. They could now see the entire Receiving Room—but the view wasn't encouraging. A sea of gnomes filled the cavern. Kindle and the others were nowhere to be seen, but Uncle Wulfric and the rest of the Steadfast Lady's sailors were present.

A large crowd of gnomes and men encircled the empty throne, chanting together in harmony. Wulfric and his men used the common tongue, which allowed the children to recognize the words.

Asmodeus! Asmodeus! You saved us from ourselves!
You taught us how to see, and caught us when we fell!
Asmodeus! Asmodeus! You made us brave and strong!
Our eyes are open wide, and we'll never again be wrong!

Suddenly, Asmodeus appeared from the far end of the cavern. Making his way through the crowd, he ascended the steps of the pyramid in long, slow strides. Those closest to him stopped and retreated, afraid to touch the pale creature they called master. When he reached the top, he sat on his throne, his skeletal face brooding and cruel, resembling an ancient idol.

A moment later, Argus and Thelda were pushed through a passageway at the opposite end of the chamber, followed by the rest of the Fearless Finn's crew. Flanked by a group of gnomes, the Valmarians' hands were bound by thick rope. They were made to stop at the mouth of the tunnel from which they had appeared, and watched the assembly in dismay.

"What's to become of them?" whispered Aethelred.

"Nothing good, I'll wager," she replied.

As if in response to her words, the mob began to chant even louder. Asmodeus had risen, and was now standing on the edge of the platform, his long arms open wide as if he meant to embrace everyone at once. Aethelred noticed again the cloud of darkness that seemed to hover and swirl around the pale figure, obscuring his appearance.

"My children!" shouted Asmodeus, looking down on the host of creatures. The chanting gave way to silence as they gazed up at him, listening intently. "My children, today, we will receive others into the fold." His eyes fell on Argus. "Though they come to us stubborn, blind, we will cure them—starting with their king!"

Despite the protestations of Thelda and his people, Argus was forcibly separated from the others by two burly gnomes and led across the cavern. They stopped in front of the platform and looked up at Asmodeus.

"What say you, Argus?" asked the ghoulish figure. "Will you not join us?"

Everyone remained silent, straining to hear the king's answer.

Argus looked up at him contemptuously. "Join you?" He raised his hands, showing the bonds that constrained him. "You may have robbed me of my sword, but not my wits."

Asmodeus shook his head sadly. "Still blind." He addressed the gnomes once more. "What do the rest of you say? Shall we help him to see more clearly?"

"Yes!" they cried. "Make him see!"

"Very well," he said. "Bring him to me!"

The two gnomes grabbed Argus by the arms, and forced him up the stairs. If the king was afraid, he didn't show it. When they reached the top of the pyramid, he looked at Thelda and smiled bravely. One of the gnomes kicked him in the back of the knees, causing him to fall forward, and he landed at the foot of the throne.

He looked up at Asmodeus defiantly. "You may break my body," he said, "but you'll never break my will."

"I have not brought you here to break you," Asmodeus replied. "Only to make you *see*."

He reached down and touched Argus's forehead with two long, white fingers. At first, nothing happened. The king neither struggled nor moved. Soon, however, he began to shake, convulsing in great spasms as his eyelids fluttered. The mob roared in delight.

"See, Valmarian!" they shouted. "See—and be happy!"

Aethelred watched from the balcony as the dark shroud that concealed Asmodeus fell away. He could see him clearly for the first time. The boy's eyes widened. The creature's fingers weren't really pale and rigid. They writhed and twisted, slithering around his father's face before settling on his forehead.

They were no longer fingers at all, but snakes.

Aethelred glanced down at his hands. He remembered the Malodoi, the ancient evil that he had found on Cloud Isle. Preying upon his fears, it had urged him to do and say things he knew to be wrong. At first, he was complicit in the lies, the reckless behavior, but he had told himself that such things were necessary. As his craving for the spirit's power grew, he had begun to change, becoming darker, angrier, endangering the lives of those he loved. Though Oorano had freed him from the Malodoi's control, Aethelred was stunned to see that it had found its way into this world again.

He took a step backwards and felt Gwendolyn's arm on his shoulder. "The Malodoi," he whispered, as if the name made him physically ill. "It's the Malodoi."

"What are you talking about?" she asked.

"Can't you see them?" he said. "The serpents?"

"Serpents?" Gwendolyn's eyes darted back to the scene below but she saw only her father on his knees. "Where?"

"They're coming out of his hand," he explained. "It's not just Asmodeus. The *Malodoi* is a part of him."

Gwendolyn put her hand on her brother's shoulder. "I don't know how you're able to see it, but I believe you," she replied. "We have to do something."

Still on his knees, Argus cried out and would have fallen, but Asmodeus caught him in his arms. Aethelred watched the creature's fingers become rigid again. The king looked pale, exhausted—and different. He now bore two dark spots on his forehead just like the others. They weren't tattoos, Aethelred now realized.

They were bite marks.

Lifting Argus like a child, Asmodeus set him on his feet. The king no longer looked defiant. Instead, he stared straight ahead, lost and broken. Asmodeus gazed into his eyes. He smiled triumphantly. "You see clearly now?"

"I see . . . I see clearly," repeated Argus, his voice purged of emotion.

As the king mumbled these words, his eyes seemed to recover. Instead of appearing empty, his pupils now burned with a blazing fire. Asmodeus nodded to the gnomes, and they untied the king's bonds. "Take your place with the others."

Argus bowed to the tall figure, touching his head to the ground, before rising to his feet and descending the stairs. The gnomes cried out in celebration.

"No!" cried Thelda. Struggling against her bonds, she tried to reach her husband but the gnomes would not allow her to move. "No, Argus! You must resist!"

Asmodeus ignored her. "Give him back his weapon," he ordered. "When the rest of your people have experienced my power, Argus, they shall fight for me, too. You shall lead them as we return to Valmar, together."

The king nodded as he was handed his sword. He didn't even glance across the cavern at Thelda and the others. Instead, he stood by Wulfric and the Steadfast Lady's sailors, where he was greeted with smiles and approving nods.

"We have to kill him before he enchants anyone else," said Aethelred, his voice trembling in anger.

Gwendolyn nodded. "Right." Unslinging her bow, she reached for an arrow.

"Those won't do anything!" he replied. "Don't you remember how father's sword couldn't even break his skin?"

"Then how?"

He held up the bomb. "He's almost directly below us," the boy explained. "All I have to do is drop it."

"It's too risky," she said, gazing down at the gnomes and men who stood clustered around the pyramid. "Father and the others are too close to his throne. If you missed, you could kill them."

"Not if they're all chasing you."

At first, Gwendolyn didn't understand. Then her eyes widened. "A diversion?"

Aethelred nodded. "If you can lead them to the other side of the cavern, Asmodeus will be all alone."

"Right," she said, giving him a hug. "Don't miss."

Crouching low, she made her way down the balcony. When she appeared at the far end of the hall, she saw a few gnomes standing beneath her but most were about a stone's throw away, near the platform. She needed to draw them closer.

"Asmodeus!" she cried, popping her head up. "Let them go!"

Everyone turned and stared up at the girl.

"Gwendolyn?" cried Thelda. "What are you doing?"

Asmodeus frowned but quickly recovered, masking his irritation with a smile. "Yes, what *are* you doing?" he said. "Why don't you spare us the trouble of catching you and join us. I see you've already adopted our dress."

Gwendolyn glanced down at her cloak and realized that the disguise was no longer necessary. She also noticed a few of the gnomes below her had slipped into a passageway without a word, a passageway she was sure involved stairs.

"Join you?" she replied, pulling off the cloak and throwing it over the railing. "Why? So that you can enchant me, too?"

Asmodeus held out his hands. "I only wish to release you from the world's enchantment."

151

More of his followers entered the stairway while those who remained on the cavern floor drifted toward her, scowling. Gwendolyn realized that her brother's plan may have worked *too* well. All eyes were focused on her. The balcony would soon be swarming with gnomes but others remained near Asmodeus. She had to draw more of them away from the platform on which he stood.

"Gwendolyn!" shouted the queen. "They're coming!"

At least ten gnomes and even a few of the Valmarians had reached the balcony and approached her from both directions. Glancing behind her, Gwendolyn noticed that the crevices in the cavern walls were deep enough for her fingers and toes to find a hold. As an expert climber, she had scaled many trees and stones in Valmar more challenging than this.

"I know they're coming, mother," she shouted, fitting a toe in one of the gaps. "But they can't hold us down forever. Eventually, we rise!"

She started to climb. By the time the first gnome reached the spot where she had been standing, she was already twelve feet above him. Soon, the far side of the balcony was teeming with angry gnomes and men. They attempted to scale the wall but their large fingers made it impossible for them to follow. Others near Asmodeus walked across the room to watch her, both curious and astonished by her dexterity.

After climbing a bit higher, she looked down and smiled to herself. The plan had worked. The area around Asmodeus's throne was no longer crowded. But where was Aethelred?

"Come now, Gwendolyn, you can't go much higher," said Asmodeus, staring at her in amusement. "Unless you can fly away, someone will have to fetch a crossbow to get you down. Tell me, can you fly?"

At that moment, Aethelred rose to his feet, revealing himself in the balcony directly above Asmodeus. "No, she can't fly!" he shouted. "But this can!"

Using both hands, he heaved the bomb over the railing. Asmodeus had no time to react before the object detonated at his feet.

The explosion was deafening. The shockwaves hurled Aethelred backwards as a huge plume of smoke rose from the wreckage. When the smoke cleared, the platform was in shambles. The emerald throne itself was destroyed. Most important, Asmodeus had been blown to oblivion.

Aethelred couldn't believe it. The vile creature was no more! The enchantment would finally be broken!

He looked over at Gwendolyn and the others trying to reach her. When they had recovered from the shock, they cried out angrily and rushed toward him.

"No!" he shouted. Asmodeus was dead. Why hadn't the enchantment died with him? Before the boy could raise his blade, the gnomes tackled and disarmed him.

Defeated in spirit, he didn't even struggle as they beat him and bound him. Finally, two gnomes lifted him to his feet and forced him down the stairway. When they reached the floor below, he saw Gwendolyn, flanked by more gnomes. Her right eye was red and swollen as she tried to wriggle out of her bonds.

"How did they catch you?" he asked.

"I was coming to help *you*, but there were too many." She paused. "Did you miss?"

"No," said a familiar voice. "He didn't miss."

The gnomes separated in the center of the cavern, as Asmodeus climbed to his feet. His cloak was in tatters. The children could see the blast marks from the explosion on his skin, yet he was unharmed.

"I saw the bomb explode!" said Aethelred, confused. "How—?"

"Your people have destroyed so much," replied Asmodeus, "but you cannot destroy me." His eyes seemed to blaze in fury. "No, not anymore." He reached out to touch Gwendolyn. "Now, I will help you both to see, just like I helped your father."

To his surprise, Aethelred heard several voices speaking in unison.

No, bring us the boy. We want him first.

As he stared into Asmodeus's eyes, he saw them change. They looked afraid. Aethelred didn't know how, but he knew that Asmodeus heard the same voice.

Yes, my lord.

With a long, bony hand, he reached out and touched Aethelred's forehead.

10

KINDLE'S CHOICE

Kindle stared at the stone column, trying to understand how it could shimmer with light. The faces, carved so cunningly into the surface, stared back at him. What did they mean?

He took a step closer and squinted, shielding his eyes with one claw. It was like trying to look at the sun itself, so brightly did the column shine, sparkling fiercely in the bowels of the mountain.

"What do those faces mean?" he asked, turning to Argent. "What is this place?"

"I have one more thing to show you," she replied. "Then will you understand."

Kindle closed his eyes. It was dark but he could see the constellations. He was flying. The wind, cold but pleasant, chilled his face. The stars began to fade as dawn approached. A blanket of silver clouds stretched out below him. Soon, the stars disappeared as the sun rose from behind a spine of grey mountains. Kindle realized he was seeing out of Argent's eyes again, experiencing a memory from her youth.

"You can go higher still!" said a familiar voice. "Follow me."

Argent climbed higher. As a young dragon, she had plenty of energy but she found it harder to breathe this high in the atmosphere. She willed herself to keep going, beating her wings swiftly, as the sound of her heart throbbed in her ears.

Soon, the sky faded until it was just a thin, blue layer below, allowing her to gaze up at the vastness of space. She smiled in spite of her fatigue. She could see the stars again! Never before had they looked so bright, so clear. They reminded her of the diamonds that lay scattered across the growing piles of gold in her cave.

"Those are a poor substitute for these heavenly jewels," she thought. "Why covet diamonds when this treasure is ours to see every night?"

She heard the voice again in her head. "It's not diamonds that brings us joy," it muttered irritably, displeased with her thought. "It's knowing that we have them and others don't."

Argent looked to her left and then to her right. She saw only the streak of blue and white separating her world from a sea of darkness.

"Where are you?" She was about to glance down when she felt a sharp pain in her tail. Stifling a cry, she tilted right—then dove, looking over her shoulder.

A large dragon, mottled red and black, was right behind her, matching her every move. Kindle gasped, recognizing the dragon instantly. It was his mother. It was *Destiny*.

"Why did you bite me?" asked Argent, reproachfully.

"To teach you a lesson," chided Destiny. "If you look up, you make yourself vulnerable to what's below. I didn't live this long by stargazing."

"But shouldn't we look up once in a while?" she replied. "The stars—they're older, greater than we are. Isn't it worth remembering such things?"

"What can be greater than we are?" snapped Destiny. "We were born to rule. No, it's better to look down, down on all other creatures. Never forget that. Now come. It grows late, and your questions make me weary."

Argent followed her mother as the latter dove underneath the canopy of clouds. Soon, they reached Destiny's lair, a cave that lay hidden in a remote valley among the Daggers. As one might expect, gold, jewels, bones, and an odd assortment of weapons littered the place.

The larger dragon assumed her usual resting place, filling a depression in a large mound of gold that stank of sulphur and rotting flesh. She lay down and closed her eyes, coiling her tail around herself while Argent stood in the entrance of the cave, examining her mother pensively.

Without opening her eyes, Destiny sighed. "What is it now, my little fool?"

"The stars," said Argent, still thinking about the heavens. "Who made them?"

"We don't ask such questions."

Argent stared out of the cave's entrance. "There must be something more."

"More?"

"More than . . . this," said Argent, turning toward Destiny again and motioning to the treasure that lay glittering at her feet. "More than killing, and plundering, and hoarding."

"It's what we do," growled her mother. "If I were to abandon my gold, what then?" she asked, as if the mere thought angered her. "Some stupid creature, probably a man, would surely claim it."

"If men are as bad as you say, why not help them to improve?" said Argent. "Why not *befriend* them?"

"Befriend them?" roared Destiny, horrified. "Do lions befriend lambs?"

"Lions don't collect gold," said Argent. "How much gold is enough? How many creatures must you kill before you're satisfied?"

"All of them." Her mother laughed at Argent's shock. "What do you want? Some grand meaning? Some high and noble purpose? It doesn't exist." She laughed again, forced, it seemed to Argent. "You're beginning to *sound* like a man."

"But why—" began Argent.

"Why? Why? Why?" mocked Destiny. "It's a pointless question, posed by philosophers and saints. One cannot answer it." She looked back at her daughter with malevolence. "I tell you again. Steal treasure and guard it. That is enough purpose for one's life."

Argent was about to object but decided it would do no good. She knew her mother loved her with a fierce, instinctive love, but she felt like just another piece of gold, another jewel in Destiny's collection. There would never be a true understanding between them.

"I am leaving," she said. "Now, today."

Argent quieted her mind and erected an invisible barrier between herself and her mother.

"You've hidden your thoughts from me," said Destiny, half-pleased. "Perhaps you are finally growing up." She raised her head and stared at her daughter. "But there is no need to leave. You will find that the world is the same everywhere. The same stupid wars. The same longing for power. The same unanswered questions."

"I've made up my mind," insisted Argent.

"Very well," said Destiny, angrily. "Go make friends with the lambs. They will never accept you, nor will I save you when they betray you. Go!" She snorted and closed her eyes again, resting her head between her claws.

Argent felt tears well up in her eyes. "Goodbye, mother." She waited but there was no reply. She turned away into the cold, winter morning.

The vision faded. Kindle opened his eyes again and found Argent standing next to him. He stared into her face, the irritating, green light in the background momentarily forgotten. She had tears in her eyes that sparkled like diamonds.

"You're—you're my sister?" he asked.

Argent nodded and smiled. "Asmodeus told me you would come one day," she said softly. "And that I would no longer have to be alone."

Kindle didn't know what to say. A jumble of questions flooded his mind. How long had she known he existed? Why hadn't she chosen to reveal herself until now?

Despite his confusion, he felt happy. He had found another dragon, a friend. No, more than that—a sister. Argent's experience sounded much like his own. Destiny had always been angry. He remembered his mother's reaction when he chose not to follow her. How she had tried to kill him for choosing to help the people of Valmar. Would Argent condemn him for befriending them, too?

He looked up at her.

"I know, Kindle," she, sadly. "I have seen that memory in your mind. I was afraid our mother would meet such an end."

"Then you don't blame me for what happened?"

"Blame you?" she said, astonished. "She would have killed you. No, brother, I don't blame you. Neither will Asmodeus."

Asmodeus. The creature appeared in his mind's eye.

"Argent," he began. "This Asmodeus . . . he doesn't seem right."

"That's because *you're* not right, and neither was I," she said. "But you soon will be. You'll finally see." There was no judgment in her voice, no condemnation. She said it as if it were the most obvious thing in the world. "We need not fear others ever again, and they need not fear us. Together, we can help him achieve so much."

"Achieve what?" asked Kindle. "I saw those gnomes long enough to know they obey him without question, as if they're all afraid of him. Why follow such a creature?"

Argent smiled indulgently. "Why follow Argus?"

"He's a good man," he replied. "A good king."

"What makes him good?"

Kindle looked confused. "His actions, I suppose," he said. "He is wise and fair—and asks nothing of his subjects that he would not first do himself."

"And yet he expects others to obey his will," suggested Argent. "For isn't that what it means to rule?" Kindle nodded, unsure of what point she was trying to make. "It seems you have found a very good king, a rarity among men," she continued. "But how did Argus come to rule?"

Kindle furrowed his brow. "What?"

"Who made him king?"

"He inherited the throne," said the dragon. "His father was king before him, and his grandfather before that."

"And where did they get their authority?"

"I don't know," replied Kindle, confused. "What do these questions have to do with anything?"

"Why, they have to do with everything!" insisted Argent. "All creatures must be governed, especially men. They are selfish, taking more than they need, and seldom contributing all they can. Men will only follow those who are strong—those who force them to behave."

"Argus isn't like that," said Kindle. "He doesn't force his will upon his subjects. He leads by example. He reasons with them, and respects everyone's liberty."

"Reason," sighed Argent, shaking her head. "Liberty." She paused. "Tell me, did he reason with our mother when she attacked?"

Kindle paused. "You're mixing things up," he said. "He didn't want to kill Destiny. He was defending Valmar, defending us."

"Yes, by using violence," explained Argent. "Don't you see, Kindle? Asmodeus does not try to fool us by telling us that the gods have given him authority, or that he inherited his power from a line of kings. He makes no apologies for trying to create a world of peace."

"Our mother would have said much the same thing," Kindle replied, with the hint of a growl. He noticed that the light had begun to hurt his eyes again.

"Yes, but her goals were selfish, wicked. She didn't care about the larger problem that plagues all creatures," said Argent. "The problem of freedom."

"How is that a problem?" demanded Kindle.

"Look how much misery it causes," said Argent. "The rich hoard wealth while the poor starve. Creatures declare war upon one another for the silliest reasons. So-called peaceful revolutions turn bloody. All of this suffering will continue for generations unless one has the strength to end the madness."

"And you think that's Asmodeus?"

She nodded. "No other creature has ever resisted my breath," said Argent. "Nor provided such a simple yet satisfying vision for what the world could be."

The column's light was now pulsing so fast that it had almost become one continuous beam. Kindle gazed at his sister. She was so sincere. He didn't want to acknowledge it, but there was truth in what she said. For the first time in his life, he began to doubt his instincts. Perhaps strength was the only true authority in this world.

But what about freedom? Surely it was more desirable to be free than to be subject to another's will? He remembered the war he had witnessed at Grimstad. The trolls had attacked the giants savagely, killing many of them simply because the giants stood in their way. Could that war have been prevented if both sides had given up their mutual hatred? If Asmodeus could convince all creatures to abandoned their selfish desires in service to him, wouldn't that peace be worth the price?

Kindle looked at his sister's smiling face. She only wanted him to be happy. He knew that now. Perhaps she was right. Perhaps his love for Valmar was selfish because it made it impossible for him to see the world as a whole. Could Asmodeus really unite them?

The green light was everywhere now. It seemed to penetrate his flesh and bone, revealing everything. He stared at the column but it no longer hurt his eyes. In fact, it comforted him. He approached the source not with fear, but as a child who longs to know the truth.

"Yes, brother," she whispered. "Receive his wisdom."

Kindle wanted to be part of that light. Why had he resisted until now? It was so much easier to be told what to do, what to be. The light promised to wash away all of his former confusion. He wished only to share this feeling with the others, especially Gwendolyn and Aethelred. He paused. Where were they? He thought of the children but the light told him that they didn't matter. Nothing mattered except the light itself, and the certainty it promised.

Still, something else, the last remnants of his conscience, urged him to think. Why *had* he come here? What had become of the children that he had promised to protect?

Resisting the light's embrace, he closed his eyes and searched for Gwendolyn with his mind. Faintly, so very faintly, he heard her voice. *Help us, Kindle! You must help us!*

He opened his eyes, and found the light painful once again. The column rose up in front of him, imposingly. He could see the faces staring at him. They look displeased. His head began to throb. Despite the pain, despite his confusion, he was certain of one thing—he had to help his friends.

"The children are in trouble," he said. "I must find them."

He felt Argent's grip on his shoulder. "You must give yourself to Asmodeus, first," she insisted, her voice strangely anxious. "I would not see you hurt."

Shielding the green light from his eyes, he looked back at her, and noticed for the first time the black marks on her forehead. "Hurt? What do you mean?"

Kindle felt Argent's grip tighten. "I cannot let you go," she replied. "Not when you're so close to understanding the truth. Look into the light. You will find it easier if you just look into the light."

The light. Of course! Why hadn't he realized it until now? The light had caused him to forget the children, to forsake his conscience. The light had almost caused him to forget who he really was. Had it bewitched his sister, too? There was only one way to find out.

He brought up his tail to smash the stone but Argent dove and pushed him away.

"What are you doing?" she cried, horrified.

"Making my choice."

Argent lowered her head and crashed into him, grappling him with her arms and tail. She was not as big as him but she was surprisingly strong, and just as deadly. He didn't know if her breath could freeze him solid but he didn't want to find out. Before he could break free, she sank her jaws into his shoulder.

Stifling a cry, he looked up and saw the faces on the column. They almost looked real now. The five pairs of wicked eyes seemed to enjoy watching him struggle. If he could escape from his sister, he could smash them to pieces. But her smaller frame made her faster, allowing her to counter every movement.

Then a new thought occurred to him. Why not use his greater weight to his advantage? Reaching over his shoulder, he grabbed her head and pulled her forward as he rolled to the ground, dragging her with him. He fell on top of her with a crash, disorienting her. He looked up. There, directly in front of him, was the column, dazzling him with its harsh beams. The faces, once so confident in their malice, now looked quite different.

They looked angry.

Curling his tail around the pole, he lifted it from the ground and hurled it across the room.

When it struck the opposite wall, he heard it shatter, plunging the room into darkness. Argent screamed as if she had received a mortal wound, and went limp.

The pain in his skull disappeared but he barely noticed as he looked at his sister. Was she dead? Would he lose her so soon after finding her?

He lifted her gently. "Argent?" he cried. "Argent, please don't leave me."

She opened her eyes. The two dark spots above them had begun to fade. "Where am I?" she asked, looking around in confusion. "How did I get here?"

Tears sprang to Kindle's eyes and he smiled.

"You have been under a heavy enchantment," he replied, "but the spell has been broken." He looked up and saw the fragments of the stone column scattered about the cavern. "Do you remember who I am?"

She paused, looking around at room before finding his face. "I remember . . . I remember that you are my brother," she said softly, looking up into his eyes.

Before Kindle could respond, the ceiling began to tremble and crack. Small pebbles fell to the ground, and the noise grew louder.

"The cave is collapsing!" he cried, lifting Argent to her feet. "We must find the others!"

"Follow me!" she said.

11

AN OLD FOE

Asmodeus reached out and touched Aethelred's forehead, and the boy's world began to change. Everything seemed to shrink. He could hear his sister screaming, demanding that they spare him, but her voice faded along with the light. Soon, he could only hear the sound of his own breath, quick and shallow in the gathering dark.

He found himself staring into Asmodeus's eyes. The figure studied the boy carefully, the way a cat studies a wounded bird before it prepares to pounce. Unlike his surroundings, Asmodeus seemed more definite somehow, more substantial. It occurred to Aethelred that he had only seen a mere shadow of his enemy's countenance. Now, he saw him as he really was—but he wasn't as intimidating as he had imagined. Instead, Asmodeus looked exhausted, in decline. The skin on his cheeks, scored by many winters, sagged grotesquely while his arms looked withered and wasted. Yet he was still very much alive, driven by a force that Aethelred could not understand. Everything about him seemed spent. Everything, that is, except his large, pale eyes which glowed like lamps in the darkness. Aethelred couldn't look away. They absorbed the light, devouring it, leaving only a vast and impenetrable void.

The boy heard a voice, or rather, several voices, though he was sure that Asmodeus's lips never moved.

His blood smells . . . familiar.

The last vestiges of light disappeared. Only Asmodeus remained. He stood tall and white in the center of the cavern, like a sun-bleached tower, battered but unbowed. Slowly, his face faded, too, leaving only his eyes floating in the air.

Aethelred's chest began to pound, and the sound of his beating heart filled his ears but he could not move. More voices spoke.

Yes, we remember. The boy once showed so much promise.

A chill spread through Aethelred's skull and into the rest of his body, causing his legs to grow numb. He dropped to his knees and began to shake. It felt as though his veins were slowly turning to ice, especially in his right hand, and he struggled to breathe. When the voices spoke again, they were soothing, even merciful.

You could have been more than a boy. Yes, so much more.

Then Aethelred saw serpents grow out of Asmodeus's fingers and curl around his throat. The boy could still breathe but he knew that the snakes could change that in an instant. Five heads, all with different faces, hovered in front of him.

Do not despair! You may still be of some use.

Though he would never agree to serve the Malodoi again, Aethelred began to lose hope. Hadn't he killed this creature? Yet here it was again, taunting him, tormenting him. Then he remembered that the Malodoi was half spirit. It couldn't be defeated with swords or arrows. He needed Oorano's help.

As if sensing his thoughts, the snakes constricted around his throat. The voices became hard.

If you beg for your life, perhaps you can serve us once more.

Aethelred began to grow faint. He had to answer. Taking one last, shallow breath, he spoke. "You can do no worse . . . than kill me," he replied. "Oorano taught me . . . that I should not fear death."

The serpents wavered at the sound of Oorano's name. Suddenly, Aethelred felt his hand grow hot—the same hand that Oorano restored after the Malodoi had tried to consume him two years ago. As the boy lifted it to his face, he realized that it was filled with blue flames, yet they did not burn him. The snakes feared this fire. The mere sight of it caused them to recoil and disappear.

Instantly, the darkness lifted and he could see his surroundings again. He was still on his knees in the middle of the cavern. The others watched him in silence—everyone except Gwendolyn. He could still hear her, screaming and cursing as the gnomes struggled to restrain her. The darkness had passed, and even Asmodeus seemed smaller.

Unlike the Malodoi, though, he didn't fear the blue flames. "Oorano?" said Asmodeus, his voice filled with hatred. "There were some gnomes who once called on that name." He raised his fingers to the boy's neck, and Aethelred felt his sharp nails. "I fed their bodies to the bats, just as I'll do with you."

The boy closed his eyes and prepared himself for death. Instead, he heard a low rumbling sound as if the mountain itself had awakened from a long slumber. He glanced up to see Asmodeus stumble and cry out as though he had been struck blind, and then fall to the ground.

A cry of surprise and dismay ran through the cavern. Many of the gnomes surged forward, anxious to see what had become of their master. The two gnomes that had been standing behind Aethelred abandoned him and rushed to Asmodeus's aid. Soon, the ring of clashing steel filled the Receiving Room.

Aethelred rose to his feet and looked around. Everything was in chaos. Wulfric and the Steadfast Lady's sailors had drawn their swords, and were attacking the gnomes who guarded the rest of the Valmarians. Argus, meanwhile, approached the two gnomes who held Gwendolyn. In two strokes, the creatures lay dead at the king's feet. Soon, both children were free, their bonds cut by his blade.

Unlike the Valmarians, the gnomes looked adrift, lost. Only a few chose to fight. Most of the others, still reeling from Asmodeus's collapse, lifted his body and retreated to the edge of the chamber, anxious to avoid Wulfric and the rest of his men.

Gwendolyn looked at her brother. "What did you do?"

"I didn't do anything," he replied. "He just collapsed."

"Well, whatever happened, the spell seems to have been broken."

It was true. With the marks on their foreheads fading, the men of the Steadfast Lady were themselves again. Led by Wulfric, they made quick work of the gnomes who opposed them before freeing the queen and the other members of the Fearless Finn. As they made their way back to Argus, they moved warily, expecting the rest of the gnomes to attack. Instead, the creatures remained near Asmodeus's body, and stared at them dumbly. They had taken orders for so long, most couldn't determine what to do next.

Argus's voice broke the impasse. "To me! To me!" he cried. "All Valmarians to me!"

"Come on!" said Gwendolyn. She grabbed her brother's hand and they followed him.

When Thelda met the children in the middle of the cavern, she gathered them into her arms. "Gwendolyn! Aethelred!" she cried, clutching them tightly. She noticed Gwendolyn's face was swollen. "Your eye!"

"It's nothing," she said, looking around the cavern. "We need to find Kindle."

The queen nodded. "Of course, but do you have any idea where he could be?"

"You still can't hear him?" asked Aethelred.

She shook her head. Where *was* he?

The mountain groaned again, only this time it was louder. A few cracks snaked across the ceiling, sending dust sprinkling down, covering everyone in a fine, gray powder. A moment later, a large chunk of rock separated from one of the columns that supported the cavern, and shattered at their feet. Skarsgaard, a city without equal, seemed to be falling apart.

Still too stunned to move, most of the gnomes remained where they were, but a few came to their senses. "To the surface!" they cried in alarm, and disappeared up the passageway at the far end of the cavern.

"Quick!" shouted Argus, pointing toward the fleeing gnomes. "We must follow them!"

"But Kindle—" began Gwendolyn.

"We won't be able to search for him if we're all dead," he cried. "Now come!"

As the Valmarians began to follow the king, a small party of gnomes, led by Kaag, stepped in front of them.

A few held spears, and one even had a crossbow, but most were unarmed.

"You may not leave," said Kaag, hefting a spear on to one of his broad shoulders.

"Fool!" cried Argus. "Can't you see this place is collapsing?"

"No, it isn't," he replied. "It's just the mountain settling, nothing more."

Wulfric strode forward. "You don't owe Asmodeus your allegiance," he said, "nor do you have to die here. Come with us!"

Kaag furrowed his brow. For a moment, he looked as if he was seriously considering the Valmarian's proposal. Then his expression hardened and he tightened his grip on his spear. "You can't leave without permission." He glanced over his shoulder. "Naradi! Bar the way!" About twenty gnomes did as he ordered.

"Very well," muttered Argus, raising his blade. "We'll do it the hard way."

The men charged, swinging their swords in long, ferocious arcs, forcing the gnomes backwards. As they fought, the mountain rumbled and the ground began to shake. Another one of the massive pillars splintered and fell to the floor, crushing the gnome who held the crossbow underneath its vast weight.

"Why are they fighting?" asked Gwendolyn. "The enchantment has been broken!"

Another column began to crumble, falling to the ground in great pieces as men and gnomes scrambled out of the way. The fragments crashed to the earth, shaking the chamber and sending everyone sprawling.

Dazed and frightened, many of the gnomes looked around stupidly, still trying to comprehend how this could be happening. They had carved these caverns out of the earth itself. They were master engineers, expert craftsmen. How could Skarsgaard be falling apart?

Argus helped Thelda and the children to their feet. "Come on!" he cried. "We have to get out of here!"

The Valmarians ran through the archway and into the tunnel. Pieces of debris lay here and there, slowing their progress, but Argus had seen some of the gnomes flee this way. He hoped it led to the surface.

They moved carefully, glancing up at the ceiling often. Before they could go further, they heard shouting from behind them. Wulfric and a few others stopped and turned as more gnomes came running into the tunnel. There were fifteen of them, and they all carried spears.

"Go, Argus!" said Wulfric, drawing his sword. "We'll hold them off!"

As he spoke, another tremor rumbled in the distance.

The king shook his head. "We're not leaving anyone behind," he said. "If we must fight, we fight together."

The Valmarians raised their swords. As the gnomes drew closer, the children recognized the leader.

It was Jorgan.

"Please!" cried the gnome. "Take us with you!" Argus and Wulfric looked at each other. Was it another trick? Were the gnomes trying to delay them? "We were deceived—but no longer," he said.

Wulfric raised his sword to strike. "Liar!"

"Wait!" shouted Aethelred, stepping in front of his uncle. "He's telling the truth."

Argus glanced at the strange creatures. They looked scared, desperate.

"Very well," he said. "But if you betray us—"

"It is we who have been betrayed," said the gnome. "Betrayed by our own fear, but for the first time in years, our minds are clear."

As he spoke, they heard more voices. Kaag and others had recovered and were passing through the archway. "There they are!" shouted Kaag. "Don't let them escape!"

"Come!" said Argus. "We have to reach the surface!"

They moved quickly, avoiding the large rocks that littered the tunnel. The air was filled with dust, making it difficult to breathe. As they ran, they could hear the dull thump of a crossbow being fired from somewhere behind them. Suddenly, Wulfric cried out in pain. Pierced by an arrow through the shoulder, he fell to the ground.

As Jorgan stopped to help, a great roar sounded from above. They both looked up. The ceiling, already cracked, began to disintegrate. Pulling Wulfric to his feet, the gnome toppled backward as a giant piece of stone smashed into the ground. When the dust cleared, they were both still alive. The rock had missed them by a few inches.

Gwendolyn noticed her uncle's wound as he stumbled toward her. "You're bleeding!"

"I'll live," grunted Wulfric. "Thanks to Jorgan." Flinching, he pulled the bolt out of his shoulder. "But we mustn't delay."

Argus shook his head. "The tunnel is sealed," he said, motioning to the massive pile of debris behind them. "They won't be able to dig through that."

Jorgan sighed. "You don't know Kaag," he said. "He's probably got the others digging already. They'll be through sooner than you think."

"It's not them I'm worried about," said Thelda, appearing behind her husband. She looked up at the ceiling nervously. "This place could collapse at any moment."

They continued down the tunnel in good time until the path split into three different directions.

Argus stopped and stared at Wulfric, breathing heavily. "Which way?"

"I don't know," he replied. "We were never allowed to go above ground."

"We go right then," decided Argus. "Follow—"

"No," said Jorgan. "We must go left if we want to reach the open sky."

They followed Jorgan and his companions up the tunnel, turning corner after corner, not knowing if they ran to freedom or their doom. Despite the gnomes' assurances, doubt began to creep into the king's thoughts. Were these creatures trustworthy?

The mountain trembled again, only this time the rumbling didn't stop. Instead, it grew in intensity. They quickened their pace as the earth throbbed underneath their feet.

Soon, they turned another corner and smelled the crisp scent of the tundra. The children looked at each other wearily as the cold air stung their faces. Jorgan and the others had proven true. They saw daylight ahead. Gwendolyn and Aethelred had never grown accustomed to the harsh, green light of Skarsgaard. What a joy it would be to feel the sun again!

They rounded the final bend and saw the opening. A great, stone archway framed the grey sky. It was morning.

Argus looked tired but hopeful. "We're almost there!"

A crossbow bolt whizzed by Gwendolyn's head. She turned and saw Kaag and the others filling the tunnel behind them.

More bolts filled the air. Most fell short or glanced off the walls. But one found its target in Argus. The shaft entered his leg just below the knee and he fell to the ground. In an instant, Thelda was by his side. She lifted his arm over her shoulder and pulled him behind a large rock that had fallen from the ceiling.

"You mustn't!" he said, gritting his teeth. "This place is going to collapse!"

"Yes, but I'd rather we not be here when it does," she said. "Now move!"

Together, they hurried toward the archway. Argus hopped on one leg while he leaned heavily upon Thelda, as most of the others reached the opening. A few more bolts whistled through the air, and the shouts of their pursuers grew louder.

They were close now. Just a few more feet. But Kaag and his companions had not been idle. They sprinted forward and caught up to the stragglers on the threshold of the entrance. Argus and Thelda turned to face the creatures.

There was no time to think. There was no time to flee. The king and queen of Valmar raised their weapons and prepared to fight, hoping to give the others a chance to escape.

Suddenly, the sunlight dimmed, and a large shadow crept across the tunnel. Kaag and the other gnomes halted and looked up, frightened. Argus and Thelda turned and followed their gaze.

Beyond the opening, stood Kindle. His body filled the top of the archway, and he did not look pleased.

Kaag gazed up at the dragon. "It is forbidden to leave without—"

Before the gnome could finish, Kindle opened his mouth and turned him into ash along with a few others. The rest dropped their spears, screaming, as they fled back down the tunnel. A moment later, the ceiling above Argus and Thelda buckled and would have collapsed but Kindle rushed forward and propped it up.

"Go!" he grunted, clenching his teeth.

They hobbled through the archway, followed quickly by the dragon. Without Kindle's support, the ceiling crumbled, sealing the entrance.

The rest of the Valmarians huddled together a short distance away, while Jorgan and his friends looked up at the sky. It was cold. The ever-present wind whistled in their ears, chilling them where they stood, but they rejoiced to see the sun and breathe fresh air.

Nearby, the king grimaced as Thelda removed the bolt from his leg. Unlike arrows, crossbow bolts weren't barbed, and could be drawn out slowly without doing more damage. Still, blood flowed from the wound before the queen made a crude tourniquet out of the ropes that had been used to bind her hands.

When Gwendolyn saw Kindle, she strode forward, arms crossed. "Where have you been?" she asked, indignant. "Why didn't you respond?"

"I'm sorry," he said. "I—I was focused on another."

"Another?" asked Gwendolyn, a hint of jealousy creeping into her voice.

As she spoke, Argent descended from the sky. Despite her relatively short wings, she moved with great dexterity, checking her speed before landing gracefully on the mountainside. She folded her pale wings and addressed Kindle. "Are these the humans you told me about?"

He nodded. "These are my friends."

"Kindle?" asked Gwendolyn, regarding the other dragon in wonder. "Who is this?"

"This is Argent," he said. "My sister."

The ice dragon nodded solemnly but the others were too stunned to return her greeting. Kindle examined their faces, guessing their thoughts. "She was a prisoner here just like the gnomes," he said. "Asmodeus bewitched her but I broke the source of his power, a stone column deep under the mountain."

Gwendolyn and Aethelred looked at each other. "That solves one mystery," said the girl. "But why didn't you come sooner? Couldn't you hear me calling you?"

"It wasn't his fault," admitted Argent. "I filled his mind with my own thoughts to block out all others, but it wasn't enough. His love for you allowed him to hear your call, and defeat the power that had misled me."

Still leaning on Thelda, the king hopped forward. "It seems we owe our lives to you yet again, old friend." Kindle bowed in acknowledgement as Argus turned to the white dragon. "As the king of Valmar, I am pleased to welcome you to our country." He looked around, a bit embarrassed. "That is, if we can figure out how to *return* to our country."

Argent smiled. "I will go with you gladly."

The king addressed the gnomes. "What of you strange folk? Were you under his power, too?"

"Yes," explained Jorgan. "But there are those like Kaag who have always thought his ideas were noble."

"Noble?" exclaimed Gwendolyn, disgusted. "How could they think that?"

"Asmodeus was like a god to us," replied Jorgan. "But now that our minds are clear, we see that it has all been an illusion." The other gnomes nodded.

"Whatever he was, he's dead now," said Wulfric, looking up at the mountain. "He lies buried in the world's largest tomb." He smiled grimly. "The only things he can enchant now are the stones."

Jorgan looked up at him. "Yes," he admitted. "He was not what he claimed to be." His expression turned to sadness. "Still, he brought my people a measure of peace. Surely, that is good?"

"To impose one's will on another doesn't make the world a better place," said the queen. "It only makes it more violent."

Without warning, a bolt whistled out of the sky and landed at her feet. Then another. She stumbled backwards, dragging Argus with her. They looked up at the mountainside. Gnome archers peered out of a few circular windows far above.

"Take cover!" shouted the king.

Unfortunately, there was no cover to be had. They stood exposed on the side of the mountain with no shields to defend themselves. Everyone looked around wildly. Pine trees filled the valley below but that was more than a mile away. How could they reach the forest safely if projectiles continued to fill the air?

More gnomes appeared from above, sending another volley of shafts raining down upon them. Rising on his hind legs, Kindle sent a jet of flame into the air, turning the bolts into ash.

"Make for the trees!" cried Argent. "We will protect you!"

The Valmarians fled down the path to the forest while Kindle and Argent rose into the sky. More bolts filled the air. But as the dragons hoped, the gnomes were now aiming for them. They smiled as their scaly hides turned away the shafts with ease.

"Now it's our turn," said Argent. Hovering near one of the openings, she breathed a torrent of ice into the small gap, freezing the gnomes instantly.

A hundred feet up the mountain, Kindle scoured a small opening with fire, sending those who occupied it fleeing into the interior. Before he could turn away, he was stunned by an explosion. The sound and the heat sent him reeling, and he crashed forward into the ice. Before he could recover, another explosion struck his head, disorienting him. Toppling over, he landed near the crumbled archway from which the Valmarians had escaped.

Though his head throbbed, he wasn't seriously hurt. He looked up, and was forced to duck as a round, black projectile missed his face before exploding nearby. Determined to end the assault, Kindle spread his wings and rose into the air. After searching the mountainside, he spotted them. Two gnomes were firing explosives at him from a hidden opening. One was placing the bombs in the barrel of a cannon while the other lit the fuse. He shook his head and growled. *So that's what it was.*

They fired again but he dodged it easily and raced toward them. Screaming, they turned and tried to flee into the mountain—but dragons move quickly, especially when angry. Swinging his tail, he crushed the face of the mountain that protected them. He didn't know if they were dead, but they wouldn't be using that opening again.

Another bomb exploded. The mountainside seemed alive with gnomes now. They all shot crossbows or hurled bombs from dozens of openings concealed in the rock. Kindle glanced down. Below him, Argent was doing her best to dodge the blasts, but for every one she avoided, another exploded near her, doing no great damage but still causing her pain. She continued to bathe the openings in ice, forcing the gnomes to find other places from which to fire. Unfortunately, there seemed to be no shortage of such holes.

Kindle looked down into the valley. With the gnomes distracted, the Valmarians had reached the forest, and were now well out of range from the projectiles.

Using his mind, he called to Argent. *Our friends are safe.*

For how long? she asked. *If the gnomes don't get them, the cold will.*

Kindle sighed. *One problem at a time.*

They wheeled about and glided into the forest where they soon found the others. Though the trees offered them protection from the wind, it was still bitterly cold. The children and the rest of the Valmarians stood together for warmth in a large grove of trees as the dragons landed nearby. Jorgan and the rest of the gnomes were not among them.

"Where are the others?" asked Kindle.

Gwendolyn came forward. "I don't know," she said. "In the confusion, they ran east."

Farin, the young sailor, glowered. "Perhaps we were wrong to trust 'em."

Aethelred shook his head. "They helped us escape. Why would they do that if they meant us harm?"

"Maybe they just ran away . . . from us and from Skarsgaard," said Wulfric. "We'd probably just slow them down."

The Valmarians hated to admit it, but that sounded like a more plausible explanation. Everyone stood shivering in silence, wondering if they could reach the ships by nightfall before the temperatures became deadly. Without the proper clothing, it seemed unlikely.

Argus cleared his throat, and was about to suggest they begin walking south when they heard a rushing sound in the trees. Three large sleighs, each pulled by a team of polar bears, emerged from the forest driven by a small group of gnomes. Jorgan and his friends had proven faithful.

"You came back!" cried Gwendolyn, running up to the foremost sleigh.

Jorgan stepped down. "Of course!" he said. "There is another passageway near the one that collapsed that leads to the stables. It was badly damaged, but we were fortunate enough to find the polar bears still alive. We returned as quickly as we could." He motioned to a large pile of fur coats that the gnomes had also thought to bring with them. "You will need warm clothes for the journey." He looked at Argus hopefully. "Do you still mean to take us with you?"

The Valmarians looked at one another, ashamed of their doubts.

"Take you?" cried Argus. "Why, I could carry you!"

As everyone piled into the sleighs, they heard the sound of horns in the distance.

"What's that?" asked Wulfric.

"Survivors," explained Jorgan. "They will keep coming until they are killed—or they kill us."

"Let them come," growled Argent. "I'll freeze them all."

"No," said Gwendolyn. "If we hurry, we can still escape back to the ships before any more fighting is necessary."

"I suppose that is wisest," said Argus, looking at his daughter with pride. "You're growing up, my dear." He turned to the others as Gwendolyn blushed from the compliment. "Perhaps in time, they will also see through Asmodeus's lies like our new friends here. For now, we should make for the ships."

Soon, they were through the trees and racing across the tundra, leaving the horrors of Skarsgaard far behind.

12

A GIANT WEDDING

It was a cheerless morning, cold and grey, as the Steadfast Lady and Fearless Finn approached Valmar's northern coast in early winter. Despite the dreary weather, the sailors rejoiced to see the familiar cliffs, the old castle, and the crowd of villagers rushing toward the beach to greet them.

"Is it always this nice?" asked Jorgan, gazing up at the overcast sky.

When the children realized he wasn't joking, they laughed.

"I think you're going to like it here," said Gwendolyn.

***

Nine months later, the horrors of the White Waste were a distant memory. With everyone home safely, life on Valmar had returned to normal—except that "normal" now included a few new residents that made for a more interesting place.

Unable to remain idle, Jorgan and the other gnomes got to work immediately, helping Wulfric and his men repair the damage that the ice had done to the ships. By spring, they had finished ahead of schedule, and had begun constructing a fifth vessel, which promised to be the largest yet.

For Argent, Valmar was a strange, new land full of possibilities. Unlike the White Waste, everything here seemed so alive, so varied. She had left a world of black and white, and discovered a place where colors blossomed like flowers.

The way Valmar changed with the seasons fascinated her the most. Argent had become used to the cold mountain wind, the tundra's permafrost, the ever-present winter. Now, she had come to love the thin, green shoots emerging from the moist earth in spring, and the sun that blazed so brightly in the summer sky.

Aethelred volunteered to help her discover the island's beauty. Clinging to the dragon's back, he showed her the red-winged blackbirds flitting among the grassy plains, the grey foxes peeking out from behind the oaks, and the wild boars that trotted along the foothills of the Skeldings at twilight, searching for food. All of it captivated and charmed her.

The boy couldn't wait to show her how the trees changed when autumn arrived. Unlike the evergreen forests of the White Waste, most of Valmar's trees shed their leaves each year. The ash, for instance, would cast its strange, barbed seeds on the wind, sending them to float like dragonflies for hundreds of feet before falling gently to the earth. Then there was the sturdy oak, with its thick limbs and strong branches, yet with leaves meek and mild, like a child's hands. But the beech was by far Aethelred's favorite tree. Its red and gold leaves reminded him of sunken treasure.

Most important, Aethelred taught Argent that it was possible to trust men, and even love them. Finding

Kindle had given her hope that she was right to have rejected her mother's philosophy. Kindle did not covet gold or use his great strength to bend other creatures to his will. He did not mistake wealth and power as things to be stolen and hoarded. Instead, Kindle saw what all creatures could become—valiant, honest, kind—if they had the courage to do so.

***

On a fine summer day, Argent and Aethelred lounged on the cliffs near Ballan á Moor that overlooked the beach while Kindle and Gwendolyn played in the surf below.

"I don't know how Kindle stands it," said the ice dragon.

"Stands what?"

"The sand," she replied. "It gets so hot in the afternoon. A dragon's feet can be quite sensitive, you know." They both gazed down at Kindle. He was chasing Gwendolyn up the shoreline, pretending to fall clumsily while she ran, shrieking and laughing, toward the base of the cliffs.

"Well, he *was* born in a volcano," said Aethelred. "I suppose everything feels mild compared to that."

Argent rolled over on her back and looked up at the sky. "I was awakened by heat, too, but of a different sort. My mother's breath was the first thing I ever felt."

Aethelred knew that Kindle was an exception to the rule. Most dragons were born through dragon fire, which consumed the seed's tough shell.

"Does it hurt?" he asked. "The fire I mean."

"Yes," she admitted, "but our hides are thick enough to withstand a great deal of heat."

They looked up and saw Kindle racing overhead with Gwendolyn clinging to his shoulders, howling in delight. The dragon turned and swept past Argent and Aethelred before landing gracefully on the grass beside them.

"There you are!" said Gwendolyn, sliding to the ground. "Where have you been?"

Aethelred leaned back on Argent's shoulder. "We've just returned from the mountains," he replied. "Argent likes the cool air near Grimstad."

"Grimstad?" she asked. "You visited the giants?"

The boy nodded. "I introduced her to them," he replied. "They were delighted to meet her. In fact, they begged us to stay longer."

"We'll see them again soon enough," said Argent, giving the boy a knowing glance.

Gwendolyn raised an eyebrow. "You're going back?"

"We all are," explained Aethelred. "King Orion is getting married next month, and we've all been invited to attend the ceremony."

She clapped her hands in delight. "Oh, how wonderful! I've never been to a giant wedding. I wonder what the ceremony will be like. I hope there will be music, dancing!"

"What does Orion's bride look like?" asked Kindle.

"She's tall," Aethelred said, trying not to smile. The dragons laughed.

"Obviously!" said Gwendolyn, rolling her eyes as she smiled in turn. "What's her name?"

"Ocwen," he replied. "We met only briefly but she seemed very kind. She is certainly beautiful. I've never seen Orion happier."

"I know a wedding gift that would make him happier still," said Gwendolyn.

Aethelred nodded. "I think I know just the thing."

***

When giants have a wedding, it is typically a grand affair, and this ceremony was no exception. Broad pavilions had been built outside of the castle's walls to shield the guests from the fierce, mountain sun. Musicians played enormous harps, filling the air with music. Wild mountain flowers, native to the surrounding slopes, lined the terraces and walkways. In short, Grimstad had never looked finer.

There was only one problem. Two days before the wedding, Orion returned to the castle with a wounded leg. He had been gathering violets in the forest (giants traditionally exchange flowers on their wedding day) when he surprised a boar that had been rooting for mushrooms in a pile of rotten leaves. He had tried to avoid the beast as it charged him, but it left a nasty gash on his calf before disappearing into the undergrowth. Chiding himself for his carelessness, he cleaned the wound, gathered a few more flowers, and limped back to Grimstad.

Two days later, the vows that Orion and Ocwen made to one another were solemn and beautiful, but I am afraid I cannot tell you what they said. You see, the ceremony differed from a human wedding in one peculiar way. While a man and a woman proclaim their love for one another openly for all to hear, the giants believe such things boastful, and prone to exaggeration. Such important words, they believe, are too sacred to be shared publicly. Therefore, after exchanging rings and flowers, Orion and Ocwen quietly knelt before one another, held hands, and whispered their vows. When they were finished, they rose, still holding hands, and faced their guests as husband and wife.

After the ceremony, the giants began a celebration that was to last seven days and seven nights, with singing, dancing, contests, storytelling . . . and eating. The latter required a lot of food, and there was plenty to be had. Massive wheels of cheese made from sheep's milk and infused with truffles were enjoyed by all. The wine, too, was excellent, gleaned from the vines that surrounded Grimstad, crisp and clear like the mountain air itself. But the parade of fruit was considered by far the greatest delicacy. Strawberries, blackberries, raspberries, kiwi, cantaloupe and more were arranged and served ornately on large platters. Crowning it all was a prized delicacy—blueberries—most of which were supplied as a wedding present by the people of Valmar.

Since giants are vegetarians, there was nothing to tempt Kindle and Argent at the banquet. But they didn't mind. The idea of eating cheese or fruit offended them as much as eating raw lamb offends us. They left the party from time to time to hunt in the valleys for stag and wild boar, returning, bloody but full, as they landed and slept outside of the castle walls.

As honored guests, Argus and Thelda made toasts to the health and prosperity of King Orion and Queen Ocwen, recalling how the giants had shown Valmar great bravery in a dark time, which drew cheers and loud applause. Orion, in his turn, rose and thanked the Valmarians for coming. He recalled fighting beside Gwendolyn, Aethelred, and Kindle only a few short years ago, an event that was bittersweet, for it had led to his father's death but had allowed men and giants to become friends once more.

"Now that the Low Road is open again, we can come and go in each other's cities, as in the days of old," said Orion. "Polonius has done much to repair the ancient highway, and for that, we owe him a great debt."

He rose and lifted his glass to Polonius, followed by the other guests. Before he could bring it to his mouth, he swayed and would have fallen if Ocwen hadn't caught him around the waist.

"Are you not feeling well, husband?" she asked, examining his face.

Orion smiled weakly. "Too much wine."

She felt his forehead. "You're running a fever," she replied. "Perhaps we should get you to bed."

When the next morning arrived, it was clear that something was wrong. The guests sat under the pavilions. Breakfast had been prepared. The musicians stood ready to play their instruments. Only, Orion and Ocwen had not emerged from the castle. They typically came in last, greeting each guest as they entered, before taking their place at the high table. As the minutes passed, it became obvious that they had been delayed.

"Where are they?" asked Aethelred, shifting in his seat. "I'm hungry."

"Hush," said Thelda. "A few more moments won't hurt you."

One of the giants of Orion's household entered the tent and approached Thelda. "My lady," he said, quietly. "I have been told that you have some skill in healing?"

The others became silent, straining to hear his words.

She looked up, surprised. "I do."

"The king's fever remains high, I'm afraid. The wound he received from the boar wasn't cleaned properly, and it's become infected. Our healers have tried everything, but it has festered. Queen Ocwen has bid you come."

Thelda rose. "Of course."

"In the meantime," he said, turning to the others and raising his voice for all to hear, "please stay and eat. I have no doubt that King Orion will soon recover."

***

When Thelda returned a short while later, she looked concerned. She found Argus and the children sitting under an oak tree outside of the castle enjoying the cool mountain air, accompanied by Kindle and Argent.

"How bad is it?" asked the king, rising to his feet.

"Bad enough," she replied. "His leg is swollen and his fever has grown quite hot. Ocwen is very worried." She looked back at the castle. "I promised to return soon, for I believe my presence provides a small amount of comfort to her."

"What do his healers say?" said Gwendolyn.

"They have tried several remedies, even going so far as to lance the wound, but nothing brings relief," replied Thelda. "They are keeping the fever down by applying cold water to his neck but that only treats the symptoms of the infection."

"What about Eldon?" asked Aethelred, remembering the gryphon who lived in the mountains. "Could he recommend a cure?"

"He nests in places unknown to us," said the queen. "I doubt we could find him in time."

"Then what is to be done?" said Argus, growing alarmed. He began pacing. "Are we to simply wait here while the illness consumes Orion?"

"There is one plant that Eldon told me could cure all manner of infections," said Thelda. "I believe he called it *garnica*. It is a white flower, almost like a daisy but much larger, which grows on tall, green stalks, near water."

Argus's eyes widened. "I know the flower well," he said. "It was once plentiful in the lakes near Ballan á Moor when I was a boy, but it's now quite scarce. I've heard that it's still common in the Solitary Marshes, but it's been years since I've been there myself."

Thelda was about to respond when a giantess appeared. The children recognized her as one of Queen Ocwen's servants. "Excuse me, my lady," she said, "but I've been sent to ask that you return to King Orion's chamber at once."

"Has his condition changed?" asked Thelda.

The giantess looked down, unwilling to meet her gaze. "It's worse, if anything," she said, hiding her tears. "Orion begins to rave, as if he doesn't know where he is."

"I'll come immediately."

"As will I," said the king, taking his wife's hand.

After watching her parents follow the giantess through the castle's gate, Gwendolyn looked at Kindle. "How long would it take us to reach the Solitary Marshes?"

"An hour or so, I'd say, with a good tailwind," replied the dragon.

"Well?" she asked. "Orion needs that flower—that garnica—if he's to get any better. If we left now, we could be back by nightfall. They wouldn't even miss us."

Kindle furrowed his brow. "Have you forgotten that the trolls still make their home there?"

Aethelred walked over and stood next to his sister. "Yes, but they're only active at night," he said, crossing his arms. "Besides, Orion is our friend."

Gwendolyn nodded. "We're running out of time."

Argent looked at Kindle. "It *would* be less dangerous if we all went," she said. "You can take Gwendolyn and I'll carry Aethelred. We can search twice the area that way. If those marshes are infested with trolls, I think they'd just as soon run at the sight of two dragons."

"Very well," replied Kindle. "But we return before nightfall . . . no exceptions."

"No exceptions," agreed the children.

Aethelred ran to his room to retrieve a small satchel in case they found any of the garnica. He also grabbed his short sword and scabbard as well as Gwendolyn's dagger, bow, and quiver of arrows before returning to the edge of the forest outside of the castle.

"I doubt we'll need these given our company," he said, handing Gwendolyn her weapons. "But it won't hurt, either."

After mounting the dragons, they rose into the air and streaked away south.

Little did they know that something ancient brooded in those brackish waters far more dangerous than trolls.

13

DARK WATERS

When Valmar was young—before men built farms along the island's northern coast or the giants mined the stone to build Grimstad's high walls deep in the mountains—another creature had made its home there. This creature had no name for it had no language. There was no history, no record of how or why it chose the vast marshes in which to live. In fact, very few knew of its existence at all, only a few wary trolls who guessed that the deepest parts of the marshes were best left undisturbed.

They were wise to keep their distance. Occasionally, the marsh water would boil and froth as something large moved underneath the slimy surface, sending them fleeing toward higher ground. Other times, a wrinkle would appear in stagnant pools with no explanation. If some trolls went missing, never to be seen again, the others shrugged and asked no questions. They were, after all, trolls, lacking the empathy most creatures have for one another. Nevertheless, a rumor had grown that something lived in the middle of the marsh, a creature they called the Marsh Shadow.

The name was fitting, for though they lived in the Solitary Marshes, the trolls never saw the monster directly. They only caught a glimpse, a fleeting glance of something vast and slimy in the moonlight. Still, in the last few months, more and more trolls had disappeared even at the shallow edges of the marsh. Worse, a foul mist, which had come and gone in the past, now settled over the wetlands like a black fog, making the moon seem like a dull, silver coin floating in the sky.

As the children and dragons crossed over the mountainous peaks and flew along the foothills that bordered the marshes, they wondered at the dark clouds below. They didn't look like rain clouds. Rather, it was as if the marsh had polluted the sky itself.

Aethelred leaned down and clutched Argent's shoulder. "Can you get closer?" The dragon nodded, descending slowly into the mist.

Like his sister, Aethelred had grown accustomed to flying on a dragon. Gripping Argent's scales with his hands and knees, he had learned to press his chest against her back for warmth. While he didn't have the same telepathic connection that Gwendolyn shared with Kindle, Argent could still easily hear him if he spoke loud enough.

Aethelred sniffed the air as the marsh rushed by underneath him. "The stench of this place makes me sick."

"It smells of decay, death," said Argent.

"Decay is typical in a marsh," replied the boy. "But this scent is particularly foul."

"It is," she said. "Yet I feel somehow lighter here."

"Lighter? What do you mean?"

"Haven't you noticed?" answered the dragon. "I haven't had to beat my wings for quite some time. We've just been gliding. It's the strangest thing. I feel like I'm riding an ocean breeze, yet there is no wind."

"I wish there were a breeze," he muttered, "if only to blow this stench away."

By the time the dragons landed on a small patch of earth in the middle of the wetlands, the sun was directly overhead. The children jumped down and explored the shallow water and thick tufts of grass nearby.

Unlike a swamp, the Solitary Marshes did not have many trees, only vast stretches of lakes, interrupted by all manner of shrubs, tall reeds, and large, green lily pads that floated on the surface of the water. Thick clouds of mosquitos were everywhere, hovering above them, harassing child and beast alike. It was a lonely place, made even lonelier by the dark clouds scattered across the sky.

As the children crept across a small hillock, they explored the reeds and surrounding bushes, disturbing a heron who stalked the shallow water. Despite searching diligently, they saw no white flowers matching their mother's description.

Gwendolyn picked up a dead reed and approached the edge of the lake. "I'd guess it's about three feet deep," she said, taking a few steps forward. The water rose around her ankles as she probed underneath the surface. "Do you—ah!"

She disappeared under the slimy, algae-covered water.

"Gwen!" cried Aethelred, drawing his sword and rushing toward the edge.

A second later, her head reappeared, covered in mud. She was laughing and wiping the water out of her eyes. "I'm fine," she said, paddling back to her brother. "I suppose the depths of these lakes can be deceiving."

Sheathing his sword, Aethelred pulled her out of the water and helped her to her feet. It was soon obvious that the lake contained more than just muddy water. Long, tendril-like stalks clung to her legs, which she had uprooted as she fell.

"They must be the stems that anchor the lily pads to the bottom of the lake," she said.

"Here," he replied. "Let me help you."

Reaching down, he pulled at the plants and freed her from their grasp. As he did so, he noticed the stalks were covered in strange, translucent bulbs, which had been hidden by the water. He picked one of the bulbs to examine it—and immediately regretted his decision.

It stank horribly.

"Yeesh!" he said, covering his nose. "So this is why everything around here smells so foul."

"The bulbs on the water lilies?" she replied, swiping at the cloud of mosquitos that hovered just beyond her reach. "I think they're rather pretty."

"They don't *smell* pretty," he said. "Watch." He picked another and tried not to gag. "See?" he said, casting it into the water. "Maybe we should call them stink lilies."

Aethelred expected her to laugh. Instead, he found her looking above his head. "What is it?" he asked, turning to follow her gaze.

"The mosquitos," she said. "Didn't you see them? When you picked the bulb, they fled. Perhaps they find the scent as repellent as we do."

Aethelred looked puzzled. "Let's try it again," he said. The boy waited until the cloud of insects descended toward him before plucking another bulb from the green stalk. Instantly, they shot up into the air. He laughed triumphantly.

"What are you doing?" she asked, covering her nose. "Trying to drive us away, too?"

"Don't you see?" He glanced at his sister before turning to Argent. "It's as if the mosquitos are *riding a breeze!* That's why we could glide over the marshes so easily. The vapor these bulbs produce is lighter than air."

"What a strange phenomenon," said Kindle.

Aethelred removed the satchel from his back and began placing some of the bulbs into the bag, careful to make sure they remained attached to the long, sinuous root.

Gwendolyn frowned. "What are you doing?"

"Collecting samples," he replied. "Polonius will want to see this for himself."

She rolled her eyes and adjusted the bowstring strapped across her chest. "Come on!" she said. "We can't afford to waste time. We must keep looking."

When Aethelred had finished, they mounted the dragons once more and soared along the marshes, scanning the ground for any sign of garnica. The place smelled ghastly, but it was also teaming with life. Herons and frogs, hidden in the weeds below, made a strange chorus while alligators peeked at them from the dark water. The plants, too, were odd and beautiful. Moss and algae seemed to grow on every bush and tree they passed. Still more striking were the flowers that bloomed among the tall reeds. Yellow petals and crimson blossoms crowded against one another, making the marsh appear to crackle in flame.

Unfortunately, they searched for garnica in vain. The wetlands stretched on for hundreds of miles but they still hadn't found the white petals they sought. By late afternoon, the children began to worry. Not only would it be impossible for them to see in the dark, but this was the time when trolls began to emerge from their holes.

The dragons landed for a brief rest on a soggy hill while they decided what to do next. Nearby floated more of the stink lilies, their green pads bobbing along the surface of the water.

"I don't understand," said Kindle. "Your father said it was common here. Shouldn't we have found it by now?"

"We have to keep searching," said Gwendolyn, slapping a mosquito on her arm. "Orion's life may depend upon it."

The dragon sighed and looked at the horizon. "He is my friend, too, but the light is fading, and the flower remains hidden. We'll have to return in the morning."

Aethelred spied something in the lake. "Perhaps it's so common that it's hiding in plain sight," he said.

Taking a few steps into the shallow water, he reached down and grabbed one of the many lily pads that floated on the surface. He picked one of the buds attached to the round leaves, and pulled its green casing apart, revealing white petals underneath.

"Garnica!" Gwendolyn gasped. "It was here all the time?"

Aethelred smiled. "We just couldn't see it because the flowers hadn't yet bloomed."

"You're brilliant!" she cried. "Now, let's grab as many as we can before these mosquitos finish us off."

The children waded into the lake and harvested the buds from the long, slimy stalks, carefully peeling each open to ensure it was garnica. A short time later, Aethelred climbed on to Argent's shoulders while his sister remained in the water.

"That should do it, Gwen," he said, patting his satchel. "We have plenty."

"Just a few more," she replied. "Giants are big. I want to make sure we have enough."

She was up to her waist in the water, looking for more of the bulbs when she felt something cold and slimy coil around her foot. Mistaking it for one of the stalks that had entangled her legs earlier, she attempted to shake it off.

It constricted painfully.

She barely had time to scream as something pulled her underwater. Kindle lunged forward, splashing into the lake as he frantically searched the surface for some sign of her. Aethelred jumped off Argent's back and they followed Kindle into the water.

"Do you see her?" shouted the boy, drawing his sword.

Kindle shook his head.

Aethelred waded in deeper. "This had better not be a trick or I'll—"

He never finished his sentence. A thick, black tendril sprang out of the water and grabbed him around the waist. He cried out and tried to stab it with his sword but the blade had little effect. He may as well have been trying to pierce the trunk of an oak tree with a butter knife. Another limb coiled around his legs and pulled him into the lake.

Kindle dove toward him, attempting to grab whatever held the boy before it escaped. Like so many places in the Solitary Marshes, the water was deceptively deep. It rose up to Kindle's shoulders as he waded into the center, dredging the muddy bottom with his claws—but it was too late. Aethelred had disappeared along with his sister.

Kindle was just about to dive underneath the water when he felt something coil around his legs. Its skin was soft, but its muscles rivaled those of the mightiest dragon. Digging his claws into its flesh, Kindle began to pull it out of the murky, green water—and marveled at its hideous appearance.

The Marsh Shadow seemed like something out of a nightmare. It resembled a giant, black octopus, only it had dozens of arms radiating from its oily body, all slippery and incredibly strong. Six great eyes stared at him just below the water's surface as the beast opened its mouth, revealing two rows of sharp teeth. Before he could move, more tentacles coiled around the dragon's chest, trying to pull him underwater.

Argent watched, too stunned to move. If she used her breath, she feared that she would do more damage to Kindle than to the creature that threatened him—but she had to do something. Leaping into the air, she beat her wings a few times and dove in after him. Though she felt arms curl around her body, she was able to pull the creature toward the shallow water. Using their combined weight, the dragons reached the edge of the earthy knoll, and began to drag the beast on to shore.

Sensing that it had lost the advantage, the Marsh Shadow slackened its grip before releasing them completely as it attempted to flee into deeper water. But Argent wasn't going to let it get away so easily. She caught one of the beast's great arms in her mouth and listened with satisfaction as it groaned in pain. Free from its grip, Kindle grabbed another limb, and pulled more of its body into the light.

The water erupted in tentacles. The Marsh Shadow didn't simply have dozens of arms. It had hundreds. Needing all of its strength to fight the dragons, the creature released the children, and attacked.

When Gwendolyn and Aethelred surfaced, they began to swim away but the churning water slowed their progress. The creature roared as Kindle bit one of its limbs in half. But for every limb the dragons severed or injured, three more took its place.

Gwendolyn found Kindle's mind. *Use your breath!*

No, you and Aethelred are still too close.

She glanced at her brother. He was treading water next to her with one hand while holding his sword with the other. She had lost her bow and quiver in the water, but she still had her dagger strapped to her waist. Grabbing the blade, she watched as the dragons struggled to keep part of the beast's body on land.

"We have to do something!" she cried.

"Like what?"

"Attack!"

"Attack?" asked Aethelred as he struggled to keep his head above the surface. "Are you nuts? I stabbed it as hard as I could. My sword did nothing."

"Its limbs are strong," she said. "Its *eyes*, however—"

Another roar interrupted them but this time it came from Kindle. The Marsh Shadow had wrapped many of its limbs around both dragons, and had succeeded in pulling them into the water. It appeared that the creature's tentacles could do more than batter and strangle. The tips of the limbs opened and closed, revealing tiny mouths with small but sharp teeth of their own. Some of these mouths had found Kindle's throat.

"We must help!" said Gwendolyn. "Come on!"

The children dove underneath the water and swam back to where the beast sat on the muddy bank. When they resurfaced, they found themselves directly behind its great head. The lake was calmer now. Caught in a web of countless limbs, the dragons could no longer resist its strength. The Marsh Shadow pulled them both slowly but inexorably toward its great maw. Gwendolyn and Aethelred scrambled closer, and looked up at its face but its attention was fixed on the dragons. All six of its luminous brown eyes sparkled with malice.

It would eat well tonight.

Communicating silently as only siblings can, the children gripped their blades and struck together. The steel pierced the beast's eyes easily, going through them as if they were made of mud.

Never before had the Marsh Shadow felt so much pain. Its screams could be heard for miles, causing the trolls to stir uneasily in the foothills. Thrashing and spinning, the beast convulsed a few times before fleeing into the deep water.

Kindle plucked the children out of the lake and leaped into the air. When they were clear, Argent blasted a torrent of ice on the spot where the creature had been, freezing the surface instantly.

"Are you both okay?" asked Kindle, beating his wings, and climbing higher into the air.

The children nodded, still stunned by the attack.

"And I thought *trolls* were bad!" said Aethelred.

Whether the Marsh Shadow died that day in the lakes and bogs of southern Valmar or whether it fled to some remote sea to nurse its wounds and hunt again, this story doesn't tell. But for years afterwards, the trolls fancied that they could hear a beast moaning from time to time among the foggy waterways of the Solitary Marshes, though they never could be sure if it was a real creature or just the wind.

14

SWEET DREAMS
AND FLYING MACHINES

When they returned to Grimstad later that evening, Orion was delirious. His pulse had slowed and his lips had become cracked and pale as he lay in bed, drifting in and out of consciousness. The wound on his leg was still swollen, and had turned an angry shade of red. Sometimes he would start up, his eyes wide open, and mumble incoherently before drifting back to a restless sleep. With each hour that passed, he labored to breathe and his fever seemed to boil his brain.

Ocwen sat by his bedside, cooling her husband's forehead with a damp cloth, while Argus and Thelda stood nearby, watching helplessly.

"You should get some rest," said Thelda. "We'll stay with him while you sleep."

Ocwen shook her head. "How could I sleep?" she asked, irritably. "How could I rest knowing that his fever grows worse and worse?"

Thelda was about to insist when she heard a knock upon the door. Opening it, she saw Gwendolyn and Aethelred, wet and muddy, standing in front of her, holding a satchel filled with garnica. "I hope we brought enough!" said the boy.

Her eyes widened. "How—? Never mind. You can tell us later."

As the others looked on, Thelda peeled back the green bulbs and ground the petals into a thick paste. After rubbing some of it into Orion's wound, she mixed the rest with hot water, creating a tea that Ocwen carefully spooned into her husband's mouth. He muttered something unintelligible but swallowed the tea and returned to his dreams.

Cradling his head in her arms, Ocwen looked up at Thelda. "You're certain it will work?"

"Alas, there are few things in this world of which I am certain, but Eldon is seldom wrong," she said. "It should reduce Orion's fever. The rest is up to him."

The next morning, the giant's eyes flickered open. A look of disgust filled his face as he propped himself up on one elbow. "This is horrible," he gasped, licking his lips as some of the liquid dribbled down his chin. "What have you been feeding me?"

Ocwen, who was sitting by his bedside, nearly fainted in relief. Those were the first words he had spoken that she could understand in almost two days. "Something that will make you feel better," she said, wiping tears away with the back of her hand. She filled another cup and put it to his lips. "Here, take more."

The garnica worked—but worked slowly. Most of the Valmarians returned home while Argus, Thelda, the children, and the dragons remained behind in case more help was needed. Over the next few days, the color returned to Orion's face, but he was still weak, and continued to sleep for long stretches of time. After a few days more, he had the strength to stand, and regained his appetite. By the end of the week, he appeared on the royal balcony overlooking Grimstad's courtyard.

A host of giants filled the square below, remaining there in silent vigil, anxious but hopeful, as they waited for news of the king's health. They had been told he was feeling better but, understandably, they wanted to see him for themselves. Now, flanked by Gwendolyn, Aethelred, and their parents, Orion emerged with the help of his queen, while his subjects shouted for joy.

He looked down at them and nodded in gratitude. "Thank you, my friends. I am sorry for spoiling what should have been a time of celebration and merriment for all of us," he said. "But I will make up for it by extending the feast for another week . . . and boar will be on the menu for the Valmarians!" Everyone roared in approval.

Kindle and Argent, who had been dozing beyond the gate, were awakened by the sound. Opening their eyes, they rose into the air and perched on top of the castle's battlements. (Perhaps it had to do with the words "boar" and "menu," for dragons love eating roast pig.)

Orion looked at them and nodded before gently squeezing his wife's hand. "Ocwen told me that I wouldn't be standing here if it hadn't been for Thelda's healing skills, Argus's memory, the children's initiative, and the dragons' bravery." He bowed. "Today, we honor *you*."

"Long live the Valmarians!" shouted the giants. "Long live the dragons!"

Gwendolyn and Aethelred looked at one another sheepishly, pleased that Orion had recovered, but embarrassed by the attention.

The giant king held up his hands. "I declare the six of you Knights of the Mountain Fortress of Grimstad. Your courage, ingenuity, and faithfulness will always be remembered." Orion and Ocwen bowed again, followed by all of the other giants.

"I just hope they don't expect us to become vegetarians," whispered Aethelred to his sister.

"Don't worry," she replied, suppressing a smile. "I don't think dragons eat vegetables."

***

When they returned home, the children spent their days together playing on the beach, exploring the forest (Aethelred had become an accomplished tree-climber like his sister), and helping Polonius with his latest project.

Ever since the children had returned from the White Waste, telling the old man tales about the gnomes' airships, Polonius had tried to create a flying machine of his own—with miserable results. First, there was the feather vest. Strapping an intricate system of feathers to his arms and chest, he had jumped off a small cliff near the beach, flapping his arms wildly before falling to earth. Fortunately, Kindle was there to witness the experiment, catching the old man before he hit the sand.

Undeterred, Polonius continued to develop new ideas. While feathers alone wouldn't work, the shape of a bird's wing was, he still believed, structurally sound. He set to work immediately. Stitching together a dozen tanned sheep hides, he stretched the material over a large frame of dry reeds until it was smooth and pliable. Next, he slowly bent the structure, adding more and more tension until it curved, resembling a falcon's wing. Placing his arms through the frame, he found that he could manipulate the material quite easily. Gripping the reeds, he experimented by turning the frame up and down at different angles that would, in theory, allow him to glide through the air, at least for a little while.

On a warm, windy day, he asked Argent to take him high above the ocean before releasing him into the sky.

"I'm almost certain it will work," said Polonius. "This glider is much stronger than feathers. Besides, with the wind at my back, I should stay airborne."

"I'm not so sure," said the dragon, examining his invention with skepticism. "Your device looks rather like—forgive me—a kite."

"A kite?" said Polonius. "This isn't a child's toy. If the gnomes can build a flying machine, so can I."

Argent sighed. "Very well. Are you ready?"

Polonius nodded.

Soon, they were soaring over the ocean, with Argent carrying him in her claws. The old man clutched the glider firmly even as his long, white beard blew into his eyes. The children and Kindle observed from the beach.

"I don't think I can watch," said Gwendolyn.

Kindle looked down at her. "He's certainly brave," he offered, diplomatically.

Aethelred rubbed his hands and smiled. "This is going to be *good*."

When Argent had reached the proper height, she looked down at Polonius, wondering if he still wanted to go through with the experiment. The old man looked up at her and winked.

She released him. As expected, he plummeted toward the sea, but to everyone's surprise, he adjusted the angle of the glider, catching the sea breeze and floating upwards. For one glorious moment, he was flying. He looked at Argent excitedly as she soared alongside.

"Do you see?" he cried. "It's working! It's wor—"

In his excitement, he allowed the nose of the glider to dip ever so slightly, and the wind forced him sharply downward. Losing control, Polonius spiraled into the sea, doing the best belly flop the children had ever seen.

"I hope he's okay," said Gwendolyn, shielding the sun from her eyes as she waited for him to reappear in the water.

Kindle nodded. "Argent sees him."

They watched the ice dragon glide down as Polonius bobbed to the surface. He was unhurt, but his glider lay broken and scattered on the waves.

"It's not easy to overcome one's own weight while flying," said Kindle. "And the wind changes almost constantly, demanding frequent adjustments. Even when the air rises on warm days like this, we must adjust our wings to catch the lift."

Aethelred's eyes widened. "What if we created our own warm air? Or use something lighter than air?"

Kindle and Gwendolyn looked at one another, baffled. "How would we do that?" asked his sister.

"Don't you remember how the vapor from the garnica caused the mosquitos to rise?" said Aethelred. "What if we could capture that and use it to float?"

Gwendolyn folded her arms and looked at her brother. "Those were mosquitos, Aeth," she said. "We would need vapor from hundreds of those flowers."

"More like thousands," he said as he watched Argent pluck Polonius from the sea. "If Kindle and Argent would be willing to go back to the marshes, we could do it! We would have enough to propel ourselves through the air—in an airship!"

"Assuming they don't run into that monster again, and can find enough bulbs," said Gwendolyn, "would you know how to build something to contain the vapor?"

"No," he said. "But I know someone who might."

***

Building the airship was hard work, and included many trials and challenges. Kindle and Argent retrieved thousands of the bulbs in the Solitary Marshes, ripping them up in great handfuls and returning over the mountains to deposit them on the beach where the ocean breeze carried away most of the odor.

Meanwhile, Polonius and the children created and stitched together a large leather balloon to hold the gas. Remembering that the structure had to be strong but light, Polonius used reeds to construct a basket to contain them when airborne. That is, if they were able to escape gravity's pull. For the major challenge still lay before them. How could they capture the gas from the garnica, and funnel it into the balloon without it first escaping into the air?

Thelda, who had watched them hard at work one day, came up with the answer. "The gas rises, right?" she said. "So why don't you simply puncture the bulbs with one end of a hollow reed and insert the other end into the bottom of the leather balloon?"

"Like a straw?" asked Gwendolyn.

"Exactly," said the queen. "The vapor will rise into the balloon—all the way to the top. Once it's inflated, simply remove the reed and find something to cap the hole. It should float. Just make sure it doesn't float away without you!"

It worked beautifully. Despite the disgusting smell made by the gas, Polonius and the children soon had both the balloon and basket floating above the sand. They attached sandbags to the basket to keep it from floating away.

The children grinned at one another. They had worked closely with Polonius to construct the airship. Now, it was almost ready. Only one problem remained. How would they steer it once they were airborne? Gwendolyn came up with the answer one day as she and Aethelred watched the Steadfast Lady anchored in the bay.

"Sails!" she said. "We can make our own sails!"

"Where would we put them?" asked Aethelred. "There's no room on the balloon."

"Don't think of it like a sailing ship," she said. "We could attach them to the sides of the basket, extending them and rotating them as necessary to catch the wind."

Aethelred smiled. "Let's get to work."

Using a series of hollow poles, they constructed a frame for the sails, and lashed them together with rope. But they soon discovered a new problem. The sails were so large and unwieldy that they began to sag under their own weight, causing some of the poles to snap. They were about to abandon the idea when Aethelred came up with a solution.

"What if we were to telescope the poles?" he asked.

Gwendolyn frowned. "What do you mean?"

"If we fit the smaller poles into the larger ones, we can elongate them as necessary, like a telescope."

"I see!" Polonius beamed at the boy. "By extending them, the sails will catch the wind!"

After much experimentation and several false starts, they had it working. Polonius slid the sailing cloth over

210

the scaffolding and anchored the wooden frame to the basket with rope. When they extended the poles, the sails opened, and promised to capture the wind once airborne.

Now, all that remained was the flight itself.

On a windy summer morning, a large crowd gathered on the beach to watch Polonius and the children take flight. The villagers marveled at the strange contraption designed to navigate the sky. Most of them admired the three brave inventors, but others shook their heads.

"If we were meant to fly, we'd have been born with wings," grumbled an old villager with a gap between his front two teeth.

"Nonsense!" said his wife. "We've been born with something better than wings. We've been born with *brains*—and we should use them."

The dragons were also curious to see if the balloon would really work. They had watched Polonius and the children labor for weeks to reach this point. Now, as they stood next to Gwendolyn and Aethelred, they couldn't help but feel a little sad. Would the children still want to fly with them?

Gwendolyn sensed Kindle's feelings. Looking up at him, she stroked his nose. "You have nothing to fear, old friend," she said. "I am yours to carry for as long as you will have me."

He smiled. "And I will delight in carrying you as long as I am able."

Argus and Thelda hugged the children before watching them climb into the basket, followed by Polonius. They spent a few moments checking the poles and rigging while the old man made sure the balloon was properly inflated.

"Are you certain you want to do this?" Argus asked. "There's no shame in remaining here on the ground."

Aethelred shook his head. "We've been on the ground almost all of our lives," he said. "It's time to fly."

"You must be getting old, brother," said Wulfric, coming up and slapping Argus on the back. "Were we any different at that age? Besides, the dragons will be right next to them."

"A wise precaution," admitted Polonius, "but I don't think the balloon will fail."

"I'm not worried that it will fail," said Argus, looking up at the sky. "I'm worried it will work *too* well. What's to keep you all from floating up to the moon?"

Gwendolyn smiled. "We've already talked about this," she explained, patiently. "Polonius has made a small vent in the bottom of the balloon. When we reach the proper height, he'll release some of the gas to prevent us from going too high."

Thelda smiled at them and took her husband's hand. "It looks like you've thought of everything," she said. "Now show us what you can do, my darlings."

"Uncle Wulfric," asked Gwendolyn. "Would you do us the honor of cutting the ropes?"

He bowed. "Of course," he said. Striding forward, he unsheathed his dagger—and paused. "Just a moment," he said. "Does this airship have a name?"

"A name?" said Gwendolyn.

Wulfric looked offended "Every ship needs a name."

"How about the Ocean Breeze?" she asked.

Aethelred wrinkled his nose. "Too obvious."

"The Stink Lily?"

Polonius shook his head. "A ship's name needs to be stately, elegant."

Gwendolyn folded her arms, annoyed. "Okay, do *you* have a better suggestion?"

The old man smiled. "The Charm."

"The Charm?" she said. "What's that supposed to mean?"

"When I was working on my first flying invention, I tried the feather vest, with unfortunate results," explained Polonius. "Then, the leather wings, and now—"

"I get it," said Aethelred. "Third time's the charm?"

Polonius smiled back at him. "Exactly."

"Very well, the Charm it is!" said Wulfric. "We'll have to paint that across the basket upon your return. For now, you'd better take advantage of this wind. Are you ready?" Polonius and the children nodded. "Then off you go!"

He cut the ropes. The balloon rose slowly into the air while the villagers whistled and cheered. Kindle and Argent sprang into the air, hovering alongside the airship as the Charm drifted past the cliffs and toward the forest, pushed inland by the sea breeze. The crowd grew smaller and smaller until they were lost completely, obscured by the clouds. Polonius and the children looked at each other, too delighted to speak.

They were flying.

Soon, they were well above the forest south of Ballan á Moor. As the mist separated and curled around the basket, they all wondered the same thing. Would the sails work? Could they tack *into* the wind?

Taking hold of the poles that they had built into the basket, they angled them downward on either side like oars. The interior shafts extended perfectly, functioning like small masts. The sails caught the wind, puffing out proudly, while the children rotated the poles. After a few moments, they had learned to bank left and right (and even slow their ascent) by changing the angles of the sails. In this way, they made their way forward, weaving back and forth. They whooped and laughed as they cleared the forest and skirted Valmar's northern coast before flying out to sea.

Kindle and Argent glided along with them, nodding their heads approvingly. "Well done," said Argent. "With a bit more practice, you'll be able to keep up with us."

"Hardly." Aethelred shook his head. "I know how clumsy we must look to you, but someone who hasn't been on a dragon before should find it exhilarating."

"Good," said Kindle, smiling. "I'm sure there will be many who would appreciate a slower pace." He beat his wings and disappeared into a cloud.

Polonius looked at the children proudly as the wind whipped through his white hair. "This will change everything," he said. "Imagine the possibilities—transportation, trade, surveying farmland, bypassing rough roads, exploration—"

"You're forgetting something very important," said Aethelred. "It's fun!"

As they soared higher, they cleared the dampness of the clouds and felt the delicious warmth of sunshine on their faces. The children felt like they were dreaming. The air was cool but not unpleasant, blowing past them steadily as they looked down upon the vast ocean below. A pod of dolphins swam just beneath the surface, weaving between one another, unaware of their presence. The seagulls regarded them curiously, gliding on the wind as the balloon made its way further out to sea.

Finally, Gwendolyn broke the silence. "Do you think we can travel to the Moaning Isles?"

"I don't think we packed enough food," replied Polonius, dryly.

"I didn't mean today!" she replied. Then, realizing he was teasing her, she grinned. "Next week?"

"That's up to your parents," said the old man," though I don't see why they would object. We should make a longer journey, to test the Charm's strength, of course."

"Argent hasn't been to the Moaning Isles yet," said Gwendolyn, turning and looking down at the ice dragon. "What do you say, Argent? You've seen the mountains. How would you like to see the islands to the east?"

Argent smiled as she beat her wings and glided past them. "That would be wonderful," she said. "Aethelred told me about how the Moaning Isles got its name. I would love to hear the sound for myself."

Gwendolyn was about to reply when she heard Kindle's voice boom inside of her head.

They're coming!

She couldn't see him but she knew he was somewhere in the clouds above. More alarmingly, his jovial mood was gone. It was replaced by anxiety, a sense of urgency.

They're coming!

She closed her eyes and concentrated. *Who's coming?*

Turn back! You must turn back!

Her heart began to beat rapidly. *What do you mean?* she demanded. *Turn back where?* There was no response. *Kindle? Kindle!* She opened her eyes and looked down upon the sea, expecting to see an enemy fleet. Had the Merovians decided to attack Valmar again? But no, there was no sign of any ships at all.

She glanced at Argent, who continued to glide next to them. "Argent?" said Gwendolyn, her voice quivering.

Before she could say another word, the dragon's expression changed, becoming grim and terrible.

Aethelred sensed something was wrong. "What's the matter?" he said, putting his hand on his sister's arm. "Where—?"

Looking past her, his mouth fell open. Following his gaze, Gwendolyn stifled a cry.

On the northern horizon among the clouds, dozens of large creatures hurtled toward them. Was it a flock of birds? If so, they had never seen birds so large or so fast. Polonius produced a spyglass and raised it to his eye.

Those were no birds. They were bats—giant, white bats like those the children had found in the bowels of Skarsgaard. The creatures moved freakishly fast, cutting through the clouds like scythes. More troubling, they carried gnomes on their shoulders who had been fitted with silver lances designed to pierce a dragon's hide.

Argent saw them, too, and increased her speed.

"No!" shouted Aethelred. "There are too many!"

"It doesn't matter." The ice dragon turned her head. "Asmodeus mustn't be allowed to reach you."

Asmodeus?

The children turned back to the approaching horde . . . and then they saw him.

Asmodeus was still alive.

Straddling the largest bat, a particularly evil-looking creature that carried him with ease, he led the assault, urging the others onwards. He held no weapon, but he bore a white scar that ran down his face diagonally, making it seem as if he had two faces that had been forced together.

Aethelred looked into his furious, empty eyes. Though he couldn't be sure, he thought Asmodeus was smiling.

15

THE TIP OF THE SPEAR

When Asmodeus awoke under a pile of rubble in Skarsgaard, he was in a great deal of pain. A fragment of falling rock had scored his face, peeling back the flesh on both cheeks to reveal the skull beneath. Though he could not see the damage, he knew that he had been badly injured. But that was not what had rendered him unconscious.

He remembered standing over Aethelred with his hand raised when, inexplicably, he had felt the power that sustained him—the power on which he had come to rely—waver and disappear. Now, lying in a small cavity under tons of rock, Asmodeus felt cold, mortal, vulnerable. He waited to die there alone beneath the mountain, but the gnomes refused to abandon him. After digging for nearly a week, they pulled him from the rubble, tended to his wounds, and waited for his orders.

He learned that the Valmarians had escaped, along with the dragons. Many of the gnomes had been less fortunate. Hundreds had perished when most of the tunnels collapsed, their bodies still entombed in the rock and ice, but others had survived. Miraculously, most of the bats had escaped, and clung to the broken side of the mountain like locusts, feeding on the dead.

Determined to endure the disaster, the gnomes worked busily to salvage what was left of Skarsgaard. It was terrible work. Digging through the debris, they recovered countless bodies, which they burned on the surface. The workshops and tools had also been largely destroyed. But the gnomes were nothing if not industrious—and loyal. Despite the odds, they still trusted that Asmodeus would guide them to victory. What else could they do? To admit otherwise would mean they were in some part responsible for this tragedy.

Asmodeus, meanwhile, watched the gnomes with indifference. Survival seemed as meaningless as death. What had become of his power? What had happened to the mysterious spirits that made him strong? Wishing to know the truth, he ordered the gnomes to burrow into the heart of Skarsgaard. It took months to remove layer upon layer of rock from the bowels of the mountain, but they finally reached the chamber that Argent had once guarded.

When Asmodeus entered the cavern, he found what he had most feared. The stone column that had always glowed with power lay at his feet in small fragments, dark and impotent. All was lost.

In despair, he cursed his fate. How could he take his revenge on Valmar now? Even if he could reclaim his army and the war machines the gnomes had built, he no longer had the strength to lead them.

He dismissed the gnomes and lingered among the ruins. Picking up one of the small pieces of the stone column, he rubbed it between his claws. It was cold and dead, like the White Waste itself. He was about to cast it away when he heard a voice.

Do you doubt us so soon?

Asmodeus looked around. There was no one else there. Was he going insane? Another voice spoke, different from the first but no less wicked.

No, you're not insane. You're finally ready.

The fragment began to sizzle in his fingers. Before he could drop it, the stone came to life, stretching and expanding like a vein of quicksilver, burning his skin. Stranger still, it became a snake. The creature twisted up his arm, slithering along his shoulder and around his neck. Asmodeus clutched at his throat and tried to free himself from its grip, but the snake was too strong. It constricted around his neck, and became a metal collar, black and cold. He could still breathe but not without effort, as if it wanted him to know that it ruled him.

You must give yourself to us.

"Give myself . . . to you?" He hesitated. "I don't even know who you are."

Yes, you do. You've always known.

He shuddered as he clutched his collar. "What do you want from me?"

Your devotion.

"You have it!"

No, not completely. You have given us your mind—now we want your heart.

His heart? Asmodeus felt like he didn't have one to give, not since he had been forced to kill his sister. He remembered fleeing into the woods all of those years ago, lost and frightened. When he found the column under the mountain—and heard the voices—another feeling had replaced everything else.

Vengeance.

That power had kept him alive, giving him the strength to subdue other creatures, and control them. He touched the scar on his face. He had come so close to taking his revenge on the Valmarians, but the boy had somehow resisted his will. Still, Aethelred was mortal. They all were. He would make the Valmarians bleed just as his sister had bled.

Asmodeus narrowed his eyes. "Revenge," he whispered. "Together, we can still take revenge?"

As one.

Kneeling in the darkness, he glimpsed the thoughts of those who now possessed him. They had once been creatures of light called the Old Ones, given dominion over the earth. But they were unsatisfied. They wanted more. In an attempt to overthrow Oorano, they united with primeval dragons to become a new kind of creature, a being half-spirit and half-monster that called itself the Malodoi. It made war on the heavens, and attempted to rally other beings to its cause, but Oorano could not be defeated. He banished the Malodoi from the physical world, but it had found ways to manifest itself in others.

Unspeakable images filled Asmodeus's head. He saw muddy battlefields full of strange creatures who, at the Malodoi's urging, slaughtered each other in great numbers. He saw a small group of children, dirty, hungry, their skin stretched across their little bones, crouching in a doorway, and heard the Malodoi's laughter. He saw a village infected with plague, its people weak and deformed, and felt the Malodoi exult. Asmodeus smiled. It was ancient, spanning time and place, able to provoke all manner of suffering—and now he was part of it.

"Give me your strength," whispered Asmodeus. "Give me your cunning." He felt the Malodoi's scorn, as if he had said something foolish.

Could you bear it?

"I can bear anything!"

He felt a stabbing pain in his chest, and he fell on his face as it spread into his arms. When the sensation reached his legs, he grew weak, nauseous. He writhed on the ground as great spasms of pain washed over him. Had he displeased it? Was it killing him? Just as he was about to lose consciousness, he felt the pain subside. He lay there, breathing heavily, wondering what he had done to suffer this way.

Rise.

He climbed to his feet, and felt stronger, more agile, as if he had the power of ten gholgors. His vision had improved, too. He could see the small pores in the rock twenty yards away. The Malodoi was part of him in a way that it hadn't been before. He could feel it moving, slithering beneath his skin, and peering out of his eyes.

A new thought entered his mind. He must rally the gnomes. He must go to Valmar and destroy its people, every last one of them. Only then could he triumph over the legacy of Edubard and his sentinels. Only then could he finally have his revenge.

When he returned to the surface, he ordered the gnomes to rebuild the airships and prepare the galleys for the long voyage across the sea. They hadn't been defeated, merely delayed. The world still needed to be ruled. In the meantime, he would be patient. He had waited years for this moment; he could wait a few months more.

As the gnomes prepared for battle, a new thought troubled him. What about the dragons? If his army was to be successful, Argent and Kindle had to be killed.

The bats are swift.

Of course! He would lead a vanguard of his fastest bats and best riders south to search for the dragons. He would lose many but that didn't matter, not as long as he was victorious. Once the dragons were dead, the Valmarians would be defenseless. The airships would soon follow, free to bomb Valmar from the air without resistance. It wouldn't be a battle. It would be a massacre.

***

The children watched helplessly as Asmodeus streaked toward them, his eyes blazing in fury, as the great bat on which he rode punished the air with its wings.

"Move!" shouted Polonius.

Pushing Aethelred aside, he unfurled every sail, causing the airship to lurch sharply sideways. When the wind caught the fabric, it propelled them back toward shore. Still, the bats were faster. Soon, they would reach the basket and tear them apart.

Cursing herself for not bringing her bow, Gwendolyn could only watch Asmodeus and the others approach. She looked down at the ocean and wondered if they could survive the fall from such a great height. It seemed as though they were going to find out.

But Polonius had other ideas. Changing the angle of the sails, he caused the balloon to climb into the billowy, white clouds. In seconds, they disappeared in the mist.

Hanging on to the swaying basket with both hands, Gwendolyn looked up at the old man. "What are you doing?"

"Hiding," he whispered. "We're in no position to fight, and the clouds should provide us with some cover until the dragons can drive them off."

With its sails full, the Charm raced back towards Valmar. Unfortunately, the dense clouds made it impossible to be sure that they were going in the right direction. The children could see almost nothing.

Silently, they floated through the mist, expecting to be attacked at any moment. It was like a bad dream. They couldn't see the bats that hunted them but they could *hear* them. Screeching and howling, the creatures snaked through the mist, needing no encouragement. If they found the balloon, they would tear it apart.

Somewhere in the clouds, they heard Argent roar, followed by a scream. She had frozen a bat along with its rider, sending them both plummeting into the sea. Before she could draw another breath, however, more creatures swarmed her, biting her flanks, as the gnomes tried to stab her with their spears. She caught another beast in her great jaws, crushing its skull and flinging it away along with its rider. But others filled the void, forcing Argent to retreat.

If they damaged her wings, she would be no use to her friends. It would be better to lead the enemy away from the Charm where she could kill them one by one, using her greater speed and strength. With her mind made up, Argent roared again, kicking the bats and their riders away before flying eastward. As she expected, many followed.

Aethelred heard Argent retreat, followed by the angry cries of those who pursued her.

"Where is she going?" he asked.

"Isn't it obvious?" whispered Polonius. "She's leading them away from us."

The boy sighed. "Can't we go any faster?"

Polonius shook his head as he clutched one of the poles in his great hand, turning it slightly to keep the canvas rigid. "We are at the mercy of the wind."

"No!" A familiar voice rang out. "There will be no mercy for you."

Asmodeus materialized out of the mist, straddling his great bat. His skin was as pale as the clouds themselves, and he looked as gaunt and sickly as ever. But the children weren't fooled. They knew that despite his ghastly appearance, he possessed great strength.

His bat hovered out of reach as he leered at Polonius. "Give me the children, and I promise you a quick death."

The old man stepped in front of them, shielding Gwendolyn and Aethelred with his body. "Begone, demon!" he cried. Begone! Or I'll—"

"Or you'll what, fool?" snarled Asmodeus. Prodding the bat closer with his heels, he reached out for Gwendolyn with his long, skeletal arm.

Polonius never hesitated. Still gripping the pole that he used to manipulate the sails, he brought the rod up quickly just underneath the bat's wing. The children heard a sickening crunch as the creature's bone broke at the shoulder, sending it hurtling into the sea.

Realizing his mount was lost, Asmodeus leaped. He grabbed one of the thick ropes that connected the basket to the balloon, tipping the structure forward. Polonius released the pole and punched him in the stomach, hoping to dislodge him before he could tighten his grip. But Asmodeus was too strong. Absorbing the blow with ease, he found a foothold on the edge of the basket, forcing the children to retreat.

"Steer!" Polonius cried. "Get us over land!"

Gwendolyn and Aethelred each grabbed a pole while Polonius flung himself at the creature. Asmodeus growled as he avoided the brunt of the old man's kick while trying to maintain his grip. Snaking his legs around the ropes, he lunged forward and grabbed Polonius with his long arms, drawing him closer to his colorless body.

It was a terrible struggle. The children could tell by Asmodeus's breathing that the old man's strength surprised him. Without a weapon, though, Polonius's only hope was to knock his enemy clear from the balloon. Prying the creature's legs from the ropes, he forced Asmodeus to scramble along the rigging like a giant spider.

Just when it looked as though Polonius might be successful, Asmodeus changed tactics. Holding the ropes with both hands, he used his legs to pull Polonius *toward* him. This caused the basket to tilt dangerously to one side, forcing the old man to grab hold of the rigging, too, or risk falling to his death. With his adversary thus preoccupied, the pale figure slid down and landed on top of his back. Polonius tried to bring his hands up to defend himself, but he was too late. No living thing had ever escaped Asmodeus when he had caught it from behind.

The children watched their tutor's face turn white as the tip of one of Asmodeus's claws emerged from his chest. Moaning, he slumped over the basket, mortally wounded. Before they could react, Asmodeus pushed him overboard, and watched him fall through the clouds.

Overwhelmed by grief and anger, the children attacked Asmodeus, striking him repeatedly with their bare fists. It did little harm. He picked them up each by the throat and stared at them, his eyes glinting with malice. Gwendolyn realized that fighting him was useless. Only one thing could save them now.

Kindle!

She looked around desperately at the dense clouds that surrounded the balloon. Tears filled her eyes. He was either too distracted by the bats to respond . . . or dead. Either way, it was clear Kindle wasn't coming.

Aethelred struggled next to her, trying to free himself from the gholgor's grip, but he was running out of air. He didn't know what to do. Polonius was dead. The bats outnumbered the dragons many times over. If they were defeated, there would be no hope for Valmar.

"Why are you doing this?" whispered the boy, laboring to breathe. "We meant you . . . no harm!"

"No harm?" cried Asmodeus. "Look—at—my—face!" The scar seemed to glow as his temper increased. He tightened his grip on Aethelred's throat, his claws drawing blood. "You did this to me," he snarled. "You and your kind."

Gwendolyn's words were barely audible. "You attacked us . . . first."

Asmodeus shook his head. "No," he said. "It was your people—it was Edubard—who hunted us nearly to extinction. I can't kill him but I *can* kill his descendants."

He squeezed even harder and both children began to turn blue. His face swam before them even as their arms and legs went limp. As she was about to lose consciousness, Gwendolyn heard a roar approaching from below. It sounded like the waves crashing along the beach. They must be closer to the water than she had realized. But how was that possible when they were still in the clouds? Then she heard a familiar voice.

I'm here.

The world seemed to explode. Something enormous struck the balloon, ripping through it like a child's toy, and sending its occupants flying through the air.

Kindle had arrived. He had heard Gwendolyn's plea and emerged from the clouds, smashing the airship before the gholgor could do more harm. With a hiss, Asmodeus disappeared into the sea while Kindle grabbed Gwendolyn and Aethelred and dove earthward.

As they struggled to fill their lungs with air, they looked about wildly. Below them was Valmar's rocky coast. They were almost over land. The Charm, broken and ruined, spiraled into the shallow waves but there was no sign of Asmodeus. They looked up. Dozens of bats filled the sky. Some still carried gnomes but others had set them down near the castle to pursue the dragons more easily.

When Kindle and the children emerged from the clouds, the beasts attacked, diving toward them, trying to cripple one of the dragon's wings. He greeted them with a stream of flame. Those lucky enough to avoid the fire veered away sharply, while others plunged to the beach below, smoking as they fell.

As the creatures died, the sound of horns filled the air. "Look!" cried Gwendolyn.

Ballan á Moor was surrounded. More giant bats hovered over the courtyard, attacking those inside, while others stalked the battlements, snatching up men with their talons. One rose into the air, clutching a soldier.

The man screamed and struggled, but it was too late. The bat released him and he fell to his death.

A group of gnomes swarmed the gates while others ran across the northern ramparts. The strange, misshapen creatures fended off several volleys of arrows as they approached Valmar's archers on the eastern side of the castle, hurling explosives at them, forcing the men to retreat. The Valmarians needed help.

Kindle put the children on his shoulders. "Hold on!"

Taking a deep breath, he dove toward the castle's walls, flying along the battlements until he was eye-level with a column of gnomes. They stopped and raised their shields, huddling together as they watched the dragon warily. It did them little good. Kindle opened his mouth and bathed the gnomes in flame. Those who weren't incinerated, jumped from the ramparts, never to rise again.

Suddenly, a giant bat appeared from above, determined to sink its teeth into the soft membrane of Kindle's wing.

"Look out!" screamed Gwendolyn.

In a blur, the dragon brought up his tail and crushed the bat against the north tower. "Is there no end to these foul creatures?" he growled. "Where is Argent?"

"The last time we saw her, she was leading the bats away from us," said Aethelred.

"There are too many for her to fight alone," replied Kindle. "I must find her—and I'll need all of my speed."

Gwendolyn understood immediately. "Of course! Put us down inside of the castle."

The dragon glided over the north wall and landed behind the battlements. The courtyard was filled with soldiers. Some of the men were putting out small fires made by the explosives. Others hurried to resupply the archers on the walls with more arrows.

A bat's cry pierced the air as the children jumped from Kindle's back. Gwendolyn looked up at the dragon. "Good hunting."

He nodded, and prepared to spring into the air when she remembered something. "Wait! Polonius is . . . well, you'll bring him home, won't you?"

Kindle nodded, seeing the tears in her eyes. "I'll try." Then he was gone.

Gwendolyn turned to her brother. "Come on!" she said. "We have to find mother and father." He stared back at her blankly. "Aeth!" she continued. "Come on!"

His voice broke. "Do you really think Kindle will find him?" he asked doubtfully as he glanced up at her. "You saw what happened. How could Polonius survive such a wound?"

She sighed and looked at the battlements. "I don't know," she admitted, "but right now, we have to go. If we stay here, we'll just be in the way."

As if proving her point, a soldier bumped into them, carrying a basket of arrows.

"You there!" she cried. "Where are the king and queen?"

He stopped and stared at the children. His face was bleeding, but if he was in pain, he didn't show it. "I—I don't know my lady," he said. "Your father ordered us to guard the north gate until he returned."

"Did he say where he was going?"

Raising his chin, he motioned behind them. "Last I saw, he was leading a group of knights beyond the walls of the south gate, fighting on horseback."

The children thanked him and ran in that direction. Weaving around soldiers, they tried hard not to imagine the worst. Though they could no longer see bats in the sky, the castle was still under attack by many gnomes. They heard explosions and the occasional cry of men in pain. What chance did they have against such weapons?

When they reached the south gate, they came upon two dead soldiers, who lay crumpled on the ground next to a giant bat. The creature's white fur was matted with blood. The children couldn't be sure, but it looked as though the bat had picked up the men in its claws but before it could drop them they had drawn their swords and stabbed the creature to death, sending all of them crashing to the ground.

Covering the fallen soldiers with their capes, Gwendolyn and Aethelred picked up the blades that lay nearby and were about to leave when they heard a moan. Thinking it might be a third solider who had survived the fall, they rushed to the other side of the bat's carcass and found a gnome, bruised and bloody, lying on the ground. He was still conscious but his injuries were severe. A bone protruded from his thigh and he lay in a pool of his own blood. Nevertheless, he had managed to hold on to his lance, and clutched it to his chest.

When he saw the children, he smiled weakly. "So much for the mighty people of Valmar," he croaked. "The dragons will soon be dead, and then what will you do? Hide behind these feeble walls while our fire falls from the sky?" His words ended in a fit of coughing.

Aethelred observed him a moment before responding. "Kindle and Argent seem to be doing just fine," he said. "You'll have to do better if you expect to kill them with the likes of these stupid beasts."

The gnome chuckled, even as blood dribbled down his chin. "You think this is it?" He coughed again but now seemed unable to stop. "Of course . . . how could you know? You have but seen . . . a *tenth* of our strength."

The children looked at each other, confused. "There are others?" demanded Gwendolyn. "How many?"

It was too late. The gnome's coughing worsened until he could no longer breathe. After a few last gasps, he exhaled and closed his eyes forever.

As Gwendolyn and Aethelred watched him die, a cheer erupted from the battlements. They looked up and realized that the archers had stopped shooting. A few men came streaming down the stairs, and headed for the south gate. The children followed.

When they reached the archway that led beyond the walls, they found that an explosion had destroyed the gate's wooden doors, and had badly damaged the portcullis. The iron bars were still there, but they were twisted and useless. Squeezing through the soldiers, the children surveyed the scene in front of the castle walls.

A brief but deadly battle had taken place here. Dozens of bodies, mostly gnomes, lay strewn among the grass, filled with arrows. Valmarian soldiers stepped over them, swords still drawn, looking for survivors. The children recognized their uncle as a member of the search party.

"Uncle Wulfric!" they shouted as they ran toward him.

He looked up. "Gwendolyn! Aethelred!" he cried, gathering them into his arms. "Thank goodness you're alive! But where—?"

"Kindle rescued us," said Gwendolyn, releasing him and gazing around in wonder. "Where is everyone? Where are mother and father?"

"The battle only just ended," he said, nodding toward the field beyond. In the distance, they could still see the gnomes fleeing across the meadow that separated Ballan á Moor from the forest. A group of knights followed them on horseback, including the king. "Your father is pursuing what's left of them with the cavalry. He asked me to stay here in case the bats return."

"And mother?" asked Aethelred.

"When the gnomes were spotted on the horizon, she left with a garrison of soldiers to take the villagers to the Low Road," he explained. "It's easily defended, especially from bats. They could escape to Grimstad if we were killed."

The boy looked around at the dreadful scene. "But that didn't happen."

Uncle Wulfric shook his head. "No," he said. "The gnomes dismounted here, expecting to overwhelm us. They fought well, but our archers are deadly at such close range. Still, we haven't accounted for the bats. They seem to have disappeared."

"Can't you guess why?" said Gwendolyn.

Aethelred nodded. "The dragons haven't been idle."

"I should have known," said Wulfric, looking relieved. "It wouldn't be the first time we were in their debt."

He was interrupted by more cries from the battlements. "What do you see?" he shouted, looking up at one of the archers on the wall.

"The king has cut off their retreat, my lord!" said an archer. "The gnomes are surrounded!"

Wulfric exhaled. "Your father and the others will make short work of them. Come, I'll take you to your mother. It will put her mind at ease knowing you're both safe."

He led the children to the center of town where they found the queen and a group of soldiers standing in front of the domed entrance to the Low Road. The villagers were frightened but Thelda assured them that they would be safe underground. Most had already passed through the archway, and were hiding in the tunnel below when Uncle Wulfric and the children appeared.

Seeing Gwendolyn and Aethelred, Thelda rushed to greet them. "By the seven stars!" she cried, inspecting the children before hugging them. "When we saw the bats approach, your father and I feared . . . but Polonius must have protected you." She looked around. "Where is he?"

She glanced down at the children. "Where—?" The words died on her lips as she noticed the tears in their eyes.

"He fell," said Gwendolyn, quietly.

She recounted what had befallen them in the balloon, and watched as her mother's expression changed from anxiety to grief. The girl explained that Kindle had promised to look for him, but the queen shook her head. "And if something happens to Kindle?" She turned to Wulfric. "Take a ship," she said. "Search the water."

Wulfric nodded. "At once."

He was about to leave when the dragons appeared on the horizon. They flew slowly, battered and bruised from dozens of bites they had received from the bats, but they had been victorious.

As she landed carefully among them, Argent held a figure in her talons. It was Polonius.

"I caught him as he fell," she said. "I would have returned sooner but there were too many—"

"The bats are dead now," said Kindle, his voice filled with disgust, as he landed beside her. "We made sure of that, but I could not find Asmodeus."

Argent set Polonius down gently on the ground as everyone gathered around him. His face was ashen, and blood covered his chest. Thelda examined the wound and looked up at the children grimly. To everyone's amazement, his eyes flickered open and he smiled weakly when he recognized them.

"Polonius!" cried the children, kneeling before him. Overcome by grief, Gwendolyn raised the old man's hand to her face.

Aethelred's face seemed to harden. "Asmodeus will pay for this, even if I have to kill him myself."

"Careful, child," whispered Polonius. "Hatred is a sickness, and the desire for revenge only makes it grow."

"How can you say that—after what he's done to you?" asked the boy.

"That is . . . why I say it," said Polonius, laboring for breath. "You must guard your heart against such things."

"But he has made war on us," said Gwendolyn, bitterly. "They all have."

Polonius shook his head. "Not all of them," he replied. "Those who do, follow Asmodeus because they are weak, afraid. Show them a better way."

Thelda knelt and cradled his head in her lap. "Rest now," she said. "I will make a healing tonic—"

Polonius smiled. "Nay, lady," he said, his voice fading. "I go to a different rest." He looked at the children and squeezed their hands. "To . . . Oorano's country."

Thelda put her hand on his shoulder. "I will never forget the lessons you have taught me." She looked up at the children and smiled, wiping away tears. "Taught us."

When she looked down again, the old man was dead. The children wept openly but they were not alone. Most of those assembled around Polonius had learned from him or experienced his kindness in some way over the years. Fittingly, he left them with one final challenge.

As they mourned, Thelda felt a hand on her arm. She turned and saw Aethelred standing behind her.

"What is it?"

"Forgive me," he said, "but we are still in danger."

"What?" said the queen. "Do you know where Asmodeus is?"

Gwendolyn shook her head. "No," she said. "But we spoke to one of the gnomes before he died. This is only the first wave. More are coming."

16
TABLES TURNED

The following day, Valmarian sentries took up watch along the coast while the rest of the people buried Polonius and twenty-three soldiers at dawn in a cemetery that overlooked the sea. It was a somber affair. Still recovering from the shock of the battle, the family members of the fallen sprinkled rose petals on the graves while everyone else looked on, honoring their sacrifice. Argus, who had been fighting the gnomes when Polonius died, placed a familiar axe in his old friend's hands.

"I don't think you'll need this, but I could think of no better place for it," he whispered.

When the ceremony was over, the people gathered the bat carcasses, nearly forty in all, and piled them on the beach where Kindle set them ablaze. The fallen gnomes were given a proper burial in a small field near the village, much to the surprise of Jorgan and his friends.

Later that morning, they found Argus.

"They tried to kill you," said Jorgan, "and yet you honor them in this way?"

"We honor who they might have been," explained the king. "They are not trolls. If not for Asmodeus, they might have led decent, honorable lives."

"That's just it," said the gnome. "They didn't. Why give them a proper burial?"

"I would ask a different question," said Argus, rubbing his beard. "Did you not once serve Asmodeus, too?" The gnomes looked at one another uncomfortably. "Yet here you stand, no longer deceived by his lies. Perhaps others will choose to think for themselves again, like you have, once they're reminded they always have a choice." He put his hand on Jorgan's shoulder. "Now, if you'll excuse me, I must prepare for war."

The gnomes were astonished by the king's words. "Let us help you," said Jorgan. "We know how they think, how they're likely to attack."

"Very well," he said. "Come along."

That afternoon, the king called a war council, and spent the day in the Great Hall debating how to prepare for the invasion. After much talk, Argus realized his military choices were limited. The castle's ramparts were not defensible from the air; the bats had proven that. More disturbingly, the gnomes' use of explosives had made the walls obsolete. Where would the people hide if they were breached? The villagers could use the Low Road again, but it hadn't been built to shelter so many.

When Jorgan and the others described Asmodeus and what they knew of his plans, everyone grew even more dismayed. Skarsgaard contained thousands of gnomes, all trained to fight, and some had clearly survived its destruction. In addition to breeding bats, they had constructed a massive number of airships. Each had a crew of six gnomes, responsible for locomotion, steering, and weaponry.

"What kind of weaponry?" asked Wulfric.

"Cannons," said Jorgan. "They will destroy the castle from the air, well beyond the range of your archers."

Another gnome, Broba, stepped forward. "I've also heard rumors of a naval fleet being built on the coast, though I never saw it myself. Asmodeus didn't like us talking to one another about the invasion, and we were careful to obey orders."

Argus studied him. "That must have been some enchantment."

"We were enchanted—but not by magic alone," replied Jorgan, rubbing the middle of his forehead where the marks used to be. "Asmodeus inspired us with tales of order, equality. We were willing to die to see those things achieved." He sighed. "We now know that hope is an illusion."

"Be careful, Jorgan," cautioned the queen, "that by avoiding one error you don't make another."

"My lady?"

"Stoicism is fool's gold," she explained. "It may seem like wisdom, except it doesn't answer the longing in your heart. You have been deceived, yes, but that doesn't mean the things you desire are not true and noble still."

After lunch, the king asked Argent to remind them of her tale. She lowered her eyes, still ashamed of how she had been used by Asmodeus. "As magical creatures, dragons are vulnerable to many different spells, especially if we are young," she said. "When Asmodeus found me in my lair, he bewitched me, and took me to Skarsgaard. There, he led me into a room that housed a stone column which glowed with an unearthly light."

"The one I smashed," said Kindle, "and which I suspect was the source of his power."

Argent nodded. "It had many faces," she said. "If I watched them closely, they looked like they were moving, whispering to one another. Of course, I was frightened at first but I became less so as I stared into the light. Eventually, I was allowed to wander the White Waste to look for my mother, but she must have departed, for I could not even sense her thoughts. One day, Asmodeus told me that I had a brother—and that he would visit us."

"How would he know such a thing?" asked Wulfric.

"The Malodoi," declared Aethelred. "It must have told him."

Argus and Thelda looked at one another, confused. "What?" said the king. "You mean the creature that you killed near Cloud Isle?"

Aethelred glanced at his sister, ashamed. She had urged him to tell their parents what he had seen in Skarsgaard, but he told himself it no longer mattered. He thought Asmodeus had died when the mountain collapsed, and that the Malodoi had died with him. In fact, he simply didn't want to remind everyone, especially himself, of the power the spirit once had over him. Now, he knew he had been wrong to remain silent. He had never seen the faces on the stone pillar that Argent described, but he didn't need to. The Malodoi must have helped Asmodeus survive.

"I saw it—or at least I think I did—when Asmodeus tried to enchant me in Skarsgaard," explained the boy. "His hand became . . . ." He swallowed hard. "Well, it looked awfully familiar. The Malodoi must have told him about Destiny—and Kindle."

The king saw the shame in his son's eyes, and did not press the matter further. "It appears we are fighting both the physical and spiritual," he declared. "Even if we could defeat such a creature, I wouldn't know where to begin."

Gwendolyn crossed her arms. "If Aethelred beat the Malodoi once, we can do it again by slaying Asmodeus."

"How can we do that when he has proven immune to steel—and even Argent's breath?" asked the king.

"I don't know," admitted Aethelred, "but the scar on his face suggests he can be hurt, doesn't it?"

Gwendolyn nodded. "Hurt and even killed."

"We'll need help," said Wulfric. "Have we sent an envoy to Grimstad?"

"Good idea," said Argus. "We also need to provide shelter for those who cannot fight. If the gnomes come in strength, our walls will not hold. Still, I worry we ask too much of the giants."

"They have little choice," said Thelda. "If we are defeated, Asmodeus will come for them next." She paused and smiled slightly. "But it doesn't hurt that some of those here found the garnica for Orion."

Argus kissed his queen's hand. "Don't forget that you knew it could heal him."

"It's settled then," said Gwendolyn. "Aethelred and I will leave for Grimstad with the dragons at first light. We will be back before noon tomorrow with an answer."

"Very well," said Argus, rising and rubbing his wounded arm. "Do not tarry, for though we do not know the day or the hour, another invasion *is* coming. I feel it in my bones."

***

As the children and dragons arrived at Grimstad, the giants greeted them warmly. Orion and Ocwen led them through the main gate and into the courtyard as the children described the attack on Ballan á Moor, including Polonius's death. The king and queen looked at each other, stunned by the news.

"We mourn with you," said Orion. "Polonius was a good man . . . and a good giant." He paused, stroking his beard. "This happened two days ago, you say?" The children nodded. "When he was last here, your father told me that this Asmodeus had been killed, buried underneath the mountains in the White Waste, along with many who served him."

"We were wrong," replied Aethelred, "and it seems more are on the way to Valmar."

"But you did not come here merely to tell us this news," said Orion, guessing their intentions. "You need our help, do you not?"

Gwendolyn and Aethelred glanced at one another. They knew that it was asking much of him, especially since Orion had his own people to think about.

"Do you remember the day we met?" asked the king.

The children looked at each, puzzled by the question. "Yes, I remember," said Gwendolyn. "Destiny had just attacked Ballan á Moor. We saw you during the battle on the beach. You fought bravely, and—"

The giant shook his head. "No," he said. "I met you in front of Grimstad's gates. You stood before our castle for the first time, frightened but determined to rebuild the peace between our two races."

"Forgive me, your grace, but that was your father, I believe—" began Aethelred.

"It was my father with whom you *spoke*, but there were two more giants, if you recall, who stood behind him."

The children looked up at him, amazed. "You were one of them?"

Orion nodded. "I was, along with Ogrom, the captain of the guard," he said. "At first, we were skeptical of your intentions, since you arrived unannounced, and with a dragon on our doorstep. We thought you meant to intimidate us but when we saw your faces, when we understood that you wanted peace—and were ready to prove it by fighting alongside of us against the trolls—it changed everything. So you see, there is no question we will help you." He looked from the children to the dragons. "Once you have bled for a giant, a giant will always bleed for you."

Kindle smiled. "If it's all the same to you, I would rather the enemy did the bleeding."

Orion roared with laughter, causing the others to grin in turn. "It's been too peaceful here since the trolls fled to the south. I wouldn't mind wielding a spear again."

"Thank you, your majesty," said Gwendolyn. "We will never forget this act of friendship."

"Friendship?" said Orion, looking down on her. "Yes, it is friendship, but is it not also wise to stand together?"

Aethelred stepped forward and bowed low. "In that case, we have one more request of you," he said. "There are those among us who are too weak or too old to fight. Would it be possible for them to take refuge here until the fighting is over?"

Orion and Ocwen looked at each other.

"You have become true diplomats," laughed Orion again, "extracting one promise from me before asking for another!"

"Don't mind him," said Ocwen. "We will gladly receive your people," she said. "Tell them they are welcome to come."

Orion put his arm around his wife and looked at the children. "Of course they are welcome. We will keep them safe," he said, his eyes growing serious as he looked at Kindle. "And we will make the gnomes bleed if they are foolish enough to attack."

The next morning, Orion and his best warriors hastened to Ballan á Moor using the Low Road. Dressed in heavy armor, and carrying shields and spears, the earth shook as they marched. On the way, they met hundreds of Valmarians—women, children, elderly, and the wounded—coming from the opposite direction, desperate to escape the coming battle. Most were in boats, paddling up the river that ran parallel to the path, while others drove livestock along the road in case Grimstad itself came under siege. The people hailed the giants as they passed. Orion nodded, acknowledging their words, but he wondered how many of his warriors would return home safely if the war came.

***

It had been nearly a week since the giants had reached Ballan á Moor. No attack had come but something else had arrived—a huge thunderstorm. The clouds darkened the skies and heavy rain pelted the castle and surrounding town, turning the roads into mud. After a few days of such foul weather, the sun seemed like a memory.

Despite the rain, Argus was determined to be ready. His soldiers worked hard to make the necessary preparations, storing food and cattle behind the castle's walls. Valmar's stonemasons and ironsmiths also labored night and day, repairing the damage the gnomes had done to the castle's gates.

As some watched the horizon from the battlements, others kept busy by making thousands of arrows. On the beach below the cliffs, Wulfric and his crew stocked Valmar's ships with gunpowder and cannonballs, storing them below deck to keep the materials dry. If it came to a battle at sea, they would be ready for that, too.

Now there was nothing left to do but wait. Men and giants sat idly under the eaves of the castle to avoid the rain, talking quietly together to pass the time. Others, unable to sit still, trained in the courtyard despite the storm, practicing their swordsmanship with blunted weapons. The dragons, meanwhile, patrolled Valmar's northern coast to look for any sign of Asmodeus, and to prevent the enemy from approaching unseen. The king brooded in silence by the fire in the Great Hall, wondering what was worse: war or the maddening, gut-wrenching anticipation of it.

The children sat in the north tower of the castle, trying to pass the time by gazing out to sea. It had stopped raining for the moment but the storm clouds still obscured the sun, making the ocean look dull and gray.

Gwendolyn was drafting a design for the rudder of a new airship, when a thought occurred to her. "Maybe they changed their minds," she said, looking up at her brother.

"What?"

"The gnomes," she explained. "Maybe they decided not to attack us after all."

"I doubt it," said the boy. "Don't you remember how many of them tried to kill us even as Skarsgaard crumbled? No, gnomes like Kaag and Norr will always do what Asmodeus tells them to do."

Gwendolyn thought for a few moments. "Perhaps," she said. "But what gives him his power? For instance, how did he manage to resist father's sword or Argent's ice?"

The boy paused, remembering Asmodeus's hand as it hovered above his face. Each finger appeared as a separate snake, something Aethelred was only too familiar with. "It's protecting him," he mumbled.

"Huh?"

"The Malodoi," he explained. "It's lending him its power. That's the only explanation."

"Then how do we defeat it . . . or them?"

Aethelred pulled on his lower lip. "When I was under its influence, I drew the Malodoi's power from the wand."

"It was incinerated, remember?" said Gwendolyn. "I placed it on the stone platform in Kairos and it was consumed by the flames."

"And Asmodeus's staff—"

"Was shattered by father's sword," she said. "Not to mention the column that Kindle smashed to break Argent's enchantment. We destroyed each of those things, yet he still retains his power."

Aethelred looked frustrated. "There must be something else, something we're overlooking. There must be a way to kill—"

He was interrupted by the sound of horns. Three long, deep notes resounded from the walls, followed by the clamor of rushing feet. The children ran to the tower's window. Men and giants stood crowded together along the battlements and pointed to the horizon.

The gnomes had arrived.

Scores of airships glided toward Valmar's shore. Driven by propellers, the machines belched flame into the balloons, heating the air to keep them afloat. Using levers to control the rudders, the pilots kept the vessels in tight formation while more gnomes stood ready to operate small cannons. The weapons were mounted on the side of each basket, allowing them to target enemies on the ground and in the air.

Flying alongside the balloons, more giant bats darted in and out of view. They each carried a gnome, and showed remarkable dexterity, diving and climbing between the airships, ready to fight anyone or anything that threatened them.

The children looked down and realized that a navy accompanied them. At least twenty large galleys sped toward the coast, driven through the waves by dozens of oars as the gnomes labored below deck to reach land. Even more daunting, the ships were fitted with cannons several times larger than those mounted on the airships. Many gnomes stood on deck, clutching their spears restlessly as they prepared to storm the beach.

"That's what must have delayed them," said Gwendolyn. "The airships have been pacing the navy."

Wulfric, Melko, and others rushed to the docks to meet the gnomes at sea. But what could five ships do against so many? The enemy fleet outnumbered them four to one. The children's hopes faded as they looked from sea to sky. The airships would soon be overhead, dropping bombs on the castle while the ships landed on shore. What chance did Valmar have?

Then the children saw Argent and Kindle streaking towards the enemy. At least the dragons would make it difficult for this armada to reach Valmar unscathed. But could they destroy the airships with so many bats harassing them?

It didn't take long to find out.

The dragons flew directly into the heart of the squadron, dodging the bombs that exploded around them as the air filled with black smoke. Just as Kindle and Argent appeared to have broken through the barrage, they changed course, veering sharply upwards and disappearing into the clouds. The bats and their riders gave chase, vanishing into the mist behind them as the balloons raced toward land.

"What are they doing?" said Aethelred, confused. "Where did they—?"

The dragons appeared from out of the clouds and descended like lighting on the airships. Then the children understood. By attacking from above, Kindle and Argent made it difficult for the gnomes to see them—and impossible to shoot at them. Kindle set one balloon on fire and watched as the canvas burst into flames before plummeting into the sea. Nearby, Argent entombed another airship in ice, causing the ropes to snap from the added weight as it sank like a stone into the waves.

Gwendolyn and Aethelred watched gleefully as airship after airship was destroyed in this way. The bats soon reappeared, attacking from all sides, forcing Kindle and Argent to defend themselves. Slashing at the hideous white creatures, the dragons killed several, while deflecting the lances that sought to pierce their scaly hides.

Hearing cannon fire below, the children looked down at the sea. Valmar's ships had intercepted the enemy fleet, and the two forces began exchanging fire off the coast. All five of Valmar's ships remained closely together, their hulls almost touching, while the gnomes converged upon their position. There would be no escape. Strangely, the Valmarians continued to steer the ships toward the much larger force, letting out the sails as they tacked into the wind.

"The gnomes are outflanking them!" cried Gwendolyn in anguish. "Our people will be slaughtered!"

Cannonballs hummed through the air and battered the Steadfast Lady's sails as the two forces returned volley after volley. Despite doing moderate damage to the lead ship of the gnomish fleet, the Valmarians were hopelessly overmatched. Soon, their masts were shattered, and they drifted, crippled and listless, as the gnomes sailed closer.

The Valmarians scrambled for the longboats, letting them down over the opposite side of the decks for protection, as they abandoned the ships. Wulfric and the other captains, now defenseless, ordered their men to row for shore. The smaller, nimbler crafts sped toward the harbor while the majority of the enemy fleet prepared to take control of Valmar's damaged ships. The gnomes smiled as they watched the men retreat in the longboats. The Valmarians could certainly outrun them, but by fleeing in this way, the fools had exposed themselves to cannon fire.

The waves pitched and tossed around the longboats as the gnomes pelted them with cannonballs, trying to sink them before they could escape. Though unsuccessful, the enemy began weaving around Valmar's ruined fleet so they would be in a better position to fire.

The children saw Uncle Wulfric stand up in one of the longboats, while the others continued to row for shore. He held a bow in one hand.

"Why doesn't he keep his head down?" said Aethelred. "He's taking a terrible risk."

Next to Wulfric, Cillian held an arrow in one hand and a torch in the other. The tip must have been soaked in oil, for when the old sailor touched the arrow to the flame, it caught fire immediately. Fitting it on the string, Wulfric took a moment to aim, and then shot in a high arc. Its tip still flickering, the arrow landed on the Steadfast Lady, which sat in the center of Valmar's fleet.

The fire spread quickly, crawling along the boards, up the splintered masts, and into the sails. Soon, flames engulfed the ship, leaping to the Fearless Finn and the other three vessels. The sailors in the longboats paddled even more furiously, increasing the distance between themselves and the gnomish fleet.

"Fire doesn't travel that fast," said Gwendolyn, watching the flames consume Valmar's fleet. "They must have covered the ships in oil."

The vessels began to blaze furiously, sending out embers in all directions. The gnomes in the ships closest to the inferno ran here and there along their decks, scrambling to extinguish the small fires that threatened their sails. Suddenly, there was a deafening series of explosions as the Steadfast Lady detonated. Then another ship exploded—and another, decimating the gnomish fleet that surrounded them.

As they watched the fireworks, the children realized that Wulfric and the others must have planted a huge cache of gunpowder in the cargo hold of each ship. The Valmarians had never intended to fight the gnomes. Instead, they had lured them toward the fleet before igniting the barrels of gunpowder that the ships carried.

Within minutes, six of the enemy galleys had sunk, taking the heavily armored gnomes with them to the bottom of the sea. Wulfric and the rest of his men watched with grim satisfaction as the gnomes battled the effects of the explosions.

When the Valmarians reached the sand, they pulled the longboats to shore and prepared to defend the beach. Though part of the enemy's fleet had been destroyed, more ships continued to approach. The gnomes who had survived were furious at the trick, and swore horrible oaths at the sailors. It promised to be a ferocious battle.

Knowing that Wulfric and his men would soon be outnumbered, most of Valmar's army, led by Argus and Orion, left the castle and raced toward the beach. Gwendolyn and Aethelred looked at each other and nodded in silent agreement before grabbing their weapons to join them.

"Where is Asmodeus?" said Gwendolyn, gazing up at the sky anxiously. "Why isn't he leading the others?"

Aethelred shook his head as he ran alongside of her. "I don't know," he said, "but it's somehow worse that we haven't yet seen him."

When they reached the others on the beach, the airships were directly overhead. The gnomes pelted Valmar's defenders from above with explosives, leaving ugly craters in the sand, and forcing everyone to retreat toward the cliffs. The giants repelled the bombs with their shields, but they too, had no answer for the assault. Some of the men fired arrows into the sky, hoping to pierce the canvas of the balloons, but they shot in vain. The gnomes were much too high to reach.

As abruptly as it had begun, however, the bombing ceased. The children looked up and saw that Kindle and Argent had escaped the bats, and had reached the airships. Kindle smashed one of the vessels with his tail, sending it crashing to earth while Argent blasted another with ice. The remaining ships directed their cannon fire at the dragons, trying desperately to hit their wings. But the gnomes simply weren't fast enough. Kindle and Argent dodged the bombs with ease as they wove through the sky, destroying ship after ship.

Along the coast, hundreds of gnomes, eager to do battle, jumped into the shallow water before the galleys landed on shore. The surf, combined with the weight of their armor, made it difficult for them to reach dry land. As the gnomes waded through the breakers, they were met by Valmar's army.

Argus and Orion led the charge, cleaving shields and helmets, and preventing the enemy from leaving the water. Nearby, Wulfric dodged a gnome's spear before finishing him with his sword. The children, too, fought bravely. Aethelred parried blow after blow from a particularly savage gnome before Gwendolyn shot him through the eye with an arrow.

As the surf turned red, the gnomes attempted to rally but the men and giants fought so fiercely and with such discipline that soon the battle became a rout. The gnomes turned and ran. Some panicked and fled into the waves, only to drown in their armor, but most ran north along the beach, followed closely by Valmar's army.

The children smiled as they tried to keep up with their father. The gnomes were retreating. The dragons would soon destroy the airships. Valmar would be victorious!

Something flashed on the precipice that overlooked the sea near the castle, causing the children to turn and look.

The smiles died on their faces. On the cliffs above, stood Asmodeus.

Behind him stood an army of trolls.

17

VENGEANCE

When Asmodeus saw the balloon floating a few miles north of Valmar's coast, he couldn't believe his luck. He had come to kill the dragons, the only real threat to his army, but as he spotted the children—Edubard's heirs, no less—it seemed that his patience had been rewarded. They would be the first to die, slowly, painfully.

Spurring his bat forward, Asmodeus raced toward the balloon but it disappeared into the clouds in a pathetic attempt to escape. By the time he found it again, he had to contend with a stubborn old man who insisted on standing in his way. Asmodeus had never understood why some chose to die so that others could live, but he was happy to oblige the fool. When the fight was over, he held each child by the throat, and began to squeeze.

Then the dragon had appeared, robbing him of his revenge.

As he splashed into the sea, Asmodeus cursed himself for not concentrating on the beasts first. If Kindle and Argent survived his bats, they would decimate the airships that followed. Still, the Malodoi's power hadn't abandoned him. He felt it throbbing in his veins, willing him to finish what he had started.

Bobbing to the surface, he looked up at the cliffs of Ballan á Moor. Victory was still possible. If he could reach the castle and capture Valmar's rulers, he would force them to call off the dragons—or at least kill the king and queen if the beasts refused to surrender. As he began to swim toward shore, he heard one of the voices whisper in his ear.

No, fool, it is too late.

"Then what shall I do?" he asked, petulantly. "I have come too far to turn back."

There are other ways to succeed, and other creatures to rally.

Guided by the voices, Asmodeus made his way south into the Solitary Marshes. He called the trolls out from their muddy villages and waited as they assembled before him in the twilight, compelled by a power they didn't understand. Hundreds of the dirty creatures regarded him warily as he introduced himself before reminding them of their humiliation at the hands of men. Had they given up so easily? Why should they be content to hide in the wetlands when all of Valmar could be theirs?

"Have you come here to mock us?" one snarled. His name was Slubgut, an older troll known for killing many creatures, including some of his own kind. "We know well what we have lost. Most of us here barely escaped with our lives during the last battle while many never escaped at all. What hope do we have? Men and giants work together now. We cannot defeat them alone!"

"You will not *be* alone," said Asmodeus. "A great host of gnomes is approaching Valmar. They will reach Ballan á Moor soon, enough time for you to assemble and march north to meet them. You can either share in the spoils of war or die here by my hand when I return."

The trolls murmured to one another, unsure of what to do. It had been too long since they had tasted the flesh of their hated enemies, but would the gnomes really aid them in battle? That would certainly even the odds. If they didn't act now, what would stop the men from one day building settlements near the Solitary Marshes, and driving them into the sea? But if Asmodeus was lying, another loss would be disastrous.

Slubgut spat on the ground and glanced up at the sky uneasily. The sun had disappeared behind the mountains but its hateful rays still lingered. If the trolls followed Asmodeus, they would have to travel during the day, which would hurt their eyes and sap their strength.

"Even if we agreed to help you," said the troll, "we wouldn't be able to reach the battle in time for we cannot abide the sun."

"Can you not?" asked Asmodeus. "Then I shall smother it—just as I will our enemies."

He closed his eyes and held up his hands. Almost instantly, the clouds in the west gathered and thickened, extinguishing the last rays of sunlight. Lightning flashed and thunder roared in the distance as a light rain began to fall. In a stroke, darkness had fallen. The trolls looked at one another in disbelief. If this strange creature could control the weather, surely he was capable of leading them to victory.

That night, they agreed to follow Asmodeus to war. They travelled slowly at first, hampered by the watery bogs and fens of the marsh. When they reached the mountains, they made much faster progress. Weaving through the deep canyons and ravines, they avoided the watchful eyes of the giant sentries who guarded the passes to Grimstad. A day later, they came to the banks of the Restless River, following it upward across the plains before approaching Ballan á Moor from the south. All this time, the sun remained hidden, shrouded by storm clouds that kept the world covered in a gloomy twilight. But as far as the trolls were concerned, it was perfect weather for war.

***

After nearly a week's march, the time for fighting had arrived. The trolls looked down on the spectacle from the cliffs of Ballan á Moor, sneering at the gnomes who fled from the army of men and giants below. The trolls would not flee. They would fight or die.

"Cowards," muttered Asmodeus, regarding the gnomes with contempt as they escaped up the beach. "Cowards!" he said again, his voice rising in anger. "Turn and fight!"

His words had no effect. If the gnomes heard him, they made no sign. Then a familiar voice whispered to him. It seemed to be laughing at him.

They are more afraid of men than they are of you.

Asmodeus bristled. "Give me all of your power, and I will show them what it means to be afraid."

No, we will.

Blinded by pain, Asmodeus cried out and fell to the ground. Was he being punished? Had the Malodoi decided he was no longer useful? To his surprise, he felt something move and grow beneath his skin, as if his very bones had become serpents, writhing restlessly inside of him. Then his back seemed to explode, and his screams split the sky.

Two pale, leathery wings erupted from Asmodeus's shoulders. His limbs, too, grew longer and thicker, making him appear like an enormous locust. Most disturbing of all was his face. As he rose to his feet, the trolls recoiled. Still scored and wasted, his countenance had changed. The eyes that stared back at them seemed vacant, cold, as if he no longer saw them at all.

Unfurling his wings, he examined his new body, overwhelmed by the Malodoi's gift. He no longer needed the airships. He could pursue the dragons into the air himself. Turning to the trolls, he pointed at the men and giants running across the sand. "There are your enemies!" he thundered. "You have only to kill them—and Valmar will be yours!"

The trolls roared in delight and rushed past him.

As he stared up at the cliffs, Aethelred grabbed his father's shoulder. "Look!"

The king's face sank as he watched the trolls streaming down the sandy trail that led from the castle to the beach. Where did they come from? Weren't the mountain passes guarded by the giants? Then he remembered. Most of Orion's warriors were either here or protecting Grimstad itself. No one else could be spared to patrol the highlands, especially when they expected the enemy to approach from across the sea.

Argus called out to his men. "Form a line! Turn back and form a line!"

Obeying his command, the Valmarians allowed the gnomes to flee and began to gather along the beach. Orion and the rest of the giants also abandoned the pursuit and assembled on the king's left flank.

Argus glanced at his men wearily through the rain. Some were injured—all were wet, tired. Did they still have the strength to fight this new enemy?

He looked back at his children. "Stay close," he said.

Gwendolyn raised her bow. "But I can—"

"Do as I say!"

The first wave of trolls had reached the bottom of the cliffs, and now lumbered across the wet sand, bellowing in rage. They were almost as large as the giants, but unlike Orion and his warriors, they would show no mercy.

"I think they've spotted us," Orion quipped.

Many laughed, encouraged by the joke, but Argus remained serious. He wiped the rain out of his eyes as he watched the enemy draw near. "Let them come," he said, speaking to the soldiers closest to him. "Just hold your position, and remember your shields. After you absorb the first blow, go for the tendons behind their knees. You'll find they fall quite easily without those."

"Aye," said Wulfric, standing next to the king. "Just don't let them fall on you."

A few of the soldiers chuckled but most remained stoic. Then each man took a deep breath, raised his shield, and waited. What else was there to do? When one realizes that he cannot avoid a fight, everything becomes quite simple. Many would call this brave—to stand firm as an army of trolls approaches. Indeed, it is. But if you ask the men who have lived through such battles, they would not say they fought for honor or glory. They would tell you they fought simply to survive.

After a few more deep breaths, the armies met.

The ring of steel echoed off the cliffs, drowned out by screams of anguish. Argus and his men met the first group of trolls courageously. Parrying blow after blow, the Valmarians waited patiently for an opening before slashing fiercely at the enemy's legs. Many fell. But a second wave of trolls, then a third, forced the men and giants to give way. As they fell back, a score of men, and two giants, lay dead.

The children remained behind the line and watched their father and uncle fight a large troll. With incredible speed, the king evaded countless strokes before Wulfric delivered the killing blow to its belly. On the right flank, they saw Orion skewer two creatures with a single thrust from his spear. Even Cillian, the sailor, had done his part, piercing a troll's foot with his sword. The creature stumbled backward and impaled itself on another's blade.

Despite such bravery, the trolls pressed forward in great numbers, forcing the others to retreat further. With a shriek, one cut down a Valmarian and burst through the line. The creature tumbled to the ground but sprang to his feet, panting furiously as the rain mixed with the spittle that ran down his chin. He lifted his eyes and saw the children standing in front of him. A few yards away, Argus tried to extract himself from the line, but he realized he would be too late. The troll, his face pocked and hideous from some unknown disease, smiled as he lifted his blade. He expected them to run. Instead, Aethelred brought up his sword and stood in front of his sister, giving her time to put an arrow on her bowstring.

"Come on, then!" shouted the boy.

The troll laughed. "Brave," he grunted. "Stupid, but brave."

As he charged them, Gwendolyn released her arrow. It ripped into the troll's shoulder and he howled in pain, but he kept coming. She fumbled with another arrow as he lifted his scimitar above Aethelred's head—but before he could bring it down, a fireball engulfed his body. The troll fell backward into the sand as the raindrops sizzled on his flesh.

The boy looked up at Kindle. "I could have handled him," he said. "Where's Argent?"

"Fighting the bats," replied the dragon, "and needing less help than you."

Kindle landed in front of the men and giants, crushing several trolls beneath his feet, and sending the rest scattering. With his friends safely behind him, he used his fiery breath to consume dozens of the creatures. Those who escaped the flames regrouped along the base of the cliffs, uncertain about what to do next.

The trolls had taken heavy losses, but so, too had those who fought for Valmar. The men and giants limped slowly backwards, dragging their wounded with them as they reformed the line. Weary from battle, everyone breathed heavily, awaiting the next order.

Before Kindle could pursue the trolls across the beach, he felt something land on his back, followed by a stabbing pain in his shoulder. He turned his head. It was Asmodeus—and he had somehow grown wings. Worse, the creature seemed intent on tearing apart Kindle's wings with his claws.

Roaring in agony, the dragon shook his great body, attempting to dislodge him, but Asmodeus would not let go. Next, Kindle covered his foe with flame. When the fire subsided, not only was Asmodeus unharmed, he tightened his grip even more, piercing Kindle's flesh.

"How does it feel?" he said, as the dragon thrashed in the sand. "How does it feel to have something taken from you—something you rely upon?"

Ignoring him, Kindle rolled on to his back, forcing Asmodeus to soar into the air, where he regarded the dragon with amusement. Kindle tried to follow him but was too weak to fly. Seeing Kindle falter, the children raced to his side. Gwendolyn shot an arrow at Asmodeus but he simply swatted the projectile away.

Still wary of the dragon's breath, the trolls watched Kindle from a distance. Asmodeus had the power to change the weather, even the power to fly. But could he slay a dragon?

As if reading their thoughts, Asmodeus pointed down at his wounded foe. "You need no longer fear this one," he cried. "The girl is more dangerous now!" Aiming carefully, Gwendolyn shot another arrow at him but he caught it before it reached his chest and snapped it in his hands. "Finish the others. I'll see to the dragon!"

Emboldened by his words, the trolls surged forward, careful to give the beast a wide berth before converging on the rest of Valmar's army. If Asmodeus could kill Kindle, they could certainly do the rest.

Argus and Orion watched the trolls approach. Even if they were victorious, how could they kill a creature impervious to dragon fire? But there was no time to create a plan. They reformed the line, and prepared to sell their lives dearly.

"Stay together!" shouted Argus. "They cannot break us if we stay together! Show them what happens to those who invade Valmar!"

As the armies prepared to clash once more, something appeared out of the dark clouds. The trolls looked up, and hesitated as they watched a pale creature descend upon them like an avenging angel. It was a white dragon, and out of her mouth came death.

Argent scoured the trolls with her icy breath, freezing the foremost creature solid before smashing two more with her tail. The others cried out and raised their shields but it did them little good. She circled back and met them with another arctic blast, freezing metal, flesh, and bone.

One troll, a great hulking brute with several tattoos, jumped up and slashed at Argent's leg with his scimitar as she passed. The dragon simply smiled as the blade glanced off her scales before turning to face him. Clutching his weapon, he retreated slowly, waiting for her to strike. However, he forgot about the other dragon in the sand directly behind him. He sensed the danger too late, his scream cut short by Kindle's jaws.

Ignoring the pain in his wing, Kindle prepared to pursue Asmodeus into the sky. Gwendolyn scrambled on to his shoulders with her bow, unwilling to let him fight the creature alone.

"Come on, Aeth!" She looked around but she couldn't find her brother. Before she could search for him among the men and giants, she realized that the trolls had rallied.

More than a hundred of the creatures advanced on Valmar's army. They no longer seemed afraid of the dragons—but they were afraid of Asmodeus. Immune to dragon's breath, he was by far the strangest and deadliest creature they had ever encountered. With such power, they were confident he would soon kill both Kindle and Argent on the beach as they finished off what remained of the men and giants.

Charging with a ferocity that startled even Argus, the trolls rushed forward, screaming in fury as they brought their scimitars crashing down on Valmar's defenders. Argent and Kindle savaged their flanks, but the trolls still did great damage to their hated enemies.

As he raced to intercept the dragons, Asmodeus heard a familiar voice.

Don't forget the children!

He looked down. Aethelred had disappeared but Gwendolyn was easy to find. Still clinging to Kindle's shoulders with her knees, she had just finished burying an arrow in a troll's eye and was reaching into her quiver for another.

One of Edubard's heirs.

She had escaped him twice now but she would not do so again. It wouldn't be difficult to dislodge her from the dragon's back, not when she was using both hands to hold the bow. Once beyond Kindle's protection, she would be easy to kill.

Beating his wings, Asmodeus dove towards her—and just missed grabbing her neck as she ducked. He hit the beach like a meteor, carving a great trench into the sand. Recovering quickly, he leaped into the air again, veering sharply as he prepared for another attack. Kindle took a deep breath, forming a fireball in his throat.

"No!" cried Gwendolyn. "That won't work, remember?"

"Do you have a better idea?"

"Fly!" she said. "Draw him away from here!"

Kindle grimaced as he tried to flap his left wing. "I'll do my best."

Strapping her bow to her back, Gwendolyn held on with both hands as Kindle struggled to rise into the air. Not far behind, Asmodeus gave chase. As they spiraled upwards, Gwendolyn grew dizzy trying to survey the scene below.

Corpses were everywhere. Argent still fought valiantly, using her breath to turn many of the charging trolls to ice. Orion and the giants battled alongside of her, thrusting their long spears into the enemy while guarding her flanks. Nearby, Aethelred and Wulfric were fighting back to back, while Argus led a group of warriors to support them.

She glanced over her shoulder. Normally, it would not have been difficult for Kindle to outdistance Asmodeus, for there are few creatures faster in the air than dragons. But with his injury, Kindle struggled to gain speed, and the gholgor was drawing closer. Flapping his powerful wings, Asmodeus held his arms out in front of him, clenching and unclenching his fingers.

"Can't you go any faster?" she cried. Kindle grunted in response. He was flying as fast as he could, and his damaged wing only seemed to be growing weaker. Gwendolyn looked back once more. Asmodeus was nearly within reach. He extended his claws, trying to grab her. Gwendolyn crouched down and screamed.

Kindle!

The dragon banked hard to the right and plunged, escaping the creature's grasp. But not for long. Asmodeus quickly recovered and matched the dragon move for move.

"I can't—" Kindle panted. "I must land!"

Gwendolyn noticed that the gash in his wing had worsened, growing wider. The sight filled her with remorse.

They had just passed the castle and were flying over the village. Almost directly below them lay the stone dome that marked the entrance to the Low Road.

"There!" she said, pointing to the structure. "He can't fly out of your reach if we lead him into the Low Road!"

Kindle grazed the trees and rooftops as he landed clumsily just outside of the domed entrance, sending Gwendolyn tumbling over his head.

Despite a bloody elbow, she jumped to her feet. "Come on!" she cried. "This way!"

Stumbling forward, he followed her into the tunnel, his left wing dragging along the ground.

As they disappeared through the gate, Asmodeus landed outside of the entrance and folded his wings. He paused, adjusting the collar around his neck. The dragon could no longer fly, and the tunnel would not save them. Nor would the darkness. Asmodeus knew both environments well.

Flexing his claws, he slunk into the shadows to kill them.

18

INTO THE DARKNESS

As they descended, Kindle used his breath to light a few torches along the walls of the tunnel. He'd never been in the Low Road before, and was confused by the many carvings that surrounded him. He expected it to be small and cramped. Instead, the vaulted ceilings and wide avenue that ran parallel to the river gave him ample room in which to move.

When they reached the main tunnel, he was dimly aware of Gwendolyn running ahead of him, but his pulse quickened when he realized why. They weren't alone.

Asmodeus walked slowly toward them.

"Did you know, Gwendolyn, I first met your grandfather in a tunnel?" asked the creature.

He dragged his claws along one side of the wall, creating a horrible scratching noise that sent a chill up her spine. "Edubard and his mighty sentinels. They were so brave to attack us underground, and without warning. I can still recall the look on my sister's face." He smirked. "She looked a bit like you do now before she died, desperate and afraid. Yes, so very afraid."

Kindle stepped in front of the girl. "You're the one who should be afraid."

Taking a deep breath, he filled the tunnel with fire, scorching Asmodeus and blackening the earth on which the creature stood. As the flames flickered and subsided, he seemed to have disappeared. Had Kindle's breath finally consumed him?

Gwendolyn peered around the dragon's flank, allowing herself to hope. Then she saw something move along the ceiling of the tunnel. Asmodeus was hiding in the shadows. When she spotted him, he crawled down the walls like a cockroach. The fire had blackened his pale skin but he remained unharmed. Now, he really did look like something out of a nightmare.

His eyes shone with cold fury as he approached. "You could have lived if you would have simply pledged loyalty to me in the White Waste, but now that time has passed."

Springing forward like a snake, he grabbed Gwendolyn's arm and pulled her close, his claws digging into her flesh. She tried to push him away but it was useless. He was far stronger than any creature she had ever met. Desperately, she reached up to scratch at his eyes, his face, and felt her hand close around something smooth and cold.

It was his collar.

Time seemed to stop. A thousand images of wrath, gluttony, greed, sloth, lust, envy, and pride flashed through her mind. Gwendolyn felt physically ill, and though she tried to release the collar, her hand wouldn't obey. To her amazement, it transformed into a snake, and began to worm its way up her wrist like a parasite searching for a new host. Sensing that it was trying to abandon him for the girl, Asmodeus flung her away. She hit the opposite wall of the tunnel with a sickening crunch and fell to the ground.

Kindle stared at Gwendolyn's motionless body. It had all happened so fast. He looked up at Asmodeus, his eyes filled with rage. The creature may be immune to his breath, but that didn't mean he was immune to his jaws. The dragon's roar filled the tunnel as he lunged forward, determined to sink his teeth into his foe. But Asmodeus was too fast. Sidestepping the bite, he leaped on to Kindle's neck, clinging to it with all four limbs.

Then, he began to squeeze.

He had killed countless living things in this way, strangling them slowly and patiently. Though much larger than other creatures, a dragon that is unable to breathe would die just as quickly as anything else. Asmodeus simply needed to hold on.

Kindle continued to struggle, trying desperately to escape the creature's grasp, but in vain. Asmodeus was too strong—impossibly strong. As the dragon's strength diminished, he called out to Gwendolyn, Argent, anyone.

Help me.

He began to see stars, and realized he was losing consciousness. The faces on the walls stared back at him, indifferent. He had to act. Summoning what little strength that remained, he lowered his shoulders and rammed into the side of the tunnel, attempting to knock Asmodeus loose. Piles of rock crumbled at his feet as he battered the walls with his body, but the creature held fast. Asmodeus simply shielded himself from the brunt of the blow by sliding in the opposite direction.

As darkness closed in, Kindle looked up. Of course! Why hadn't he thought of it before? Leaping into the air, he smashed into the tunnel's ceiling. There would be nowhere for Asmodeus to go this time. The creature gasped as he absorbed the dragon's weight against the fortified rock. Dust and fragments of stone rained down on them. The creature maintained his grip but he had slipped just enough to allow Kindle to take another breath. The dragon leaped again—this time even more forcefully—crushing Asmodeus into the ceiling. He felt the creature release him, and they both fell to the ground with a crash.

Dazed from the collision, Kindle looked around. The air was thick with dust. He was lying on his side, surrounded by rubble. His wing throbbed, almost certainly broken from the fall. Nearby lay Gwendolyn. She still wasn't moving, but there was something tangled up in her fingers. It looked like a metal ring of some sort. Where had he seen it before? Then he remembered. It was the same collar that Asmodeus wore around his neck. But something was wrong. The object was cracked, broken.

Suddenly, he felt a searing pain in his ribs. Asmodeus had recovered from the fall, and had plunged his nails between the dragon's scales. Kindle cried out in agony as the creature pushed his claws deeper into his body.

"Time to die," he hissed.

Despite his own cries, Kindle thought he heard Argent's voice.

Don't give up.

He lifted his head and looked up the tunnel. Argent and Aethelred were coming. The boy was shouting something.

"Push him away!" screamed Aethelred. "You must push him away!"

Kindle roared and kicked Asmodeus with the last of his strength. The creature tumbled backwards but spread his wings, landing nimbly on his feet. He crouched and prepared to leap toward Kindle again when a rumbling sound filled the tunnel.

Asmodeus looked up—too late. The portcullis came hurtling down, directly on top of him, impaling his head with one of its metal spikes, as the rest of the contraption crushed him underneath its tremendous weight.

Unable to believe that the creature was dead, Kindle glanced around the tunnel. He was in a great deal of pain, but he would survive. He looked back and noticed that Aethelred and Argent were staring at him from the other side of the portcullis. They were calling out to him. He tried to focus on the words.

"—badly are you hurt?" cried Aethelred, his fingers clinging to the gate. "Where's Gwendolyn?"

Before he could answer, Asmodeus's body dissolved, transforming into black smoke, and disappeared.

Kindle grimaced as he turned over on to his feet. Using his tail, he gently picked up Gwendolyn and drew her near. She didn't respond. Then, he felt her heartbeat and looked at the others, relieved. It was strong like the girl's spirit. "She's alive," he croaked.

Argent froze the ruined portcullis and shattered it with her tail. Soon, Aethelred was holding Gwendolyn in his arms. He looked down at her face. It was pale and matted with blood, but her quick, shallow breaths concerned him the most.

"Gwen," said Aethelred, softly. "Gwen, wake up."

She remained limp but he noticed something in her hand. A metal collar. He removed it and held it up to the torchlight. As he did so, he felt her breathing become even more ragged.

A familiar sensation ran up his arm. He felt stronger, more definite, as if he was the only real being in the room and the others mere shadows. Before he could drop the collar, he heard a voice in his mind.

Aethelred.

He remained silent, uncertain of whether or not he should respond.

Aethelred, there is still time for us to grow together.

Slowly, the object began to change. The collar rippled in his hand as five small heads struggled to emerge from the surface. He had already seen the faces of the Malodoi. He did not want to see them again.

"I know what you are," thought Aethelred, "and what you tried to do to me."

He tossed the collar away in disgust. It didn't matter. He continued to hear the voice.

We can save her.

Aethelred paused and glanced at Gwendolyn. Though her chest still rose and fell, she remained motionless. Could the Malodoi really save her? It was unquestionably evil. Even so, if it could heal his sister, should he not try?

His eyes were drawn back to the collar and he realized it had grown in size. Along its edge, five distinct faces now appeared. They seemed to be looking at him. Only, the object was no longer a collar. It had become a crown.

If you declare yourself king, you can heal her.

Aethelred rose and picked up the crown. A thrill of electricity ran up his arm, reminding him of its seductive power. The serpentine faces seemed to smile hungrily as he walked back toward Gwendolyn.

The dragons watched him curiously. "What are you doing?" asked Argent, fear creeping into her voice.

"Saving her."

The boy lifted the crown with both hands but instead of setting it on his head, he whispered Oorano's name.

Almost instantly, small, blue tongues of flame appeared on his fingers and crawled up the crown. As the fire grew, it became brighter, hotter, searing everything it touched—yet Aethelred's hands were unharmed. Soon, the crown changed, becoming a small hydra. Twisting and writhing in the flames, it snapped at his hands but could do nothing to hurt him. Finally, a dreadful wail pierced the air as it disintegrated. The fire had consumed it, leaving behind a charred, iron collar.

As he flung it to the ground, Gwendolyn groaned and her eyes fluttered open.

"Gwen!" he said, kneeling beside her.

She looked awful. Her scalp was caked with blood, matting a few strands of hair to the side of her face, and her dress was torn. Asmodeus had also injured her arm, leaving behind several deep scratches. But Aethelred didn't care about any of that. She was still alive.

"Do I look as bad as you do?" she asked, weakly.

Despite all that had happened, Aethelred couldn't help but laugh. "Worse!" he shot back. "But it doesn't matter." He reached down and touched her scalp. "How's your head?"

She rubbed it gingerly. "Throbbing," she replied. "What happened?"

He explained how he and Argent had been fighting the trolls on the beach when she heard Kindle's plea for help. Grabbing Aethelred, she flew to the Low Road where they found Asmodeus and Kindle in a deadly struggle. As Kindle separated himself from the creature, Aethelred used the hidden crank to bring the portcullis crashing down on him.

"So he *could* be defeated," she said.

"Only after you removed his collar," he replied. "I found it in your hand."

Gwendolyn smiled. "What happened to it?"

Before he could reply, Kindle spoke. "He destroyed it." The dragon motioned to the blackened ring of metal nearby. "He destroyed it—and what it represented."

Aethelred blushed. "The battle isn't over. The others need our help." He nodded to Argent and Kindle. "Especially yours."

19

HIGH TIDE

It was no longer raining when the children and the dragons emerged from the Low Road in the middle of the village. The dark clouds that had settled over Valmar like a funeral shroud were almost gone. Gwendolyn and Aethelred paused to stare at the patches of blue sky, and feel the sun's warmth on their faces, but they did not linger. Asmodeus was dead but the trolls still had to be defeated.

Hurrying past the castle and toward the cliffs, they were amazed by what they saw, or rather, by what they didn't see. Only a short while ago, throngs of men, giants, and trolls fought desperately on the beach in a battle that would be long remembered as one of Valmar's darkest hours. Now, there seemed to be no survivors.

"Where is everybody?" asked Aethelred.

Corpses were plentiful. Hundreds of bodies lay on the sand, twisted and broken, along with the remnants of the ships, pushed slowly but unceasingly ashore by the waves. Only the seagulls stirred.

Argent rose into the air with Aethelred to explore the area, while Gwendolyn and Kindle travelled slowly down the sandy trail on foot. Kindle's wing trailed behind him like a broken mast, but his breath was still deadly, and Gwendolyn knew better than to ask him to rest if more fighting remained.

When they reached the beach, Aethelred and Argent were waiting for them. Scores of trolls lay dead. Valmar's men had slain many but the giants had slaughtered an even greater number by forcing the creatures against the cliffs, and impaling them with great spears. The large bodies of bats also lay here and there, either frozen or burned beyond recognition. Gnomes, too, could be seen among the carnage, though most had fled when the dragons approached.

Still, a number of men and giants had also died. The children recognized Cillian and Farin among them. The sailors had perished next to one another, fighting a group of trolls until the creatures had overwhelmed them. Cillian seemed to have given his life trying to save Farin; he lay across the younger man, still gripping his sword.

"We must honor them," said Kindle, gazing down at the fallen sailors. "All of them."

But where were the others? Though they could not find them among the dead, it gave the children little comfort. Just as they began to lose hope, Argent cried out.

"Look!" she said, nodding westward. "There!"

Far up the coast, they saw movement. A host of men and giants had gathered along the shore, but there didn't seem to be any sign of the enemy.

"Come on, Argent," said Aethelred. "Let's take a look." He jumped on the dragon's back and turned to the others. "We'll be back."

When Argent and Aethelred landed among a cluster of Valmar's soldiers, the men greeted them enthusiastically. They had gathered near a stony bluff along the coast where the waves lapped the sand, though for what purpose, it wasn't clear. Aethelred climbed down from the dragon's shoulders. Before he could ask why they were here, several of the men slapped him on the back and received him warmly. Many, he noticed, were injured. Some had even been pierced by arrows, yet they remained standing, refusing to abandon their comrades. They held their swords as if some danger were still near.

A soldier limped up to Aethelred. His head was roughly bandaged, and he appeared to be favoring his right leg. "Welcome, young master," he said, smiling. "You're a pleasant sight to see." He glanced up at Argent. "Both of you." Then he frowned. "But where are the others? The princess, that is, and Kindle?"

"Near the castle," said the boy. "Kindle's wing is injured." The soldiers looked at one another, worried. "He'll be alright," Aethelred continued, hastily, touching the old soldier's arm. "We all will."

"And the demon?" asked another soldier, expectantly. He was young, perhaps a few years older than Aethelred himself. "The one they call Asmodeus?"

The others grew quiet as they awaited his answer.

"Dead," replied Aethelred. "Dead and gone."

The Valmarians cheered. "Thank the gods!" cried the old soldier. "For when we saw that creature, we doubted if even the dragons could defeat him."

"But why are you all here?" asked Aethelred, looking around. "Where is the enemy?"

"Most of the trolls are dead," said the young soldier. "After Asmodeus abandoned them, they seemed to lose hope—and we killed many on the beach near the castle. Others fled into the woods, and they're being hunted as we speak by a large party of men and giants."

"And the gnomes?" asked Argent.

The older soldier motioned up the beach, near a large outcropping of stone against the cliffs. "Most are still alive," he grumbled. "Hiding in there like a bunch of crabs."

The boy looked up but he couldn't see beyond the men who surrounded him. "In where?"

"The cave," said the old soldier. "It's tucked in the foot of those bluffs. That's where they've taken refuge. They'll shoot at anyone who comes near them."

"Your father has been trying to convince them to surrender, but time is running out," said another. "When the tide comes in, the cavern will flood. Still, they think we mean to kill them. Maybe we should. They deserve death." He looked over the boy's shoulder. "If the tide don't flush them out, the dragons will. Fire or ice, it don't matter to me."

"Dragons—?" Aethelred turned and saw Gwendolyn and Kindle walking up the beach. Facing the soldier once again, he shook his head. "Perhaps there is another way."

He shouted out to Gwendolyn. "I think father still needs our help," he said. "Come! I'll explain on the way."

As they approached the base of the cliffs where the gnomes were hiding, a throng of men and giants gave way, allowing them to pass. Like the others, these soldiers looked weary but resolute, like those who had reached the finish line of a marathon only to be told they must keep running.

"The gnomes must be made to realize the battle is over," said Aethelred. "With Asmodeus dead, what more do they have to fight for?"

"Be careful not to underestimate the stubbornness of these creatures," replied Argent. "I have often found that reason alone is not enough to change another's mind."

Seawater washed over their feet as they made their way up the beach. The tide was indeed coming in. If the gnomes remained in the cave too much longer, they would have to choose between surrendering, fighting their way out—or drowning.

When the children reached the cave's entrance, they saw their parents standing nearby. (To stand in front of it was to risk being hit by a gnome's arrow.) The king and queen were speaking to Wulfric, Orion, and Jorgan.

"Is this a private conversation or can anyone join?" asked Aethelred.

They turned and gasped. "Gwendolyn! Aethelred!" cried Thelda, as the children ran up and hugged her tightly. "We sent riders to look for you!" She raised Gwendolyn's chin with her hand and looked alarmed at her daughter's bloodstained face. "What happened?"

"It could have been a lot worse," she replied, pushing a few strands of hair behind her ear.

Argus looked up at Kindle and saw his damaged wing. "And you?" he said, laying a hand on the dragon's flank.

"I did no more than anyone else on this day," he said, looking out at the men and giant surrounding him. "The real heroes stand before you. If not for the children, we would all still be in danger."

"Is Asmodeus dead then?" Wulfric asked.

Aethelred nodded.

"Then it's true," said Jorgan, pensively. "Asmodeus wasn't immortal after all."

Orion smiled grimly. "Tell them that," he said, looking at the cave's entrance. "Jorgan and your father have been trying to convince the rest of the gnomes to surrender, but they've refused. They won't even talk to us." He snorted angrily. "Perhaps Kindle's breath could coax them out."

"No," said Argus. "I would not see them hurt unless necessary. They are not wicked . . . just foolish."

Thelda nodded in agreement. "Asmodeus has been ordering them around for so long, they've forgotten how to think for themselves. They just need time."

"I'm afraid time's running out," said Wulfric, glancing out to sea. "Look at the tide. Water is already filling the cave. If we can't convince them to lay down their weapons, they might come out fighting. We may be forced to kill them."

"Then let Aethelred and me talk to them," said Gwendolyn, looking at her brother. "We can tell them of Asmodeus's fate."

Argus frowned. "What makes you think they'll believe you?"

Gwendolyn smiled mysteriously. "It's not what we'll say," she said. "It's what we'll show them." She looked down at the water that swirled around her feet. "Preferably before they drown."

"Very well," said the king, "but take a couple of shields with you—as well as Jorgan. His presence will prove that gnomes and men don't have to be enemies."

When Jorgan and the children approached the stony entrance, they found that the opening was narrow but the cave was deep, the perfect place to defend against large numbers.

A quick peek around the corner revealed that the gnomes had taken refuge behind several large rocks near the back of cave. The creatures glanced nervously out from the mossy outcroppings, holding their crossbows, waiting for an attack that they believed was inevitable.

Gwendolyn took a deep breath and looked at Jorgan. "Ready?"

He nodded. "Perhaps it will help if I speak first."

Splashing through the water, they raised their shields and followed him into the entrance. A voice sounded from the back of the cave. "Another step and we'll shoot you where you stand!" The children glanced at each other. They recognized Norr's voice immediately.

"As you can see, we are unarmed," said Jorgan, slowly raising his hand. "I have brought Gwendolyn and Aethelred with me." He paused. "They wish to speak with you."

"There's nothing to talk about," said Norr. "We've already heard enough lies."

"The tide doesn't lie," said Jorgan, looking down at the surf around his knees. "Soon, the water will fill this cave. Then what? Will you not at least hear them out?"

The gnomes murmured amongst themselves. The children couldn't make out the words, but the tone suggested that the creatures were debating the matter. Finally, they heard Norr's voice. "Speak then!" he said, sounding displeased. "But if you think we'll beg for mercy, you'll be disappointed. Our master will come! You'll see!"

Gwendolyn shook her head. "I'm afraid that's quite impossible. Asmodeus is dead."

Some of the gnomes cried out in dismay, but others simply scoffed. "More lies!" cried Norr. "He is invincible!"

"It's *not* a lie," replied Gwendolyn. Lowering her shield, she held out her hand, revealing Asmodeus's blackened collar. Though it was now scorched and lusterless, there was no denying it had once belonged to him. "Asmodeus may have seemed invincible, but in the end, he lost everything—even himself."

"What are you talking about?"

"He was possessed by a demon," explained Aethelred. "The Malodoi."

Norr forced a laugh. "There are no such things!"

"Yes, there are," continued Aethelred. "I know because . . . well, because it once tried to possess me, too. I understand what it means to be afraid—to take comfort in lies—because sometimes the truth can be harder to face."

Norr was still reeling as he stared at the collar in the girl's hand. He recognized it as his master's, and his mind raced as he considered what to do next.

Behind him, the gnomes began to talk uneasily. Many were beginning to believe that Asmodeus was dead. They looked down at the rising water. Perhaps it would be better to lay down their weapons and ask for mercy. But Norr still wanted desperately to believe that the children were lying.

"Demons?" he cried. "The Malodoi? Enough of your superstitions!"

He raised his crossbow and shot at Gwendolyn. Before the bolt could reach the girl, Jorgan leaped in front of her. The dart pierced his chest and he fell backwards, stifling a groan. The other gnomes cried out in alarm and tackled Norr before he could fire again.

"Wait!" they cried. "He no longer speaks for us! Please don't punish us!"

Fearing the worst, the children dropped to their knees and examined Jorgan's injury. The bolt was sticking out of his cloak, directly above his heart. They had seen several arrow wounds in their time, and knew the injuries they caused could be terrible. A crossbow bolt would be no different. Things looked grim, but to their surprise, the gnome raised himself up on one elbow, and took a deep breath.

"Save your strength!" said Aethelred.

Ignoring him, the gnome pulled the bolt out of his chest.

"Don't!" cried Gwendolyn. "You'll only hasten the bleeding!"

Jorgan smiled and held up the shaft, causing the children to gasp. There was no blood on the steel tip. In fact, there was no blood anywhere. Before they could utter a word, the gnome reached into the folds of his cloak and pulled out his book of poetry. Its leather cover was badly damaged, but its many pages had stopped the bolt from penetrating his chest.

"Who says poetry isn't functional?" he asked, laughing nervously.

As Jorgan rose to his feet, they heard a great number of feet splashing through the water. Dropping their weapons, the gnomes emerged from behind the rocks, marching in single file, with hands raised over their heads.

They no longer looked stern and proud. They looked like creatures who had become thoroughly ashamed of themselves, and were willing to accept whatever fate the Valmarians might impose upon them.

Last of all came Norr. Flanked by two gnomes, he walked with his hands bound in front of him as he looked at Jorgan and the children, more than a little frightened. "I'm not responsible for any of this," he said as he stopped in front of them, not daring to look them in the eye. "I was just following orders."

"I know," replied Jorgan. "That's the madness of it."

***

Argus and his men led Norr and the other gnomes back to the castle courtyard and placed them under the watchful eyes of Argent. Everyone else had the terrible task of collecting the dead. Already exhausted from the battle, they nevertheless spent the evening and the early morning hours gathering up the fallen.

Hundreds of dead trolls and bats littered the beach, a grim reminder of the horrors of war. Now the corpses presented a new problem. How could Argus and his men possibly find the strength to gather the beasts together and burn them? Kindle proved to be the answer. Using his great jaws, he gathered them together one by one, and placed them into piles before setting them on fire. The corpses burned throughout the night, casting the beach in a strange, infernal glow.

Jorgan and his friends collected the bodies of the gnomes who had perished in battle. The number was smaller than expected. Those who had survived the fireships were surprised by the fearlessness of their foes. Asmodeus had told them that the enemy was weak, wicked, and easily frightened. Never did they imagine that the opposite was true until they landed on the beach.

Still, some gnomes had stood and fought . . . and died. Now, the corpses were gathered up and buried in a field near the castle. Jorgan himself erected a large wooden stake in the ground where they lay. At the top he carved a series of concentric rings, one for each fallen gnome, with a small inscription in naradi that said:

Here lie people of the tool
May they rest in peace
Free from life's labors
And the world's caprice

When the sun rose the next morning, the giants had wrapped their dead in furs, and placed them side by side near the castle. Orion was anxious to take them back to Grimstad for burial but he remained to honor Valmar's fallen soldiers—and decide the fate of the gnomes. As they all gathered in the cemetery north of Ballan á Moor, Argus said a few words about each of the fallen soldiers, for he was a good king, and knew every one of them by name.

Once the ceremony had finished, most returned to the castle and slept, exhausted by what had transpired. But not everyone. Together with Orion, Wulfric, and Jorgan, the king and queen deliberated for hours in the Great Hall, discussing what was to become of the gnomes. Finally, they emerged in the early afternoon, looking tired but pleased with what they had decided.

The children had been waiting for them, but had grown so tired that they had fallen asleep next to one another outside the room.

"Gwendolyn, Aethelred!" said Thelda. The children jumped as they looked up to see their mother's face. "Would you mind gathering everyone together? We've made a decision."

Soon a throng of men and giants stood together in the courtyard while Norr and the rest of the gnomes looked around nervously. Despite the assurances that Argus had given to them, they were convinced that some horrible punishment awaited them. (As you may have already learned, those who suspect the worst in others are often guilty of the same thoughts themselves.) Finally, Argus, Thelda, and Orion entered. A murmur ran through the assembly as they approached the gnomes.

Argus stepped forward and cleared his throat. "When we left the White Waste, I had hoped that we had seen the last of you," he began. "Instead, you chose to cross the sea and make war on us." He sighed. "But I also understand you did this out of some misguided attempt to correct the world's wrongs. Asmodeus deceived you, convincing you that violence was a necessary prelude to peace." He glanced at Jorgan. "Thankfully, not all of you were gullible enough to believe his lies . . . which gives us hope for the rest of you. Therefore, Orion and I have decided to give you a choice. You can return to the White Waste on your ships and live out your days as you see fit in Skarsgaard with the pledge that you must never make war on us again."

Orion came forward and stood next to Argus. "Or you can return with us to Grimstad. We will help you to make a home in the mountains."

The gnomes whispered to one another in surprise. Instead of death, were they really being offered a new beginning?

But Orion hadn't finished. "If you choose to remain, don't think it will be easy," he warned. "The highlands can be treacherous. As this day has shown, there may be trolls still lurking in the foothills near the marshes. Nevertheless, wild fruit and game is plentiful in the valleys, and there are many mountain lakes and streams where you can fish. But you must pledge to live at peace with us and one another."

The gnomes huddled together and discussed the matter with great urgency in their native tongue.

Watching the strange creatures, the children resisted the urge to laugh. Norr and the others appeared quite comical, arguing with one another in such an animated fashion that their great noses bounced with each gesture. Finally, they seemed to come to an agreement.

Norr stepped forward and gazed at Argus and Orion distrustfully as if trying to settle something in his mind. Finally, he spoke. "Do we have your word that you will allow us to return to the White Waste, unharmed?"

Orion growled but Argus raised his hand. "Forgive me if I find it strange that you ask such a question," he said. "If anyone's goodwill should be doubted, it is not ours. But yes, you will not be harmed as long as you pledge to never attack us again."

Norr looked down, as if unable to meet the king's gaze. "Then some of us have chosen to leave Valmar," he said. "As soon as you will allow it."

"Very well," said Argus. "If that is your wish—"

A small gnome with large ears shuffled forward. "It is not *our* wish!" he said. The children recognized Crum almost immediately. Gwendolyn still felt guilty for knocking him unconscious.

"Most of us would prefer to remain here," he continued, glancing at Argus and Orion nervously. "That is, if you'll have us." The others nodded their heads in agreement. "We promise to do you no harm. In fact, we will do as you say . . . think as you think."

Argus frowned. "That's not what I meant."

Crum and the others stared at him blankly. "Don't you want us to adopt your ways?"

"I want you to think for yourselves," said the king.

"Then we are . . . free?" asked Crum.

Argus and Orion looked at each other and smiled. "You always were," said the giant. "You just needed to be reminded."

The king nodded. "You are free to come and go as you please—for it is precisely our freedom that allows us to make meaningful choices, and be responsible for those choices. If you can accept those terms, then you are welcome to live among us."

20

OF GARDENS AND GNOMES

By the time autumn had arrived, everyone was so busy with the harvest that it was easy to forget how much things had changed. The giants and gnomes had long since returned to Grimstad. The repairs to the castle were nearly complete. The Valmarians had salvaged much of the gnomes' fleet, giving the kingdom eight seaworthy ships to compensate for the loss of the others. Best of all, Gwendolyn and Kindle, save for a few scars, had recovered from most of their injuries. (Most, but not all, for, alas, not all injuries are physical, nor do they always heal.)

On a cool, fall afternoon, the girl and the dragon sat in the cemetery along the cliffs, as they often did now, where Polonius was buried. "He loved this time of year," said Gwendolyn, admiring the subtle beauty of the white clovers that grew on the old man's grave. "When we were younger, he would take Aethelred and me into the forest to teach us the names of the trees, the birds, even the wild flowers." She picked one of the clovers and smiled at the memory. "One day, as we waded through the leaves, he found an acorn, and held it up for us to see. He told us that, given enough time, it would grow into one of the oaks just like those that surrounded us. I remarked on how strange it was that such a small thing should grow so large, and become so different. 'Is it so strange?' he said. 'None of us are yet fully grown—not even me.' When I asked him how that could be, he thought for a moment. 'You mustn't judge others by their appearance, Gwendolyn,' he said. 'After all, we're much like these acorns, though many can only ever see our outward appearance. But one day, we will outgrow our shells.' I asked him what I would grow into. 'Why, yourself, of course! But what you are now and what you ultimately become,' he said with a twinkle in his eye, 'well, that's up to you.'"

"That sounds like Polonius," Kindle replied. "He was a good teacher—and an even better friend."

Gwendolyn's smile faded. "Now he's gone," she muttered, casting away the clover and bringing both knees to her chin. "Oh, Kindle! What I wouldn't give to see his face, to hear his voice again! I'd even settle for a geometry lesson."

They grew quiet as they listened to the waves break, rise, and break again on the beach below. The sky was a stunning shade of blue. The seagulls glided lazily on the wind as the sun sank closer to the horizon.

Hearing the sound of wings, Gwendolyn looked up and watched as Argent and Aethelred appeared in the sky. They circled slowly downward in great arcs before landing in the grass. "We thought we'd find you here," said the boy. "You're late for dinner."

His sister's eyes remained fixed on the ocean. "I'm not hungry."

Aethelred sat astride the dragon, studying her. Then he slid from Argent's back and sat down next to her. "I miss Polonius, too," he said, softly. "But he's not coming back . . . not to Valmar."

Tears filled her eyes. "Is that supposed to make me feel better?"

Aethelred sighed. "I just know he wouldn't want us lingering here, that's all," he said. "He gave his life for us so that we could *live*."

"Then why do I still feel so sad?" she asked, wiping away the tears and looking at him. "Don't you miss him?"

"Of course," he said, gently. "But death isn't the end."

"What do you mean?"

"Remember when Oorano rescued me from the Malodoi?"

Gwendolyn nodded, recalling how she thought she had lost her brother forever, as she watched fire consume his body. "He carried you into the flames . . . and you returned, whole."

"Did I ever tell you what I saw while in the fire? I thought it was a dream, but now, I'm not so sure." He looked out at the sea. "As the pain faded, I opened my eyes and realized I was somewhere else. I was standing in a field of wheat. It was not quite dawn. I could see the sunlight in the east, but not the sun itself. The air was cool, pleasant. The wind rustled through the prairie in great waves, like it had gone on forever, and would go on forever." He took a deep breath. "I still remember wondering how the air could smell so sweet."

He stood up and took a few steps, as if he were in the wheat field again. "Then I noticed Oorano standing next to me. Except, he looked different. Gone were the flames that surrounded him. He was a man—but so much more. He was also a lion and a lamb. They were different, yet they were all the same." Aethelred turned and saw the puzzled look on his sister's face. He smiled. "I told you it sounds like a dream."

Aethelred raised his arm. "Then I saw what I had become. My hand was gone, consumed by the fire . . . but, strangely, it didn't hurt as much as I thought it would. I remembered how the Malodoi used to be a part of me, and how it would have destroyed me if it weren't for Oorano. My hand was a small price to pay for the suffering that I'd caused."

The boy stopped and looked down. "Then Oorano said something to me that I'll never forget." Gwendolyn and the dragons leaned forward, listening intently. "He touched the place where my hand used to be, and said, 'Unless a kernel of wheat falls to the ground and dies, it can't produce seeds.' All of a sudden, I felt a warm sensation in my arm. Only, it wasn't like the fire. It was gentle, soothing. When I looked down, I'd been made whole again. Not only that, but I felt more alive than ever before."

He returned to Gwendolyn. "So you see, death isn't the end," he said. "It's only the end of the beginning."

***

When spring arrived, the dragons and the children visited Grimstad. It had been many months since the battle, and everyone was curious to see how the gnomes were adapting to the mountains under the guidance of the giants. But Orion and Ocwen told them that the gnomes had left some time ago.

"They wanted a fresh start," explained Orion. "I urged them to wait until winter was over, but they were anxious to explore the mountains, and they said they didn't want to trespass on our hospitality any longer. So we forged them some tools and provided them with food—and away they went as the first snow began to fall. Strange, wouldn't you say?"

Gwendolyn nodded. "Strange, indeed," she said. "Did they say where they were going?"

"South," said Ocwen. "They planned to settle in the mountains near the Great Desert. Now that the days are growing longer, I've been wondering if we shouldn't go looking for them."

"We can save you the trouble," said Argent.

"The Skeldings are vast," cautioned Orion. "It might be difficult, even from the sky."

The ice dragon smiled. "I lived with them for years, and they aren't the subtlest of creatures. If they're in the mountains, we'll find them."

After spending the evening with the giants, they set out early the next morning in search of the settlement. They spent hours flying across the deep gorges and over the hoary peaks that spanned Valmar. Spring had clearly arrived. The swollen rivers ran swiftly through the valleys while the melting snow in higher elevations revealed the earthy face of the mountains. Occasionally, one of them spotted animal tracks in the deep snow but by early afternoon, they still saw no sign of the gnomes.

"Orion was right," said Aethelred, as they passed by a waterfall, its spray rising into the air. "They could be anywhere." He turned his head and saw the tan plateau of the Great Desert stretch away to the west. "Perhaps they went there."

"Perhaps, but I doubt it," said Argent. "The gnomes are builders. To build, one needs materials. We will find them here in the mountains, where timber and water are plentiful."

After a short rest, they continued onwards, gliding over highlands, and admiring the swollen rivers and streams in the valleys below. The sound of rushing water filled the children's ears but the dragons heard something else.

"What's that?" asked Kindle.

Argent looked down at the mountains. "It sounds like metal striking metal."

The children glanced at each other, confused. "I don't hear anything," said Gwendolyn.

"I would be surprised if you could," said Kindle. "Not everyone can hear as well as a dragon but I think it's coming from the south."

Following the sound, they soon observed a series of flashes coming from a jagged column of spires. "Look!" said Gwendolyn, pointing.

"If I had to guess," said Argent, "that's where we'll find the gnomes."

"How can you be sure?"

"Glass doesn't occur naturally in Valmar," explained the dragon.

"How do you know that's glass?" asked Aethelred.

"Don't you remember the windows of Skarsgaard?" said Argent. "The gnomes relied on the emeralds to light the tunnels underground, but they prefer sunshine. The glass allows them to illuminate the mountain's interior naturally."

"Skylights," said Aethelred, impressed. "They're skylights."

"I haven't heard them use that term before," said Argent, "but I suppose it fits."

As the dragons descended, the children noticed three skylights fitted neatly into the face of the mountain. Nothing else had been disturbed. The pine trees, boulders, and hardy bushes of the surrounding area remained untouched. Finally, they heard the cacophony for themselves. The noise echoed in the valley, resounding from cliff to cliff, as the children saw the source of the sound below.

The gnomes had set up camp near a stream, and they looked very busy. Dozens of tents clustered together near the edge of the water, and the creatures hurried among the narrow lanes of canvas, carrying out their duties. In typical gnome fashion, everyone had a job to do. Some cooked wild game, while others smoked fish or washed linen. Another group fashioned tools on anvils near a large fire (thus, the clanking sound) while still others stood over a kiln, baking glass.

As the visitors landed near the bank of the stream, the gnomes smiled and waved as they gathered around them. Sitting astride the dragons, Gwendolyn and Aethelred looked at one another, bemused. Hadn't these creatures once been their enemies? Now, free from Asmodeus, they had changed, appearing unafraid, hopeful, even kind.

Jorgan pushed his way to the front. "As leader of the council, I welcome you!" He solemnly touched his nose and held his hand out, palm upward, in greeting. The rest of the gnomes did likewise.

"Jorgan!" cried Gwendolyn, bowing her head slightly in return. "We came to see how you were getting on. It looks like you have found a suitable home here?"

"Suitable?" said Jorgan, trying to contain his enthusiasm. Some of the gnomes twittered behind him. "Forgive me, princess, but 'suitable' doesn't begin to describe this place. Never before have we seen forests this beautiful, earth so rich with minerals, rivers so clear and clean. We have fallen in love with Valmar."

Gwendolyn smiled. "I am glad you approve," she said. "But something tells me that you've been doing more than simply admiring your surroundings."

"Yes, indeed," said Jorgan. He looked up at the mountain proudly. "We call it Sodergaard—that is to say 'Southern Fortress' in the common tongue. This mountain will soon be our new home. We will guard the southern passes so that you will never again be surprised by the trolls." He looked back at them, his eyes widening in excitement. "Would you like to see our progress? The halls are not yet finished, but a few are large enough even for the dragons to enter."

Kindle and Argent looked at one another, reading each other's thoughts. "No, thank you," replied Kindle. "My sister and I have spent enough time underneath mountains. We find being above them much more agreeable. Speaking of which, we passed by a few goats on the eastern slope as we approached and, well, we are a bit hungry."

Gwendolyn laughed. "Go on then," she replied. "We'll take the tour and meet you later."

As the dragons flew away, Jorgan led Gwendolyn and Aethelred inside Sodergaard. Despite the camp's impressive organization, it was nothing compared to what the gnomes had begun to accomplish *inside* the mountain. They had worked tirelessly all winter, digging into the earth and stone, carving living quarters, sculleries, storerooms, aqueducts, workshops, and even fashioning the skylights that had caught the children's eyes. Though the mountain was not yet quite ready for inhabitants, it soon would be.

"This is amazing," said Aethelred, admiring the arches that supported the cavern. "How were you able to accomplish so much in such a short amount of time?"

Jorgan smiled. "The giants make good tools, and we enjoy the work." He looked at them slyly. "We have also discovered something else. Would you like to see it?"

They nodded and he led them into another hall. When they saw what it contained, the children stopped, unable to believe their eyes. Heaps of gold filled the room.

"We collected it as we dug," said Jorgan, climbing up the closest pile. "I know humans are fond of gold. Do you think your people would like a few tons?"

If the children looked surprised before, they looked even more so now. "A few tons?" gasped Gwendolyn.

The gnome nodded, causing his nose to bounce. "It's a small price to pay."

Aethelred looked puzzled. "Pay for what?"

"For showing us mercy." Jorgan looked away, as he recalled the past. "After Feigaard was destroyed, we lost ourselves in a manner of speaking. We were afraid that the old disagreements between us would rise again. Asmodeus offered a convenient solution. We could remain united, happy, but only if we let him think for us." The gnome beamed. "Then we met you. You showed us that some things are more important than unity, safety—and yes, even happiness."

Aethelred climbed up the pile of gold and put his hand on the gnome's shoulder. "I think you're going to fit in just fine here."

"Then you'll accept our gift?"

The children looked at each other and smiled.

"With pleasure," said Gwendolyn.

***

When they returned home, Gwendolyn and Aethelred left the dragons in the courtyard and found the queen in one of Ballan á Moor's many gardens, just beyond the castle's walls. It had been trampled during the battle, but Thelda had worked diligently to repair the damage. Now, as spring arrived, jasmine, roses, geraniums, and many other flowers native to Valmar were thriving again.

"They're beautiful," said Gwendolyn, admiring one of the rose's scarlet petals.

Aethelred nodded. "I didn't think they'd recover."

"Roses are delicate," said Thelda, "but rosebushes are tough. They will grow even stronger now that I've pruned away the broken branches."

Gwendolyn touched her scalp, and felt the scar that she had received from Asmodeus. "I wish everything could be repaired so easily," she sighed. "Why do people behave so wickedly against one another?"

Thelda removed her gloves and looked at her daughter. "Some say that we behave in such a way because we are confused. That is, we mistake evil for good."

Aethelred frowned. "Is that what you think?"

"Sometimes people act out of a misguided sense of justice," said Thelda, "but more often, I find that most of us know the difference between right and wrong." She wiped her brow and looked up at the sun. "The hard part is summoning the courage to fight evil—especially in ourselves. It's not our heads that need taming so much as our hearts."

"Thank goodness the gnomes finally figured that out," said Gwendolyn. "They seem to be thriving in the mountains."

"I am glad," said Thelda. "We should never be so foolish as to take for granted the freedom that we enjoy here." She nodded to the flowerbed in front of her. "After all, the weeds will always attempt to take root."

"I don't see any weeds," said Aethelred.

The queen smiled. "That's because I wage a constant battle against them. We must never take an orderly garden for granted."

Gwendolyn sat next to her mother, and picked up the spade, digging it into the rich, black soil. "I just hope that Aethelred and I demonstrate the same wisdom that you and father have shown when we're grown," she replied. "You always seem to know what to do."

Thelda put one hand around each child, and drew them near. "Neither of you will be a child much longer," she said. "But you have already learned enough lessons for a lifetime. I have no doubt the kingdom's future is in good hands."

ACKNOWLEDGEMENTS

It would have been impossible to imagine the world of Valmar and all that it contains without a lot of help from an extraordinary group of people in my own world.

First, I want to thank Leighton Isaacs for creating a wonderful cover illustration. She took my rough ideas and developed an image that perfectly captured a pivotal scene in the book. The original drawing is now hanging in our home. To see more of her work, please visit www.brightshadowsart.com.

I'm also once again indebted to Judy Marc and Anne Delong for the time they took to proofread the manuscript. It pays to know teachers!

Finally, I want to thank my wife, Rachel, to whom this book is dedicated. While I benefited enormously from her edits, ideas, layout skills, social media expertise, and daily encouragement, I appreciate most of all her faith in these books, and in me. My dear, it is a privilege to experience life with you.

Roy Sakelson, December 2014

ABOUT THE AUTHOR

Roy Sakelson lives with his wife,
two children, and a cat in San Jose, California.

www.RoySakelson.com

Other works include:

Gwendolyn and the Seeds of Destiny
Aethelred and the Wand of Woe

Made in the USA
San Bernardino, CA
26 March 2015